My Summer with George

My Summer with George

MARILYN FRENCH

ALFRED A. KNOPF   NEW YORK   1996

THIS IS A BORZOI BOOK
PUBLISHED BY ALFRED A. KNOPF, INC.

Copyright © 1996 by Belles Lettres, Inc.

All rights reserved under International and Pan-American
Copyright Conventions. Published in the United States by
Alfred A. Knopf, Inc., New York, and simultaneously in
Canada by Random House of Canada Limited, Toronto.
Distributed by Random House, Inc., New York.

http://www.randomhouse.com/

Library of Congress Cataloging-in-Publication Data

French, Marilyn.
My summer with George / Marilyn French.—1st ed.
p.   cm.
ISBN 0-679-44774-1
I. Title.
PS3556.R42M9   1996
813'.54—DC20   96-10574
CIP

Manufactured in the United States

First Edition

For Barbara Greenberg with love

Part I

I

*T*hen George said: "The reason I don't want to get involved with you, Hermione, is that I don't want to end up a character in one of your novels."

My mind, or maybe my heart, stopped. We were in a cab heading crosstown to the theater. I'd gotten tickets to the off-Broadway production of *The Good Times Are Killing Me*. I was already anxious. I wanted to expose him to some northern culture but I wanted him to enjoy it—yet not be miserable myself. I knew I would enjoy this play because I'd already seen it. I wasn't sure he would. It was about a friendship across color lines. I feared his politics might be liberal in the way of other southerners I'd known, who thought they were liberal because they disagreed with their neighbors who supported caning juveniles, chopping off the hands of thieves, and burning people at the stake. On the other hand, some of the truest radicals I knew had originated in the South. I wasn't sure about George.

I wasn't sure about him because he specialized in double signals. For instance, at the very moment he was saying he didn't want to get involved with me, he was sitting half-assed on the taxi seat, facing and leaning toward me. Although this position must have been uncomfortable for him, for me it was most appealing: if the cab had stopped short, as cabs so often do, he would have been hurled right into me.

When my heart resumed beating, my mind tried to deal with his complexities. My mental wheels spun, but in different directions, leading to engine lock. I briefly considered questioning him to probe what he was *really* telling me, but I was terrified of discovering that he really meant *both*—he did and did not want to get involved with me. This conclusion I backed off from. After all, if he really meant both, we were trapped on opposite ends of a seesaw balanced in midair, unable to rise or descend. If he meant both, I should stop the cab right now, get out, and hand the tickets to the first pair of bored-looking tourists I passed.

I wondered if he was in the least bit pleased to be with me. I dredged up some jokes, blandishments, or gestures to amuse him, but discarded them all. The hell with it: if he didn't want to be with me, he didn't. Nothing I could do about it. I sat back and resigned myself. He sat back too, a smile of victory on his face. He had silenced me. From then on, the evening went well.

So it wasn't until late that night, in the quiet comfort of my lonely bed, that I considered what he had actually *said*. I sat straight up, realizing suddenly that he had lied when he said he was a fan of my work: if he had ever read even one book of mine, he would know that I couldn't possibly use him as a character.

I've written eighty-seven novels, which averages out to a little over two a year. This was because forty years ago, I had to write three or four a year just to pay the rent; whereas for the last twenty-five or so years, one a year has been enough to keep me in the highest tax bracket. Eighty-seven books may seem an inordinate number to you, but it is not uncommon for a romance writer. My publishers sometimes advertise me as the queen of romance, but the *real* queen of romance, Barbara Cartland, has published over six hundred novels. Of course, she's ninety, but even if I live that long, I won't equal her. Now that I've slowed down—indeed, taxes make it financially disadvantageous to be more productive—I'll be lucky to top a hundred.

But however many I may write, all my books are the same. My readers depend upon that. I have always modeled myself on Barbara Cartland. I repeat my plots and I stick to my myth, as she does. She's a champion of "real love." So am I, in my books at least. Cartland is even published in Russia and China, because her books are romantic but contain no sex.

All my books have three major characters; George couldn't possibly be any of them. There's the heroine, gorgeous, relatively innocent, and under thirty. I did try to stretch that a teensy bit in my twenty-sixth—no, twenty-seventh—novel, *Blood on the Sand*. (I refer to my novels by number rather than title, because it's hard to remember the titles, they are all so similar. But I remember that one because it required a lovely vacation in Morocco.) Anyway, in number twenty-seven, *Blood on the Sand*, I made the heroine thirty-three years old, and for some reason, it didn't sell as well as number twenty-five or -six. One can never be sure why these things happen, but to be on the safe side, after that I was careful to keep her under thirty. I often make her twenty-nine, a good age for a character or a real person, reusable for any number of years.

The other two characters are the hero and the villain. They are between thirty and forty-five and are almost impossible to tell apart. The difficulty of telling them apart *is* the plot, after all. the heroine shows her mettle by detecting which is the villain and which the hero. Both men are fantastically gorgeous, sexually adept, utterly in control, and full of daring, with a dangerous edge. No rational person could ever confuse my male characters with real human men. And George is eminently human-all-too-human. So how could he be one of my male characters?

The heroine of course benefits from the men's amorous expertise, but she never recognizes that, because she starts out a virgin and never becomes sexually sophisticated. To help or hinder her in her search for true love, I create minor characters: a wicked-stepmother type; a benevolent older man, an uncle or a guardian, or perhaps a threatening sexy father figure; a retainer, an old cook or gardener or housekeeper or neighbor, who is a simple uneducated person utterly loyal to the heroine. Sometimes, for a little frisson, I give the retainer a deceptive edge, making her or him apparently loyal but actually treacherous, or apparently treacherous but actually loyal. There are any number of changes a resourceful novelist can ring on this arrangement. In a few novels — numbers fifty-four and fifty-five, I think (written during a period when I was trying subtly to persuade my daughter not to marry the man she later divorced) — I created a wise kindly older woman: a grandmother, a teacher. My readers liked this figure; I got tons of mail from them, happily recalling wonderful grannies and aunties and teachers. But I didn't use her again. She made things too hard for me. After all, if a young woman took advice from a wise older woman, she wouldn't have the problems romance heroines have in the first place. A wise and benevolent older woman subverts the very fabric of the myth.

And I don't like to depart from the myth, which is the cutting edge. After all, the reason I'm the most successful romance writer in this country is that I understand the myth so well. The girl has to be alone. She has to face these men alone, to be as isolated with them as if she were on a desert island. She can't even have a good, reliable friend. She can have a friend who is true and loyal but utterly powerless and not very bright, or a strong, intelligent friend who proves false. She has to be on her own, helpless. Everything—the heroine's very survival—depends on whether she can tell the men apart, and since the beneficent older woman always can—otherwise, she isn't wise, is she?—her presence saps tension from the novel. You have to create all kinds of hard-to-believe plot ruses to explain why the older woman just can't tell her young friend the truth. Of course, in real life, older women do tell younger women the truth and are not believed. But it would undermine a fictional heroine to present her as being as stubborn and blind as real young women invariably are. Showing her as stubbornly blind introduces a note of realism that subverts the reader's reverie. Romance readers know they are in an illusory world, and that's where they want to remain.

Anyway, George didn't fit into any of my categories. So if he had read my books, he was lying about his reasons for not wanting to get involved with me. If he hadn't read my books, he was falsely claiming he had. In either case, why?

Oh dear.

I met George the first Sunday in June 1991, at a party at the Altshulers'. They have a house in Connecticut, right on the Sound, a splendid Victorian mansion with terraced gardens leading down to the water. It's a magnificent house—they've let me use it a few times when *Cosmo* or *Time* wanted to take my photograph. I try to suit my image to my work, so I pose for photographs in a hoop-skirted white dress, very low cut (the body has held up despite the years: the face has needed help), with a diamond necklace echoing the V neckline of the dress. Emulating Barbara Cartland, I wear a diamond tiara on my red hair (still red, with help), and I stand atop or below one of the Altshulers' glorious staircases, or lean gracefully on one of the terraces, flowering shrubs and trees rising beneath me. The Altshulers are flattered that I choose their house, and I'm pleased because the house makes me look like the queen I'm supposed to be—the Queen of Hearts, I'm called in the industry.

The Altshulers are rich but a little bored with each other and their lives, so they entertain a lot. They hate to be described as high society, which they associate with the old WASP world that would certainly not have embraced their Jewish selves. Rather, they think of themselves as cultured, a tinge bohemian: they do collect art, after all. So they invite mainly writers, poets, and artists to their parties. Years ago, this was easy: you could get all the poets, artists, and writers you wanted just by providing free booze. But nowadays, nobody drinks. They can guarantee an artist's presence by buying his (or her) work: they've begun collecting women, partly under my influence, I'm pleased to say. But they have to work for writers, who are not a very sociable lot. So they appreciate me, since I'm quite famous and sociable but not highly esteemed, so I threaten no one.

The Altshulers are old friends of mine. Janice Altshuler believes that I am *the* expert on relations between the sexes and confides to me all her problems and unhappiness with Leo. Leo believes I am an all-understanding, all-forgiving woman who instinctively understands men and their inchoate longing and sorrow. Leo doesn't confide in me; he just assumes I am his soul mate. And in fact, I do sympathize with Janice's complaints: I am endlessly interested in the small problems of a marriage, which are, after all, grist for my mill. My books are aimed at women like Janice, who never move to end a problem but suffer continually, year after year. And in fact I do sympathize with men like Leo, locked in their lifelong isolation cells, unable to articulate their own feelings or to understand anyone else's. I have had no difficulty remaining their friend because I have been careful not to get between them when they are quarreling. On the rare occasion when a quarrel breaks out while I'm visiting, I see to it that an emergency telegram or telephone call arrives from an old friend dying of cancer or on the verge of a divorce, demanding my presence in Arizona or Hydra. And for all these years, the Altshulers have been most rewarding friends: they offer regular invitations to weekends in Connecticut and parties at their Manhattan penthouse, and you don't have to return the invitations more than once a year or so.

The weekend I met George was a crowded one. Janice and Leo had just bought a Krakauer, and Justin Krakauer himself was going to be there. This news was a magnet for hard-to-get guests: at least a hundred people accepted for the Sunday party, and over a dozen were coming for the weekend: Justin and his lover, Mark Mahaffey, the beautiful young dancer; the writer Anita Heller and her lover, Elaine Kovatch, the theater producer; the journalist Ellis Porter with his wife, Marie; and the Moscones, a rich retired couple who were close to the Altshulers. The rest were single, like me — two painters, David Hoon and Mitch de-Wald, a sculptor, Willy Schlag, a society real estate saleswoman, Lillian Amato, and a banker, Margie Dent.

I enjoy watching people. It was a delight to see the famous, wealthy, arrogant, sophisticated Justin Krakauer twist himself into contortions trying to please sullen young Mark, and to watch Anita and Elaine spar continuously and viciously, with the venom only love generates. Marie Porter had long since been crushed into a nonentity by Ellis, who looked around in boredom for another woman to do sexual battle with and, in disappointment, found only me. The Moscones, on the other hand, really liked each other, and like the Altshulers, had long since accepted their differences. This made them peaceful and pleasant to spend time with. The voluptuous blond realtor Lillian and the banker Margie, a slim lovely woman in her forties, were also good company, and very discreet as they slid into an intimacy that was not consummated that weekend but I suspected would be in the not-too-distant future. I listened in delighted malice to two of the painters one-upping each other. David Hoon appeared to be trying to drive Mitch deWald crazy by disparaging all art before the late twentieth century; Mitch took on the task of defending the old masters.

"You are an ignoramus! You speak drivel! Giorgione is a master!" cried Mitch, holding his head with both hands, his chins quivering. "Consider just the draftsmanship!"

Over the course of the weekend, David quite wittily impaled every artist from quattrocento Siena through to Picasso (only Giotto, Goya, and Rembrandt were for some reason immune to his abuse). It seemed to me that he was really insisting that Western art—as he defined it—truly began with him, an assertion that drove Mitch wild. If he had seen clearly, even momentarily, what David was claiming, he could immediately have ended the argument by laughing. Instead, they went round and round. Rolling his eyes, Mitch appealed to all of us to agree that David was mad, a lunatic egomaniac, but no one else took David seriously and we were all enjoying his brilliant malice, as well as Mitch's outrage, so no one intervened.

The sculptor, Willy Schlag, was a soft-spoken hunched-over

middle-aged man with a tire of fat around his middle and a humble manner. He looked at me with round blue eyes and told me how much he admired and respected women. He said he was one of the folk, like Walt Whitman, part of the common mass of humanity. Eyeing David and Mitch, he said he hated artists who were nothing but walking egos.

I mistrust humble people. I believe they are monsters in the privacy of their own souls. In this case, I had some reason, because Willy sculpted winged bronze phalluses fifteen to twenty feet high and six to eight feet in diameter. Like Arp's eggheads, they were his claim to fame. I suspected that his name had traumatized him. The Altshulers owned one of his phalli. It stood in the center of the formal garden in front of the house, rather than in the back, on the water, where we spent most of our time. Thank heavens.

Willy quite took to me; perhaps he thought that being alone, I would be grateful for his attentions. But his "attentions" consisted entirely of informing me of his humility and bemoaning the failure of the art-critical world to set him beside Giacometti, where he felt he belonged. So much for humility. I had had to sigh and smile sympathetically at him for much of Friday night and Saturday. I determined to avoid him on Sunday.

George wasn't himself invited to the party, I found out later. He didn't live in the area; he was from Louisville, Kentucky, where he edited a newspaper. He had come north to a conference of journalists and was spending the weekend with his old college friend Edgar Allen, the actor, who brought him along to the party. Edgar, a southerner originally, was a tiny man with a sweet face framed by dark curls. He became famous in the sixties, playing the Merman in the counterculture play *The Little Merman.* He still appears in an occasional Broadway play or cameo film role. He lives near the Altshulers, in a tiny eighteenth-century house. Small as it is, its age gives it—and him—cachet. And in this part of Connecticut, cachet is everything.

The usual activities were planned for Sunday: sailing, boating, waterskiing, or swimming in the Sound. But most people just lolled in deck chairs making idle conversation, and drank and ate. I had an early-morning swim, then a roll and coffee on the terrace. Afterward, I went back to my room for a few hours to work on my little laptop computer. I like to work every day; it makes me feel I've exercised my insides. Besides, I cannot spend an entire day in company—I have to be alone for a few hours. Around two-thirty, when most of the guests had arrived, I put on white linen pants and a beautifully cut black linen top and went downstairs. Taking a gin and tonic and some little cheese things, I began to socialize. Willy eyed me from a corner, but I just smiled and turned to greet some people I knew.

I was standing near the huge windows facing the water, talking to Elliott Morris, the composer, when I saw a man standing alone, leaning on the railing that surrounded the balcony off the library. He was tall, with thinning blondish hair, and wore a white suit. When he turned my way, I saw he had a beautiful face, sweet and thoughtful in repose, but what struck me most was the dejection of his posture. I thought I had never seen such a disheartened human being, and my heart immediately turned over in sympathy. But then June Morris joined us, and the composer Elizabeth Harris, and I got caught up in the chatter and forgot him.

Several hours later, Janice grabbed out at me desperately as I passed her on my way to the bar. I was familiar with that particular grasp and the look on her face: she was about to foist someone who didn't mix well on her old dependable friend. She tried to pull someone forward, but he stood immobile, head sunk almost to his chest. "Hermione darling, I want you to meet Edgar Allen's dear friend—" Pausing, she turned to see if he was still there, obviously having forgotten his name. His shrinking wasn't obvious, it wasn't a physical motion, but it was palpable just the same. He didn't want to meet anyone, I thought. He was the man I'd seen leaning on the railing.

"George Johnson," he mumbled. "How're you." Janice fled and he looked around, fixing me with intense penetrating turquoise eyes. "This is a hell of a house," he announced in what seemed to be an angry tone. He was good-looking enough to be one of my heroes (if a little too old), but too intense. Heroes are never intense, only villains are. Heroes are bemused, a bit distant, given more to laughter than passion, except about the heroine, of course. But neither my heroes nor my villains are ever reluctant. They would not dream of shrinking from an encounter, as George did. They are always at the ready, sure of themselves, in control, oozing charm. Their bellies never hang a little over their belts, nor their ties askew, as George's was. But precisely the qualities that made George unsuitable as a romance hero made me breathe a little more quickly.

For if there's one thing I can't stand in people, men or women, it's a posture of control. People who act as if they have themselves and the situation completely in hand tend to take over every situation, take *you* over as if you were a child. Whenever I'm around someone like that, I tend to drift away—physically if I can, mentally if I can't. The appearance of total control is appealing only in fairy tales—adventure or military stories or romances, written or cinematic. In the make-believe world, people *can* have total control: the story makes it true. But in life, no one can possibly have total control. People who pretend to it are pretentious and fake, and I loathe them. You adore the hero who assumes control in the movies, because he really has the supernatural powers he claims: the movie gives them to him. Only godly power can make control bearable, can redeem it, and godly power is found only in fiction. George's obvious *lack* of control—his flustered manner, the discomfort he could not or did not try to mask—deeply appealed to me, a person whose social graces, painfully acquired over the years, conceal scars from self-inflicted wounds. So I challenged him with a smile.

"What do you mean, a hell of a house? A hell of a nice house or a hell of an awful house?"

"A hell of a *big* house!" he exploded, his head pivoting as he examined the ceiling, the staircases, the dining room, with its table that seated forty.

"Ah, yes, that it is." I dredged up the usual question for breaking the ice at parties. "How do you know the Altshulers?"

"Don't. Never heard of 'em. Who are they? Was that woman who grabbed me and dragged me over here an Altshuler?"

I laughed. "You sound as if you feel dragooned."

"I don't like being dragged—or dragooned," he said grumpily, looking around him warily. He returned to me. His eyes began to focus on me. "I'm visiting Edgar Allen. The actor—you know him? We've been pals since prep school. He's a hell of a good actor. Did you see him in *The Little Merman*? He was great. Terrific."

My mind, as always when I meet someone new, was whirring with deductions. That he was socially uncomfortable was immediately apparent. He had a strange vocabulary—very enthusiastic and male and American, full of *great*s and *terrific*s and *a hell of*s—the kind of language one hears from men who had problems learning to become men, who had had to learn how to speak something they consider the language of men, like boys who learn in prep school to call each other bro and invite each other to go out for a brewski. But since I had spent many years learning how to be a woman, I was not entirely without sympathy for such men. He sounded enthusiastic, sincere, and a little naive, like the open palm of a hearty handshake, suggesting good intentions, good wishes. His speech was the male equivalent of the lockjaw speech so prevalent among Connecticut matrons, or the gushing effusiveness of middle-class women in Atlanta or Charleston. I dislike fake tones of voice; I prefer voices that reflect reality, that reveal a bit of edge, bitterness, sorrow, anger. But George's display of innocence and openness seemed to me self-protective, masking and deflecting attention from the intensity that showed in his piercing eyes and the tiny, tremulous lines around his mouth. And those drew me mightily.

He'd gone to prep school. I always note class markers. That meant he'd probably prefer light chat, meaningless conversation. Most men liked to talk about sports—it was the only dependable subject, actually, with men—but I had cultivated an ignorance of sports as carefully as men cultivate knowledge of them, and I could not converse in that language. Politics was tricky, since one never knew, and I take politics too seriously to discuss it lightly. Money is a boring subject, and I refuse to discuss it *or* its markers—cars, houses, boats, acquaintance with Alan Greenspan or David Geffen. So all that was left was persons or the arts. Persons was safer.

At this point, I had merely a certain sympathy for and interest in George Johnson, a little quickening of attention, a heightening of the hormones, and it was easy enough for me, with my long, self-conscious training in party conversation, to extract the relevant facts about him. He'd been born in Louisiana but now lived in Kentucky and edited the Louisville *Herald*. He was, it seemed, in his mid-fifties (god, he looked good), and *he was not married* and *did not appear to be gay.* And—wonder of wonders in a man—he asked me questions about myself! I was always vague about my distant past and, if pressed, would lie about it. But I didn't need to lie about the past thirty-odd years. For that period, my record was socially impeccable.

"So you're a writer?" he exploded. "And you write novels! God, I respect that! I edit a first-rate newspaper, but I've always wanted to write novels. You know, in novels you can tell the truth about things. You can't do that in a newspaper, not really. You can tell certain facts, but not the truth. Well! That's great!"

I could be wrong, but I believe that around this point, his glance became a little brighter, he peered at me with more interest, even some intensity. Strangely, his way of speaking contradicted his appearance: his language suggested someone burly, muscular, red-faced, outgoing, his hand extended to greet every stranger; not a lanky, pale, delicate-limbed, slightly potbellied man.

"And I envy you your work. How thrilling to edit a newspaper! I would love to do that in my next life."

"Do it in this one. Come on down to Louisville, and I'll give you a shot." A half-smile played around his mouth.

It had been a long time since anyone had flirted with me, so long that I could not be certain that was what he was doing.

"That would be fun," I said, smiling back at him with a certain glint.

"Be great. We'd have a ball. Show you the town." His eyes glittered unmistakably. At least, I thought it was unmistakable. But then he looked around uncomfortably.

Time to backtrack, perhaps. I looked around too. "Is there someone here you'd like to meet? I know almost everyone," I offered.

He brought his eyes back to me. "Somebody said Ellis Porter was here. God, I respect him! That book of his on the CIA, that was great stuff—he really probed for that book, he broke all the taboos. I tell you, that book made him a hero of mine!"

"Yes, he is." I searched the room, finally spotting Ellis near the bar, talking to Martin Samuels, the publisher. From the look of them, this would not be a good time to interrupt them: Ellis was speaking intensely, and Martin was riveted by him. They looked as if they had just discovered mutual passionate love, although neither had previously shown inclinations toward the same sex.

"We could meander toward the bar," I suggested to George. "He's over there engrossed in conversation, but we could wait until they finish."

It took some time for us to get to the bar—the room was still crowded, although the party was several hours old. But Ellis's voice reached us even before we reached the bar.

"Fucking goddamned liar told me I was getting the highest advance any journalist had gotten since Woodward and Bernstein, and I believed him—fuck, you believe your agent!"

Martin raised his hand. "Listen, it was a damned respectable advance, Ellis! I don't know what Billy told you, but the advance was the best we could come up with—we worked the figures. I don't like to go into all this, it's so unpleasant, but your last couple of books didn't do all that well...."

Ellis's face was deep red. He seemed to be exploding and I feared he would have a stroke. "What kind of promotion did you give those books, Samuels, just how much did you extend yourself for them, huh? You didn't get me a *Time* interview, you didn't get me the *Today* show..."

"We agreed on an advertising budget of a hundred thousand,

Porter, and we abided by that agreement. We can't deliver major media, you know that, they're independent...."

Both men were yelling now, drawing the attention of half the room. I glanced at George: he was staring at them, open-mouthed. "Would you like to see the gardens?" I asked.

He nodded.

As I led him past the arguing men, Leo Altshuler stepped in between them, put his arms around them, and whispered something. But Ellis yelled even louder and smashed his glass down on the bar and stalked out. Martin stood transfixed. We moved toward the glass doors and down the terrace steps. We paused at each level while I pointed out the flowers growing there, the ones whose names I knew, anyway. We reached the dock. A breeze had sprung up. It had apparently sent everyone else indoors, but I found it refreshing.

"Ah, what a wonderful breeze," I murmured. "Would you like to sit here for a moment? Or is it too chilly for you?"

He looked at me blankly, as if he didn't know what *chilly* meant, or didn't feel anything at all and so didn't understand my statement. But he plopped into one of the gleaming white canvas deck chairs Janice kept on the dock. I sat in another.

"My god!" he said. He was quite pale.

"Sorry you had to hear that," I said. But then I burst out laughing. "And to think I thought they were making love! I should have known!"

"Love?" George repeated, horrified. "Love?"

I shrugged. "Pitching woo. You know." I giggled. "They seemed so passionate."

"And here *I* thought he was such a great guy, a great journalist!"

"Well, he is. A great journalist."

"All he cares about is money. How can he be a great journalist? He's destroyed my respect for him, I tell you that!"

"He was just talking about money at that moment. He cares about lots of other things. Writers get crazy on the subject of money. It's an occupational hazard. They work alone, the loneliness gets to them. They develop fantasies about other writers—who's earning more, who gets more publicity, sells more books, is better known. Money is the only scorecard. Don't be dismayed. Ellis is a decent man. I'll introduce you to him another time."

George shook his head. "No, thanks. Umm-umm. No." He kept shaking his head. Suddenly, he stopped and stared at me.

"You do that? Get crazy about money? Yell at publishers?"

"I've done my share of yelling in my life," I confessed, smiling, "mainly at incompetent cabdrivers, parking lot attendants, and other petty obstructionists. I've never yelled at a publisher, and I've never yelled about money—that I can recall. But I can imagine doing it, if I were ... anxious enough."

He was listening to me as if what I was saying really mattered to him. "I never heard anything like that in my life. Never. That was terrible."

I examined him with some interest. Tender soul, I thought. Better he should stay in Louisville.

It was then I realized I had already been imagining him moving to New York.

During the next hour, as George and I sat on the dock, he regularly exploded with enthusiastic invitations. Three or four times, he urged me to come to Louisville to enjoy its cultural glories, especially its theater. He invited me to the local summer theater that evening, to see Edgar in (what else?) *Our Town*.

"He's the narrator. He's really fabulous, he's great! You should see him!"

When it became clear that I did not intend to take him up on this, he fell silent. But only a few moments passed before he announced enthusiastically that at least I should see Edgar's garden. "You're interested in flowers, and he has a great garden—I don't know the names of anything, but he's a real gardener. His garden's not as big as this one, of course. But it's nice; you'd like it. I could show you the garden, then we could pick up a hamburger or something. I really want to get out of here; I don't like these people."

As the Altshulers' weekend guest, I would have been committing a social gaffe to leave the party, especially with a complete stranger. Moreover, I knew that for Janice Altshuler, the best part of a party was afterward, when a small group of trusted friends would sit around the living room having high tea— lovely little finger sandwiches and scones and oozy cream cakes, tea or coffee—and rehashing it. We all reveled in the new gossip, evaluating the clothes, the food, and any behavior that was in the least bit unusual. Tonight we would probably have to skirt the main bit of gossip—Ellis Porter's terrible breach of decorum—since he would be there. But if he had already decamped in shame, there would surely be an orgy of gossip. For me to defect from that crucial after-party session would be as close to unforgivable as any sin in the Altshuler catechism. Only a death in the family could excuse it.

But George had no idea of any of this, since I smiled in pleasure with each invitation, even the repetitions of invitations, as if I was taking them seriously. Indeed, I was: I took them as expressions of George's desire to see me again. This delighted me. Words kept running through my head: that there would be time, there *will* be time... "time for you and time for me, / And time yet for a hundred indecisions...."

Smilingly complacent, I sat gleaming at him.

He finally gave up, fell silent, and stared at the water with a furrowed brow. It was after six, and the sun was slowly lowering itself into the water, which was brilliant with reflected color. Suddenly, he turned and announced that if I couldn't come tonight, I absolutely had to visit the garden the next morning. Edgar would be home until he left for rehearsal for next week's play (*Harvey*, of course) at about eleven. George would be there until around noon. It was urgent that I see this garden.

But guesthood has unbreakable rules. Whenever I stayed overnight at the Altshulers', I returned to New York the next morning with Leo in his limousine. Leo looked forward to these sessions, the only times we were alone together. Although we always chatted easily enough, he never spoke personally during these drives. But I knew he felt they were our private times for communication. When I got out of the car at my apartment (he dropped me uptown first, then drove downtown), he would clasp my hand with particular fervor and kiss my cheek with special warmth. I could not abandon him.

"He always leaves at eight o'clock in the morning," I apologized. "He goes in every day. He's retired, but he has his hand in everywhere. He's on boards." That was all Leo did, as far as I knew. "I serve on a lot of boards, Hermione," he'd told me. I gathered that he—that some people—made money from being on boards. How, I didn't understand. The few boards I'd been on took up huge amounts of my time and money. They never *paid* anything.

"New York! You're going to New York?"

"Yes. I live there."

"Huh! I thought you said . . . what did you say? Didn't you say you lived in Bag Bar or something?"

"Sag Harbor." I laughed. "I have a summer house in Sag Harbor. That's on Long Island. But I have an apartment in New York too, and that's where I'm going tomorrow."

"Well, say! The reason I'm here, in the North—I just came to Connecticut to spend the weekend with Edgar—is to attend a conference of newspaper editors at Columbia, an international seminar. It lasts all week. So I'll be in New York too!"

His furrowed brow had smoothed; he seemed quite cheered. Eyes glittering, he gazed at me with a broad smile.

"How nice!" I glowed back at him. "So where are you staying?" I asked casually.

Columbia was putting up the participants in university housing, he wasn't exactly sure where. "Say"—he pulled out a notepad and a ballpoint pen—"give me your phone number and address, and maybe we can have lunch or something."

Edgar appeared behind George's chair. "Have to be off, old man," he said, "grab a bite before show time." He turned to me. "Say, Hermione, bunch of us're going to Donnelly's for a hamburger before the show. Want to come?"

"Yes, come!" George urged, standing.

I stood too. "Thanks, but I can't. I really can't."

"Bring the Altshulers," Edgar urged. Perhaps he knew their rituals.

"They'll be tired. They won't want to go. But thanks."

George stood there like a demand. "Ask them. Hell, *I'll* ask them! It'll be fun," he insisted.

"Please don't!" I held up my hand. I could imagine his importunacy swaying Janice to agree, thinking it was important to me, then resenting it afterward, resenting *me,* mourning the loss of the after-party gossip session, giving me the third degree about him, not all that pleasantly....

I just shook my head. "Sorry. It would be fun, but ..."

"Well, all right." George turned away reluctantly. "I'll call you in New York," he said.

The two men walked up the steps toward the house. I watched their silhouettes, one tall, one short, in the dusky light. They were talking in low voices, and their heels clattered on the stone terrace. They walked around the back of the house to the side lawn, headed for the parking area, and disappeared.

I sat down again and watched the water. Little caps of foam appeared as the breeze grew stronger, roiling the water, turning the calm Sound into a miniature ocean. It was exciting to watch, like seeing passion arise from tranquillity.

2

I lay in bed that night unable to sleep after the hashing-over session. Gossip is stimulating, and raking poor Ellis Porter over the coals (he *had* left early) had been especially so. We'd laughed ourselves silly. And I'd eaten too many sandwiches (they were delicious, and so tiny I gobbled them up without counting) and drunk too much coffee. Janice said it was decaf, but can I trust her? The food, the coffee, and the conversation all contributed to my insomnia, but the content of my awakeness was George. I couldn't get him out of my head. His urgency, his importunacy—it had been many years since a man had acted that eager, that *demanding* toward me. I tried to recall the last man who had pursued me, pressured me that way. Were any of my husbands that insistent? That doctor in Colorado, the one with the Jeep—he'd been really pushy. And the famous Greek movie director I met at the Opéra in Paris, whose name I could never remember. There had been others, but not in years, not since I'd hit my middle fifties. My experience with sexual pursuit had been unsettling: by the time I got used to men pursuing me, I was in my late thirties, when they were just about to stop. It didn't seem fair, somehow.

But it wasn't just George's importunacy. By itself, that never won me over—I never went out with the movie director, for instance. What turned me to mush was his dejection. Sad people touch my heart; they always had, women and men. Some of my best friends are deeply depressed. This has its downside, I have to admit. I get entangled in the idea that I can help them become more cheerful, and of course, I can't. A number of the men I'd married—my best marriages actually—had been on the depressed side. Charles and Mark. Even Bert, if truth be told, although no one could call that a good marriage. In his case, even depression wasn't enough....

But on the whole, I understand sadness. I sympathize with it; it is familiar to me. After all, my whole early life was spent in a depressed household, fighting off depression myself. I may be billed as the Queen of Hearts, but I am an ordinary hardworking woman. I may put on a flounced gown and a tiara and have myself photographed on the Altshulers' grand staircases, but afterward my very bones are tired. I didn't start out knowing how to behave in rooms of five hundred people—or even five, if they weren't family. In fact, I am often startled that I did learn these things: I don't know how I did. Like many of my friends, I'd created myself.

Although today I live in comfort, even luxury, I grew up poor. My family lived in Millington, a pleasant undistinguished town north of Boston. My father, Herman, was exposed to poison gas in the war—World War I, that is. He survived and returned home to marry my mother, Helen, and father five children, but he never really recovered his health, and after many years of illness, he died. Mother was left with five of us, ranging from twelve to two. I was the youngest. Father's illness and the Depression had depleted their small savings, and they had had to borrow against his life insurance and mortgage the house. Mother was in a pickle. We were too young to be left alone, so she felt she couldn't go out to work, and besides, she had no particular skills. She believed the only thing she was really good at was baking, so she started baking layer cakes and pies and other confections, and selling them for fifty cents apiece.

That was a fair amount of money during the Depression, when a pound of hamburger cost fifteen cents, but she was an excellent baker and used only the best ingredients—unbleached flour, four score butter, heavy cream, eggs, Swiss chocolate—all the things no one eats anymore. She was a mild woman who unexpectedly exploded on one or two subjects. Baking was one of them: her mouth would curl with contempt at the mere mention of bakers who used lard or Crisco. Mother's pies were as buttery as shortbread but lighter; her apple, pumpkin, lemon meringue (my favorite), and pecan pies were famous in the neighborhood. She was less imaginative with layer cakes, making only two varieties—a chocolate one with white icing and a vanilla one with chocolate icing—but she made a wonderful cheesecake and a luscious strawberry shortcake and the best cookies I have ever tasted. All our neighbors had enjoyed her baking, sampled at kaffeeklatsches or as gifts offered during illnesses or funerals; the neighbors spread her fame, and her business grew. She began to bake bread and rolls, turning the glassed-in front porch of our house into a full-fledged bakeshop. She made a counter by shirring a long piece of cloth and tacking it onto the front of an old table. At the beginning, we didn't have glass cabinets like real bakeries: the cakes and pies sat on the table on glass-covered pedestal dishes.

Our big old Victorian house had come down to Mother from

her Scots grandmother. It stood on the main street of Millington, a little Massachusetts town whose sole reason for existence, a textile mill, had long since vanished. Mother worked all day and into the night in the big old kitchen at the back of our house, baking, kneading, making dough. Jerry was twelve, and she taught him to chop up fruits and nuts, to knead dough and make frosting—a job she hated. She put my older sisters to work selling. At first, Susan, who was nine, and Merry, who was seven, were very self-important, and Tina and I complained to Mother that they acted as if they were the bosses of us. But soon enough the job became a burden to them, partly because the porch was freezing cold. Mother had storm windows made for the wide glass window panels; she put an electric heater behind the counter and moved our dining room rug to the porch floor. But the porch remained chilly. Susan's and Merry's hands and feet were always blue in the winter.

We all missed Father. Well, maybe not Father himself: "Father" was how we referred to our old life, what we called it. I have no memory at all of my father. But once in a while, when Mom went to bed early, we kids would sit around the dinner table putting off doing the dishes, and Susan and Jerry would reminisce about how it was when Daddy was there. They remembered Mom sitting at the kitchen table talking to them while they ate cookies and milk after school; and they remembered going outside to play every single day except when it rained. They had even gone to the beach. When I was five, that awed me: I'd never seen a beach. Jerry and Susan and Merry remembered Daddy walking down the long street from the bus stop after work. He repaired watches in a jewelry shop, but he wasn't working by the time I was born. In those earlier days, they said, Mom would have dinner on the table as he walked in the door, real dinners, with meat and potatoes and vegetables. And sometimes Daddy would play ball with Jerry after dinner or let Merry hold the hose when he watered the front lawn.

We children resembled our parents: Susan and Merry were square and sturdy, with pale skin, blondish hair, and brown eyes, like Mother; Jerry, Tina, and I were slim and small-boned, with darkish skin and hazel eyes (I always called mine green), like Father. Jerry's and Tina's hair was dark brown; mine was a sort of russet, which later turned quite red. Mother was taller than Father, and her height popped up in Jerry, Susan, and me. Merry and Tina were tiny.

But Daddy himself was gone, and Mother had vanished too, gone up in steam and the constant smell of baking cakes and breads. We could not live typical children's lives. But even with our help, Mom never earned enough to do more than pay the mortgage and the electric bill, buy coal and food. We didn't have a car or a telephone, we never went to a movie or had a soda at the drugstore. Most nights, dinner was canned soup or eggs. The only thing there was plenty of was unsold bread, cake, or cookies, which made up a large part of our diet. Mother invented a dish made of stale bread broken into little pieces and sautéed in butter with onions, parsley, thyme, and, if she had them, bits of sausage or chicken livers. We loved that. But mostly we ate leftover cake (we all had bad teeth), to the envy of our school friends. But with the perversity of children, we hated having cake for dinner, at least after the first twenty or thirty times.

The worst thing about our house wasn't the food or the lack of money, though: it was the mood. When I was small, Mom still smiled—she looked at us, talked to us, laughed at us. The family would often go into giggles as we worked together in the kitchen. But although her work became a little easier as we got older—Jerry took over the huge job of making bread, Susan and

Merry began to bake the layer cakes, and Tina and I helped tend the shop—Mom became sadder and quieter. I didn't understand why, and I resented it. I was a callow kid; I had no sense of how she must feel, seeing her life pass in that way. And she always told us that the only thing that mattered to her was us, her kids, our survival, our staying together. Believing her, and knowing we were trying so hard, I felt that the least she could do was be happy. At eight years old, I thought happiness was volitional.

When Jerry finished high school, he found a job in a huge commercial bakery in Bridgeport, Connecticut. Bridgeport was too far away for him to commute even if he'd had a car, so he took a room there. Mother accepted this; she seemed even to have expected it. But for my sisters and me, Jerry's defection was a terrible rending of family solidarity. All those years, the six of us had struggled as a unit to keep our family alive. We had watched our friends going to movies or football games or away on summer holidays, our faint envy offset by the conviction that we and our work were essential to our family and the family essential to each of us. Jerry's leaving breached this, even if he sent Mother ten dollars every week. And besides, we missed him. Jerry was the most fun of all of us, the one Mother loved most. He was the oldest; he'd heard the most laughter in his youth, and it was his nature to crack jokes and tease. And Mother's matter-of-fact acceptance of his leaving was silently subversive; it implied that the family was not the inviolable unit we had thought it.

Jerry's leaving had an immediate effect: in her sophomore year, Susan, who was three years younger than Jerry, signed up for the high school's secretarial course without telling Mother. And on her graduation day, as we celebrated with ice cream (a treat), she announced triumphantly that she was going to New York to get a job in an office.

This Mother did not expect. She cried, "You are what?" and

put down her spoon. Our mother, who never scolded or raised her voice, shouted, "You most certainly are not!"

Susan protested: Jerry had left, so why couldn't she?

But Mother just shook her head. "That's different; he's a boy. *Nice* girls *never* leave home until they get married.... Why do you want to leave home?" Mother continued, looking at Susan suspiciously.

Not understanding Mother's objections, Susan refused to accept them. There was a YWCA where she could stay cheaply until she got a job; Alice Morrell's sister had stayed there when she went to New York. And she said that she was a crackerjack typist and could take dictation and would get a job quickly and send money home. She would still help out, she argued.

That didn't seem to matter to Mother. She stopped speaking—to any of us. On the Sunday of Susan's departure, she lay in her darkened room with a damp cloth on her head. Merry and Tina and I alternated between tears and wild excitement as we helped Susan pack her clothes and her life's savings of forty dollars. We had never had a major conflict in our house; we kids might squabble, but Mother never scolded or got angry or even raised her voice. She had always said we were her angel children. Her rage and silence bewildered and terrified us. We went into her room just before Susan left, but Mother refused even to say goodbye. We walked Susan to the bus station, taking turns carrying her bags. I sobbed the whole way there and back. But after her bus left, we had to go home to make the bread and pastry dough. Mother never left her room at all that day.

Susan said Mother would get over it in time. She couldn't believe Mom would stay angry at her, the daughter who had worked hard and uncomplainingly in the bakery for nearly ten years. None of us guessed that our mild, sweet, vaguely anxious,

sad mother would go on regarding Susan as something un-
speakable for the rest of her life. The night after Susan left, I
found Mother sitting alone in the dark living room. I went and
put my arms around her and laid my head on her shoulder. She
patted my hand vaguely and murmured, in a voice gravelly
with rage, "Promise me you won't grow up to be a cheap slut
like your sister."

I pulled away in shock. "She's not a slut!" I didn't know what
a slut was, but I knew it wasn't good and I knew Susan *was* good.
She was my favorite sister, and if I, too, was a little angry with
her, it was only because she had abandoned me, like Jerry. I kept
thinking, Mom didn't get mad at Jerry. It wasn't fair.

The United States had entered World War II, and there were
lots of jobs for women. Susan got a job as a secretary in the pool
of an advertising agency in Manhattan. She found an apartment
with two other girls. She didn't earn as much as Jerry did in the
bakery, and her expenses were higher—a share in a Manhattan
apartment cost more than a rented room *and* meals in restaurants
in Bridgeport—but she sent twenty dollars home every month.
She always enclosed a letter with the check, but Mother never
read it or wrote back. Merry and Tina and I did, but we didn't
tell Mom, because after one terrible argument, Mother set her
lips and said she never wanted to hear Susan's name mentioned
again. Mother always wrote early to invite Jerry home for
Thanksgiving and Christmas, but she never wrote Susan, and
Susan never came.

This unforgivingness in Mother shocked us, like the discov-
ery that someone you've always known has an artificial limb you
never noticed. But it intimidated us too, which may have been
her purpose—conscious or not. None of us wanted Mother to
treat us as she had Susan. So when Merry was graduated, she

meekly asked Mother what she should do—work in the bakery, get a job in Millington, or go to a city for work. She too had silently taken the precaution of enrolling in the school's commercial course, and could type and take stenography. Mother set her lips and said it was up to Merry, that girls these days seemed to do as they pleased. Merry sighed and left the room. She never said another word, just took over as head baker.

But something went out of her. I saw her eyes that autumn as she watched her school friends go off to college or to Boston or Hartford for work. Only a few stayed in Millington; they got crummy jobs at Woolworth's or the luncheonette or the dry cleaner's, but at least in places where they could meet people (boys, that is). We met the same people every week, and they were almost all middle-aged women. We never had a full day off—on Sundays, when the bakery was closed, we had to make the dough for Monday's bread and pies. By now Tina and I were baking too. Occasionally we went to a movie, but that was our only outing.

It was after her graduation that Merry began reading romances. She found them in a little shop in town that bought and sold used books, mostly mysteries, adventure stories, and romances. She could buy a romance for a dollar or seventy-five cents, and sell it back for thirty or forty cents. Later, when paperback books came out, they were even cheaper. Merry began spending most of her allowance on them. I always knew when she'd bought one: after the dinner dishes were done and the bread dough was kneaded for the last time, she would go up to the room she used to share with Susan and get in bed, even if there was a good radio program on downstairs. Since I had already begun experimenting with my body despite my shared room (Tina was a sound sleeper), I suspected that Merry used her reading to arouse her imagination to the same end.

I had always done well in school and was pushed ahead several times, so I finished grade school and entered high school at twelve. I was younger than the other students, but I knew what I wanted. Saying nothing to anyone in the family, I enrolled in the academic course. I told myself that even if I couldn't go to college, I'd study what I was interested in. I loved Latin and French and math and English literature, and that's what I studied.

This decision probably marked the first appearance of my bad character. It didn't matter that I said nothing at home: the entire household had sunk into a somnolent state. Mother worked hard, ate meagerly, and slept; she didn't even prepare dinner anymore. On Sundays, she paid bills. We worried about her. We tried to get her to go out for a walk with us, but when she did, she would get tired fast. She'd start breathing hard and turn around and go back home. I always grimaced at her, sure she was putting on that breathlessness. She was just bored, I thought. She wanted to go home and sit in the armchair and daydream. I knew all about daydreams.

Mother wasn't the only depressed person in the house. Merry too had grown silent and sad. Our once cheerful, busy, hardworking house was bleak with depression, which hung over us all like a black umbrella. It grew even thicker after Tina was graduated and, without even discussing it, took her place in the bakery along with Merry.

Though closest to me in age, Tina was the sister I knew least. She was the quietest one in our family. Three years older than I, she was only a year ahead of me in school. I always thought she was a little slow, but her daydreams were ambitious beyond our imagining. We should have guessed, but somehow no one in the family was interested in poor Tina. She just didn't squeak loudly enough. We thought nothing of the fact that every year, she begged Mother to let her join the Drama Club. But rehearsals took too much time, evenings and afternoons too. Mother couldn't spare her, and refused. And whereas once she had refused us things sadly, with tears in her eyes, now she just forbade them in a dead hard voice that allowed no argument. Tina never complained, just looked more and more pinched.

Meantime, I went on taking academic courses and getting A's, and at the end of my junior year, when my English teacher, Mrs. Sherman, urged me, I applied for college scholarships. I told myself it was just to see, just to find out if I could win one. When, in the spring of my senior year, I got a letter informing me I'd won a scholarship to Mount Holyoke College, I wept. Somehow it was worse than if I hadn't applied at all. I knew that even if my tuition and room and board were free, I would need money for books, clothes, transportation, daily living. And I knew we were too poor to provide me with that.

After I stopped crying, I went to see Mrs. Sherman. I wanted her to know that she hadn't wasted her recommendation entirely. Maybe I wanted to brag a little. She listened with twisting mouth—a habit that I believed accounted for all the wrinkles over her upper lip. Concentrating on them got me through my recital without crying. At the end, she said, "Don't turn it down yet, Elsa. Let me see what I can do." As I walked home down the broad streets lined with trees that shimmered with just-opened little green bolls, my heart beat in little skips. Knowing it was a hopeless situation, I was full of hope. I told no one at home about it, just put on my apron and washed my hands and relieved Merry at the counter.

A week later, Mrs. Sherman called me into her office. The teachers in Millington High School, determined that I should go to college, had made a vow. First, they took up a collection, and gave me a hundred dollars for a typewriter, clothes, and books.

Beyond that, they promised to send me twenty-five dollars a month throughout my college years! I was overwhelmed by their generosity, and my predicament. My heart leaped, my tongue failed, my courage waxed and waned. Could I do it? How could I tell Mother?

All the way home, I tried to build up my courage. I had a right to a life. Didn't Jerry and Susan have lives of their own? Weren't Merry and Tina miserable sacrificing theirs? But what would become of Mother if we all did what I was doing? That was the moral problem. I wouldn't be earning anything. I'd be the only one in the family who wasn't contributing something. If Merry and Tina acted this selfishly, Mother would be destitute now that she was old (she was only in her forties, but she seemed ancient to us), after working and sacrificing all those years for us.

But I wanted wanted wanted to go. I had to go. I would die if I couldn't go. I couldn't go on living if I didn't go.

I knew that whatever I did would be a judgment upon me, would fix my character forever. I hadn't made a final decision by the time I got home— I was still mulling and weeping—but the minute I got into the house, I announced the whole thing. I crowed, I laughed, I jumped in the air and cried out for joy—I gave them no alternative but to celebrate with me, congratulate me. Mother was so touched by the teachers' act that she wept and hugged me. She was so proud of me, she said. Smiling, I swallowed their acceptance, not by a single eyelash flicker revealing my knowledge of my selfishness, my awareness that I had betrayed and abandoned them, my profound sense that my character was now fixed in stone, and it was bad bad bad.

My conviction that I had a bad character was reinforced at the end of my freshman year in college, when, like a punishment for it, Mother died. It was June 1948, and she was only forty-eight herself. Dr. McCrary told us she'd had angina for years. None of us had known about it, not even Jerry. Merry and Tina and I clung together, weeping, until Jerry and poor wrecked Susan arrived. Devastated, we all tried to comfort each other. Even when she was ill or depressed, Mother's will had held us together. For all those years, she made keeping the family together our first priority. And staying together had enabled us to survive. Now what would we do? Realizing that she must often have felt sick and weak over the past few years, we girls were overcome with guilt at the way we'd treated her or, worse, the way we had felt about her. We'd been irritable with her, sick of her depression, her constant weariness.

The night of her burial, we sat in the dark kitchen and tried to remember any moments of happiness she'd had.

"That lamb's-wool sweater we all chipped in for, three Christmases ago," Merry recalled. "She loved that, said it really kept her warm. Even when she had to go out to the porch."

"It was such a good color for her too, that light pink," Tina agreed.

We chewed cookies.

"Jerry's Christmas bonus the year after he was made floor manager. Remember, Jer?" Tina swiveled toward him. "She needed that money so badly, remember? That was the year we had to get an oil burner, when the coal furnace cracked. She was so proud of you, Jer."

Jerry smiled weakly.

"She was happy the time we went to Cape Cod for a vacation when Daddy was alive," Susan said in a nostalgic voice. "We stayed in a little cabin, and it rained, and she cooked out of cans on a kerosene stove, and the smell made me throw up, but she loved being there. She went swimming. Remember, Jer?"

He nodded.

"The day Elsa got her scholarship!" Merry announced. "She was really happy that day, and so proud of you!" All of them turned toward me with glowing faces. They were *all* proud of me. I burst into tears and ran from the room.

Yes, my name was Elsa in those days, Elsa Schutz. You can understand why I changed it. I chose Hermione for two reasons: I found it elegant, and it resembled my father's name, Herman. Since I couldn't remember my father, I was able to invent him, and over the years, I'd created a sweet loving kindly man I would want to be named for. I chose my last name, Beldame, because it meant beautiful lady— fitting for a romance writer. I have also published books under other names—Ariane Hart, Lorelei Lettice, Misty Marsh—but that was in the years when I had to write several books a year to earn enough to live, yet had to avoid seeming like a spouting faucet. But my sisters still call me Elsa.

We closed the bakery for the funeral and never opened it again. Merry and Tina packed it away, viciously dropping the fifty-pound bags of flour and sugar and baking powder into cardboard boxes to take to the orphanage a few towns away. They grunted as they lifted the heavy bags, and their teeth were set as if they were casting out something evil and cruel and dangerous. The five-pound blocks of butter and the jars of trimmings—jam for fillings, chocolate sprinkles, maraschino cherries, chocolate chips— they dropped on top, in a wild parody of a cake. I packed up all our unused cake boxes and bags and balls of string to take to the other bakery in Millington: no point in letting them go to waste. A new doughnut shop in town agreed to buy our glass-fronted counter for a hundred dollars. In a few hours, we dismantled the shop we'd spent years getting into its present near-professional shape. No one paused for even a moment of regret, except maybe Jerry, who ran his hand over the old table we once used as a counter (it was going out with the trash), a little nostalgically. But he'd had only six years of it, not fifteen, like Merry and Tina. And Mom.

When everything was gone, we sat down around the kitchen table. We didn't look at one another. I felt we'd thrown Mom out in the garbage, and I imagined the others felt the same way. It was as if Mom had become fused in our minds with misery and darkness, with boring, endless work that brought no reward beyond survival. We sat there as it grew dark. I was a little frightened: if we were capable of such rage, what else might we do?

But after a while, life roused in us. Jerry acknowledged it first. "I'm hungry," he said. There was nothing in the house to eat, so we walked downtown and had dinner out. In a restaurant. Well, a diner. It was the first time we'd ever eaten out as a family, the first time I'd ever eaten in a restaurant at all. Giggling with the nervousness of the forbidden, we ordered Coke with our dinner. For Mother, Coke was taboo: it was expensive and not nourishing, she said, a waste of money and calories. We didn't care about calories. In those days, we were all too thin. And that day, we didn't care about wasting money, either. We had gotten a hundred dollars for the counter, and even with Coke, dinner for the five of us came to only thirteen dollars.

At the diner, we began stumblingly to talk about what we were going to do now. It was a hard subject, because the truth was, Mother's death had freed all my siblings. Merry and Tina suddenly recognized that they could now do whatever they wanted to do. I saw them realize it, saw the joy, the terror, and the guilt of it hit their brains like a shot of dope. And Susan and Jerry would be able to spend their whole salaries on themselves. Susan was distraught, breaking into tears at the thought that she had not seen Mother in six years, that Mother had never forgiven her. She was grieving, but I believed she could not forgive herself for feeling happy that she could keep the thirty-five dollars a month she'd been sending.

Only for me was the new freedom lonely. Mother's death opened a door for them but brought me only a cold blast. I had selfishly chosen to have my own life, and I had it: but the center of my life had been cut out like the core of an apple. I felt like a paring.

Over the next few days, we tended to hide out from one another, each of us sunk in a new question: What do *I* want, just for *me*? We all felt selfish, wrong, defensive. We snapped at each other at the least thing.

We were especially depressed at the thought of giving up the Millington house, which had been in our family for four generations. This felt like a complete betrayal of Mother. But we could not afford to keep it, and the day after we buried Momma, we put the house on the market. Merry and Tina were whispering gleefully, plotting their futures. They were going to move to New York and get rooms at the YWCA until Susan's roommate Eleanor got married, at the end of the month. Then they would share Eleanor's room.

"After that, we're going to try to drive my other roommate, Audrey, out of her mind," Susan said.

"That's not a very nice thing to do, is it?" I asked tentatively.

"*She's* not very nice," Susan said tartly. "Ellie and I can't stand her. She never washes, and she has B.O. She leaves her clothes in a heap on the floor, and they smell up the whole apartment. I never would have accepted her, but I couldn't say no; she was Eleanor's best friend. Was. Eleanor can't stand her now. And once Eleanor leaves, it'll be unbearable. She'll be on my back all the time. Whining."

"But what will we have to *do?*" Tina asked, appalled. "To drive her out."

"Anything. Talk to her—endlessly—or don't talk to her at all. Play loud music, especially classical music; she can't stand that. Flirt with her boyfriends. Whatever."

Tina and Merry gave each other long looks. Was there a hint of a grin under their mournful aspects?

Susan would help Merry get a secretarial job. She might have to start as a typist, or even a file clerk, to brush up on her skills—she hadn't used them since high school, four years back. Susan was doing very well now: her boss was a vice president of the agency, and she was earning good money. For a woman. We were impressed with her clothes.

Tina looked vague when we questioned her, said she had no particular plans. Speaking in a low key, shrugging, she said she'd work as a waitress and take some acting classes, but when these last words came out of her mouth, they felt electrical. In an instant, we knew Tina's secret: she wanted to be an actress and had since she was in fourth grade. She had never said so out loud, but we realized we had always known. If we never acknowledged it, that was because it seemed so impossible.

Jerry seemed especially pinched and sad. His grief was the worst, maybe because he hadn't lived with Mother for nine years. He hadn't watched her progressive deterioration. Jerry did not talk about himself; it seemed he had forgotten how to talk to us. Sometimes he addressed us like hired help he could order around; other times, he spoke to us the way he spoke to Mother, with reverence and love, as if we were his superiors. He had trouble with equality. We had to squeeze information out of him. He said he was now assistant manager but that he really managed the whole bakery. Under our prodding, he admitted he'd been wanting to get married but couldn't afford it because of the thirty dollars a week he'd been sending Mother. Now he could marry. He had trouble describing his girlfriend, beyond saying she was pretty and nice and a good Catholic. After everyone else was in bed, I asked Susan why Jerry kept mentioning that Delia was a good Catholic, since we were not religious. Christened in our father's Lutheran church, we had never set foot in it again until Mother's funeral. Susan made a face, half grin, half grimace.

"It probably means she is insisting on virginity until marriage, and Jerry is going crazy with horniness."

"What's that?" I asked.

I couldn't get over the fact that for Merry, Tina, and Jerry, Mother's death was perhaps the only avenue to freedom. The cruelty of this awed me. It collapsed any notion I still had about a divine order that gave meaning to one's acts by distinguishing between virtue and vice, rewarding one and punishing the other. Momma had given up her life to enabling us to survive. She had been a saint, a martyr, the most unselfish person we would ever know. Yet her life had imprisoned us, her death had liberated us. This fact was unbearable.

It had freed them all—except me. Mother's life had centered me: her death left me homeless. I wondered where I would go summers and holidays. I was only seventeen, and a babyish seventeen at that. I felt like the orphan I was. I knew this homelessness was my punishment for being a bad person. I knew I deserved it.

3

*M*y restless body had still not managed to sleep when the birds began their clamor around five. It was too late to try to sleep now. I took a bath and packed my things. In Janice Altshuler's well-run house, coffee, toast, jam, and croissants were delivered to the rooms at six forty-five on Monday mornings, saving the morning people from having to think up conversation at that hour.

Leo dropped me at my apartment about nine-thirty. It was a beautiful June morning. I waved to Ko Chao over the roar of the vacuum cleaner, opened the apartment windows, unpacked my overnight bag and put things away, then made some coffee and sat down at my computer to work. My current novel had only a half-dozen chapters to go. I worked poorly for a while, until my eyes refused to focus on the screen. Turning off the computer, I lay down on the chaise in my study and slept until nearly two in the afternoon, when I was wakened by Lou, my assistant, announcing a seemingly urgent telephone call.

It was George. He must have called me almost as soon as he returned to Manhattan. This made my heart turn over with a shudder and a bang, like an old car being cranked up.

"Hey. How are you? Your trip in okay?"

How sweet. "Yes, fine. Very nice. A comfortable limousine and sweet Leo's company—what more could I ask?" I laughed.

"Who's Leo?" Was there a bit of a snarl in his voice?

"Leo Altshuler. The man whose house you were in yesterday."

"Oh, the little fat bald guy?" he said with (was I imagining it?) relief.

"Umm. I suppose he could be so described."

"So listen. You want to take in a movie?"

"Sure. When?"

"Tonight."

"Oh, I can't tonight. I'm busy. Sorry."

"Tomorrow night."

This was not going well. "Actually, the only night I'm free this week is Thursday. I'd love to go then if you're free."

"Okay. Thursday. You want to have lunch tomorrow?"

I laughed again. "Sure." I had to work—the book was due at the end of the month—but the hell with it.

"I'll come and pick you up," he said.

I was taken aback. In New York, no one picked anyone up. Ever. People met in restaurants, at theaters, at the concert hall. Picking someone up seemed very old-fashioned. It was far too humane and courteous a habit for New Yorkers. It seemed southern.

"That will be lovely."

If he didn't exactly act like a man in love when he came to pick me up for lunch the next day, he did act wildly excited. My apartment is on Fifth Avenue and has six rooms, three of which—the living room, the study, and my bedroom—face

Central Park. George, wide-eyed when he walked in, put on a country-boy enthusiasm as he wandered from one room to another, whistling low as he went. "What a place! What a view! I thought the apartment Columbia gave me was pretty spiffy until I saw this."

After he'd toured the entire apartment, he stopped in the middle of the living room, raised his head like a horse tensing to attention, and said in an urgent voice, "You mind if I look at your bedroom again? It is really something!" And strode off.

Now, what did that mean?

He returned bubbling with enthusiasm about the view and the room, and kept it up in the elevator and on the street. But he spoke only in general terms—how great it was, how terrific—and I had little sense of precisely what pleased him. We walked over to a little bistro on Lexington that had good light food. We both ordered salads. George was wearing chinos with a blue-and-gray-striped shirt that set off his blue eyes. I wore pale-green pants and a matching V-neck cotton sweater, hoping they made my eyes look green.

"You look really nifty, Hermione," he said, gazing at me with a broad smile. His eyes glittered.

I thanked him and asked about the conference.

"Well, it's the damnedest thing! You know, you come to New York, great liberal city, you expect to meet people who are sophisticated about race, religion, gender, but damned if these people in this seminar aren't the most uptight conservative bunch I've ever met—God, we're more liberal down in Kentucky!"

"Well, who are they? Are they New Yorkers, or do they come from all over?" I don't like to hear my adopted city slandered.

"Oh, they come from all over. A few of them are Brits, there's an Australian and a guy from Hong Kong. But the leaders are all

New Yorkers, and they sound just like the others. One guy had a cut on his head and a black eye, and someone asked him about it at the coffee break. Turns out he'd been mugged last Friday. So they got talking about poverty and cultural deprivation and single mothers, but you knew damned well they were really talking about *black* people. They talked as if blacks were the only people who were poor, or had babies without being married, or mugged people in the street. One of them even brought up the argument that criminals have a gene that predisposes them to crime. So I asked him if he thought the guys who arranged the Watergate break-in had that gene. Or Reagan and Oliver North. And he acted shocked, appalled that I'd say such a thing. He backed away from me as if he'd just found out I was carrying the plague. If you don't agree with them, they look at you as if you're a real subversive. And when they say crime, they mean street crime, not crimes committed by government figures, bankers, brokers. White-collar crimes aren't crimes—they're just common practice that had the bad luck of being caught.

"Even after a black editor, Darcy Meeks—a terrific guy— joined us, they went right on talking that way. They acted as if they expected him to agree with them. Damn!"

"Yes, I've heard that too, the new code, a whole new set of euphemisms for blackness."

"The Louisville *Herald* was the first paper in the South to hire blacks, and for our size, we have the most blacks and the most women of any southern paper today. People still talk about the South as if we were benighted, but I tell you, we're way ahead of most northern cities." He leaned back and lit a cigarette.

I somehow doubted that, but I didn't argue. I didn't even wonder why I didn't argue. "Are you going to persist in your efforts to enlighten them?" I smiled.

"Sure. Why not?"

"I wish I could hear you," I said, with what I knew damned well was a fatuous admiring smile on my silly face.

"No, no!" He sat up sharply. "You don't want to come!"

"What, are the sessions open?"

He backtracked. "There are some observers," he admitted uneasily. He looked away. "I could probably get you in. But don't come! I don't want you to come."

"Why not?"

"I'd be too embarrassed. No." He shook his head.

We moved to other subjects. I hadn't even finished my iced tea when George laid some money on the table and stood up. "Got to get back."

I wiped my lips on the napkin. "Oh! Okay."

"You can stay if you want, but I've got to get back."

"No, no, I'm finished."

He walked me to my apartment, explaining, "I'll just cross the park and get the subway on Central Park West." He stopped briefly at my building's door.

"Thanks for lunch."

"Sure. How about tomorrow? You free for lunch?"

"Yes. Yes." I nodded, confused.

He turned, striding off. "See ya then—twelve-thirty, okay?"

"Okay." I glanced at my watch. He had picked me up at twelve-thirty today, and it was one-thirty now. He had allotted exactly an hour for lunch.

I walked into my apartment excited and happy, but with just a tinge of unease. I was happy because he still seemed eager to see me, and because I liked what I'd seen of his politics, or values, or whatever you want to call them. I deeply believe you can't be close to someone whose politics you despise. But I was a little disappointed that he'd spent so little time with me. And I wondered how come he looked at me with what in any other man would have to be called desire but didn't even reach out a hand to touch me, didn't so much as brush my cheek with his lips, hello or goodbye? Men I'd met once did that much. Of course, they weren't southern. Maybe southerners had a different code of behavior. Maybe he was shy. Maybe he was a gentleman. And I hadn't made any moves toward him, either.

I let it go. I had to work that afternoon to make up for my nap the previous day, and I had a date for the ballet that night with Alicia Masterson. Maybe I could talk to her about it.

Alicia is one of my closest friends. She's a lawyer and very smart. She made partner in a prestigious law firm in only five years. We both love art and dance, and we get together every few weeks to see a ballet or go to a gallery or museum show. Alicia is stunning, thin, with high cheekbones and satiny dark-chocolate skin. Her black hair shines so, it looks silver in the light. She's had a variety of relationships—she was married to an African-American painter I never knew, and then to an Irish bard, a drunken total madman who was lots of fun. I understood why she divorced him, but I missed him. Since then she's had relationships mainly with women, usually artists of some sort. But she'd broken that pattern recently when she got involved with Adele Poniatowska, a high-flying bond saleswoman who spent her life traveling around the country giving speeches to groups of investment bankers.

Alicia and Adele were really in love; you could see it in their eyes and gestures when they were together. And because Alicia loved Adele, I tried to, but it was hard. Adele had made tons of money and was used to being truckled to; Alicia earned a lot of money herself and never truckled to anybody. It seemed to me that although Adele despised people she could impress with her wealth, she was a bit resentful when she couldn't. Because every once in a while, she'd pull a real superior act on Alicia. I'd seen it. Alicia never seemed upset by it, though. She overflowed with love; she'd laugh and hug her, say, "Give me a kiss." But Adele made Alicia unhappy by her frequent absences. When Adele was away, Alicia's eyes looked bruised.

Her eyes were bruised tonight. We met at the Joyce Theater and saw the new Eliot Feld ballet, which wasn't as exciting as we'd hoped. Still, it was a pleasant evening. Afterward, we took a cab downtown to Alicia's local in the Village, Chez Jacqueline, which served a magnificent brandade de morue, one of my favorite dishes. We began with asparagus vinaigrette, which I ate hungrily. Alicia dawdled over hers.

"Adele away?"

"Umm-hmm. Tulsa. What a place, huh?" She put a single asparagus tip in her mouth and chewed it. "Can you imagine the nerve of her, leaving *moi* for Tulsa?" She had a merry jingling laugh. She always sounded happy, and I always wondered how she managed it.

"She's a fool," I agreed. "Though I might understand her leaving you for Venice."

"If she were in Venice, I'd be with her."

"The two of you talk any more about moving in together?"

"She wants to, but ..." Her eyes teared; she wiped them with her hankie, then laughed. "I'd have to get a cat for company!"

She sent her asparagus back with only the tips eaten, and then she toyed with her main course, rare duck breast sliced thin. She talked a bit about a couple of interesting new cases she was handling—omitting names, of course—but conversation dwindled as we finished the bottle of wine, and I thought it might be all right to bring up George.

"I've met a man," I began.

She put her wineglass down hard. "Really!"

I smiled, but I knew my smile was more a self-satisfied smirk. I hated myself for it but couldn't control it.

"Well, I *think* so."

"Tell me!" Her hushed voice sounded awed.

I gave her a brief description.

"Wow, he's really pursuing you, isn't he?"

"Seems to be."

"Oh, Hermione, I hope it works out!"

"You know, I have this feeling about him. About it. As if it could really be ..."

"Really be ...?"

"Oh, you know. Serious. Long-term."

"Happily ever after," she said softly.

"Yes," I whispered.

"I know that feeling. I had it when I met Adele. I still feel that way about her. I love her to pieces. I'm mad for her. We get along so well, we like to do the same things, we both love art and dance, we even like the same books. We both like to travel—but I like it within limits!" She laughed again, even as tears sprang to her eyes. "But she's never there for me. You know, last week I had a little emergency. I had to go to the hospital—"

"*What!* Why didn't you call?"

"Oh, it was nothing, just a little ulcer attack, but you know me, great big baby." She laughed. "I thought I was having a heart attack or something...."

"Alicia, an ulcer attack isn't little! Oh, I wish you'd called me,"

I scolded, knowing perfectly well that she hadn't called me because I wasn't the one she wanted.

"It was nothing, really; they just kept me overnight. But the symptoms were unclear, so Ellen—my doctor, Ellen Langner—told me to go to the emergency room, she'd meet me there. She's really great. So I went over in a cab. Adele was in Dallas. And I thought, She's always going to be in Dallas. Or Tulsa. Or Los Angeles. And this isn't it, you know? This isn't what I want, isn't what I bargained for. Love everlasting I can promise, but only to somebody who's going to *be* there everlastingly. Or as everlastingly as anyone *can* promise to be. It's too painful. It's so painful that it poisons even the good times we have together. We do nothing but fight. She says I'm trying to control her, change her, ruin her life. She's lived this way all her life—well, anyway, for the last ten years or so. And she loves it, being on the road, meeting people." She wiped her eyes. "I'm the big bad bitch. And I start to feel like one."

I sighed. I reached across the table and took her hand. "Is there no compromise?"

"Well...," she said, a faint smile curling at the edges of her lips, "I called Adele from Saint Vincent's. But the next plane from Dallas to New York was very late; she wouldn't have gotten in until the morning. So she chartered a jet and flew back to New York. She arrived around eleven, came charging into the hospital, her arms overflowing with flowers, visiting hours be damned! She stayed with me all night, holding my hand. So"—she raised her huge warm eyes and smiled broadly—"it worked out fine!"

Little tease.

I spent another long, sleepless night, lying awake, but this time I was inventing futures, not recalling the past. I kept thinking about the warm gleam in George's eyes as he gazed at me over the lunch table, the interest he showed in everything I said, the shape of his long, graceful fingers resting on the table. I had wanted to lay my hand over his, but of course, I didn't. He was too spooky, a horse about to bolt.

My mind would not rest; it invented and discarded one scenario after another for George and me. I had us commuting, him coming north, me going south once a month, spending the time either at Fifth Avenue or my Sag Harbor house or at his wonderful, modern glass-and-wood house in the Kentucky hills. In an inspired moment, I decided he was offered a job by *The New York Times* and moved to New York. I knew he could not afford to live in my building, but he found a lovely airy studio on Central Park West, almost directly across the park from me. With binoculars, we could wave to each other across the park, like Woody and Mia. He didn't miss Louisville at all, because he found Manhattan so fascinating. We saw each other several times a week and spent most weekends together. He liked my friends and they liked him. Even my children liked him, understanding his curmudgeonly affection. We cooked together on weekends; our favorite dish was penne with a sauce of green and yellow peppers, tomatoes, onions, zucchini, and sausage.

Most mornings, I rise early, long before Ko Chao arrives at nine and turns on something noisy—the vacuum cleaner or the floor waxer or the dishwasher—long before my assistant, Lou, arrives at ten-thirty, bearing the morning mail. I have coffee and a croissant and read the *Times;* then I begin to work, concentrating without a break until noon. I keep the telephone turned off, treasuring the lovely silence. Thus I missed George's call Wednesday morning.

In fact, I didn't get his message until I stopped working, when

I picked up the pile of messages and mail that Lou had placed on the side of my desk. She had written that some unidentified man had said that something had come up and he couldn't make it for lunch that day. He left no number where I could contact him. He said he'd call later.

I felt bitterly let down. I'd been so high a moment before, about to dress for lunch, humming to myself, wondering what to wear—always such a delightful problem. I sank back in the chair and stared out over the park without seeing it. *Why* couldn't he make lunch? *What* had come up? I was not just disappointed but angry, mainly at myself. I knew perfectly well that I would stay in all afternoon so I wouldn't miss his call. I was acting like a moony teenager, something I'd never been when I *was* a teenager. I hated that. I couldn't get past my frustration that I hadn't picked up the phone when he called.

I was exhausted again, so despite my resolution against it, I took a nap after lunch. But I firmly instructed Lou to wake me if a George Johnson called. He didn't. As I dressed for dinner, I was grateful I was meeting Marsha that night. My friend Marsha Wolf loves the theater, and we had tickets for Lynda Barry's *The Good Times Are Killing Me* that night. Afterward, we would have dinner and talk. I needed to talk to someone wise and caring, who would understand what I was going through and could calm me down. Marsha is intelligent and compassionate without being sentimental. She exudes warmth. Her very voice embraces you. I was sure she'd comfort me.

Just the sight of my old friend standing in front of the theater warmed me. She's tall and so thin she's skinny. Her skin is as white as paper; her dark hair is cut short and hugs her head like a skullcap. Wearing layers of linen topped by a long, embroidered vest, she looked like a priestess for some ancient religion.

We embraced warmly, as always, and she put her hand on my

back as we entered the theater. "You look *fabulous!*" she said. "I know you haven't had a face-lift, because I saw you only a few weeks ago, but you look years younger! A new cosmetic?"

I laughed and shrugged off her question: I didn't want to launch into my problems until we could really talk.

The play was splendid, and we left the theater feeling liberated, the way you do after exposure to good art. We cabbed down to Orso, where I ordered vitello tonnato and cappellini with tomato and basil; Marsha wanted caprese and risotto with portobello mushrooms. I waited until the white wine we ordered was poured, before I said, "I've met a man."

Marsha, her glass halfway to her mouth, stopped dead. She stared at me. "You have?"

I nodded.

"Really!" she breathed.

Marsha had been married to the same man for thirty-eight years. She had hinted about flirtations, even affairs, in years past, but not recently. If she felt an occasional twinge of regret at opportunities forgone or no longer proffered, she never admitted it to me.

She smiled broadly, extended her glass. "Well, cheers! That's wonderful, Hermione! Tell me, tell me! Where, when, how, who?"

I clinked glasses with her and launched into a description of George, our meeting, his persistence and intensity.

"He sounds madly in love."

"Doesn't he? But he doesn't follow up. I mean, he asks to see me every day, but only stays for an hour. He makes dates and breaks them; he promises to call but doesn't."

Her kind forehead furrowed. "It does seem to have happened awfully fast. Do you believe in it? His . . . enthusiasm?"

"My head doesn't. My head is on vacation. But my heart and my body believe it."

"Ohh," she lamented.

"Yes."

We sipped our wine.

"I wonder if he's like that fellow Teddy Warden, the one Phyllis was sort of involved with for a while—remember him? He pursued her passionately for months, then, when she finally agreed to a relationship, he suddenly went off on an assignment in Europe that dragged on for months.... In fact, I don't know if he ever came back. Do you remember that?"

I nodded glumly. I didn't care for the comparison. I looked away and stared around the restaurant. We ordered cappuccino. She must have caught my mood.

"Or maybe he's like Martin," she suggested.

"Martin? Oh, Martin Goldberg!" I liked that much better. "Yes!"

Martin Goldberg had been married for years to a brilliant biologist, Elaine O'Hare. She developed cancer some years ago. After she was treated it went into remission for a year or two. But it returned and spread throughout her body. All her friends gathered around her, buoyed her with love for the entire year of her final illness. And throughout her illness, Martin tended her with utter devotion; he was so loving and kind and devoted that all Elaine's women friends fell in love with him, even the lesbians.

"Yes," I repeated. "But his problem was guilt at admitting he could love anyone but Elaine. There was a strong attraction between him and Annie even before Elaine died. I saw it. I think Elaine did too. I think it pleased her. She knew he'd be all right without her."

"And he and Annie are happy together now, aren't they?"

"Last I heard, she was having some trouble adjusting to mar-

riage. You know, she'd lived alone for twenty years after her divorce from Jack Steele. Said she'd forgotten how men expect to
be waited on."

"Umm."

Marsha had solved this problem, I knew, after years of strug-
gle. Stanley no longer expected her to cook his dinner every
night—or even be home for dinner—and a third party (female)
cleaned their house and did their laundry. But they had a high
income: Marsha was a highly paid technical writer, and Stanley
was a physicist.

"Your fellow might have had a bad experience with some
woman," Marsha ventured.

"Umm, I don't think George is grieving over anybody," I said
glumly.

"His behavior—his insistence—his *attraction* to you does
seem to have arisen terribly fast," she suggested apologetically.
"For people our age, I mean. It sounds adolescent, somehow.
You know, kids get crushes, but . . . how old is he?"

I tried to conceal the grimace I felt growing on my face. "Oh,
younger than I, but in his mid-fifties, I'd think. Not a kid."

She gazed at me appraisingly. I began to feel self conscious:
What was she seeing? Did I suddenly look much older? Had I
been looking older for a long time and she just noticed it? Hadn't
she said I looked fabulous, when we met at the theater? Of
course, that didn't mean anything. Women always said that to
each other. It was a euphemism for I'm happy to see you, I'm
glad you're still alive. Did she think I was a silly fool?

"Of course, you too have been"—she wiped her lips with her
napkin, searching for the kindest word, I thought—"precipitous.
You know, you don't know anything much about him, do you?"
Her voice was cool, measured.

She did think I was a silly fool.

This was my warm friend Marsha?

She put her napkin down with a kind of finality. "Well, you can only see what happens, can't you? It just feels a little unreliable to me. I hope he doesn't end up hurting you, my dear." She reached her hand across the table and placed it on mine, sympathetically.

That wasn't what I wanted her to say or do. "Umm," I mumbled, hating her, even if she was one of my best friends. I went home that night feeling battered—by Marsha, not George. Jealous, that's what she is, I thought. Nothing like this has happened to her in years. She can't stand that it happened to me. To think that Marsha would let jealousy destroy our friendship! It was devastating.

When I got home, there was a message from George on the machine, saying he'd been "dragged to lunch" by the dean. Chagrined, I thought that what he called coercion I called a better offer. He wanted to know if we were still on for the movies tomorrow night. He wanted to take me to see *Thelma & Louise,* which he'd seen with some of the editors the night before. The women had loved it, the men hated it, except for him; he wanted my reaction. The movie started at seven-thirty: he'd pick me up at seven. He didn't leave a number at which I could reach him, but said he'd call the next morning.

Why had he gone to the movie with other people if he was intending to see it with me? Why hadn't he left a number? Why did I always have to wait for him to call me? Suppose seven o'clock was too early for me? Suppose I'd already seen *Thelma & Louise?* What did he mean, the women had loved it? What women?

He wanted to keep control of things firmly in his own hands,

I thought. I could probably call the Columbia School of Journalism and track him down, but that might offend him. Besides, I was willing to cede control to him, if he'd just be a little more ... communicative. I decided to leave the telephone bell on next morning, even though this would interfere with my work.

The next day, ten people called before 9:00 a.m. George was not one of them. My irritation grew, hour by hour—irritation and anxiety. I felt helpless, a passive victim, and I cursed myself.

He finally called late Thursday afternoon, to say he was running late and could not after all come to my apartment. Would I meet him at the theater, Broadway and Eighty-fifth, at seven-fifteen? Again I felt absurdly let down, bruised, but I brushed away the feeling, concentrating on good cheer.

I saw him as I got out of the cab, before he saw me, and my hurt vanished. My heart leaped out of my body and flew to encompass him. Of course, I forced my body to walk to him in dignity.

He was wearing a white suit and a red-and white-striped shirt and was leaning against a mailbox on the corner in front of the movie house, waiting for me. His stomach hung over his belt, and his head dropped onto his chest; his whole body sank in hollow dejection. I longed to wrap my arms around his head and stroke his hair and lean my cheek against his and whisper that he was loved and could rest in that love.

I walked toward him, and while I was able to restrain myself from putting my arms around him, I could not restrain myself from touching him. I reached out and fixed his collar, which was folded up.

"What are you doing?" he barked.

I jumped a little. "Just fixing your collar," I apologized. "It's bent up." Vowing I wouldn't touch him again, I told myself not to take this personally. I recalled a lover I'd had years before, a beautiful young man with skin the color of golden mustard. He didn't object to being touched during sex, but he quite peremptorily stopped me from stroking him as we lay side by side afterward. I tried to believe that his upset had to do with his feelings about his color, not me. I tried not to take it personally.

Still, I never saw him again.

I brushed away my downheartedness, and we went in and found seats. He talked about the movie: it was great, fantastic, hilarious, he said. Later, as we left the theater, I told him I agreed with him—except I added that it was heartbreakingly true. I looked at his face, expecting him to be pleased that he'd pleased me, but he showed no emotion. We walked out into a mild summer night.

We made our way to a little Italian restaurant just a couple of blocks north of the theater. George wanted to sit at an outdoor table. I thought it was going to rain, but I did not say so. This was unlike me. I usually said what I thought. But something about him silenced me. I was so pleased he'd indicated a preference—it didn't matter what for—that I simply bowed before it.

We discussed the movie; we discussed other movies.

"What's the best movie you ever saw?" he asked.

"Oh, if I had to pick one—Bergman's *Cries and Whispers*," I said.

He was outraged. "What?" It turned out he'd never heard of it. He seemed to feel I was trying to humiliate him.

"You've never heard of it?" I was incredulous.

"We don't get those egghead films in Louisville."

I doubted that, but not out loud. Change the subject.

"So. Tell me about your life. Have you ever been married?"

"Four times," he said brusquely.

"Really! Me too," I confessed.

"Really?" He seemed dismayed.

I nodded.

"Four divorces?"

"Two divorces. Two of my husbands died. What about you?"

"Four divorces, but from one woman twice. My second wife was also my third wife. I married my first wife when I was young, in the service."

"Is that supposed to mean you were too young to know what you were doing?"

"Yeah."

"Umm."

"And you married the second twice?"

He grimaced. "She was gorgeous," he explained.

I studied him.

"And the fourth?"

"She was young—too young, I guess. She was great with my kid, my daughter. I thought Liddy needed a mother, and I thought she'd be a mother to her. But she walked out on me, just walked out. I never knew why. She just left."

As he said this, his voice edged into rawness. I would come to recognize this tone, which appeared only when he spoke of this last wife. Although she had left him over five years before, he was still apparently smarting from it. I wondered at pain that long-lasting. Maybe Marsha was right about him.

"So you have a daughter?"

His face lighted up, and for the first time, he spoke easily. He had raised his daughter himself. Liddy was a joy and a delight to him, bright, had done well in school.

"How did it happen that you got custody?"

"Her mother was crazy," he said. I would have challenged such a statement from any other man, but I said nothing. He adored Liddy, he had loved raising her, and she was terrific. She had done well at Radcliffe and then gone off and joined the Peace Corps. She was working in Ghana now; she loved Africa. She was doing good works. He was proud of her. She was twenty-four. She was great.

I smiled. "She sounds it. I have kids too—four of them." He expressed no interest in my kids. We were midway through our pasta when a sudden downpour drenched us. George handled our damp remove indoors—a test for most men, I think—with good temper. Still, once our watery dinners lay on a dry table before us, we could not face finishing them. We sat with dripping hair, shivering in the air-conditioning. I ordered a decaf cappuccino; he ordered coffee. I gazed at him and thought he looked a little tired. The evening was over, I felt. But we sat making conversation for another half hour, the way lovers do at the very beginning of an affair, when they are reluctant to part. At least, that was how it seemed to me. It was good, I told myself. Especially since, as we were saying good night in front of my building, he asked:

"You want to have lunch tomorrow?"

The entire world seems to be heating up these years—at least, compared to my youth. It was hot and muggy that Thursday night, but I didn't turn on the air conditioner because I dislike its noise. I turn it on only when there is no other way to sleep. Again I could feel myself starting to have a bad night. I lay naked on my cream satin sheets, while fantasies of George and me together played in my imagination. My body was hot, every one of my pores was open and parched, panting, noisily demanding nourishment. And what they wanted was George's hands on them. My poor starved body. My hands felt huge and empty, tingling with emptiness; they wanted to be on his body.

Then he was there, transported by magnetism. We had only to look at each other, only to *think* about the other, for our breath to come more quickly. Hot, with quick, shallow breaths, we turned our bodies toward each other. When they met, we jumped with electricity.

Each of us instinctively understood the other's body, knew where to touch: the soft places behind the ear, on the eyelids, in the crook of the neck and arm and leg, on the upper thigh near the groin. We moaned. Kissing, our mouths were unwilling to let go. Electric charges ran from mouth to groin to toes in each body in which body in both bodies. We pressed against each other, we could not get close enough to each other, we wanted to be inside each other, but we held off. We got hotter and hotter, we twisted and squirmed, we pressed and kissed and stroked, and only after a long time, when the tension was unbearable, did I rise up and sit astride him, and when I put him in me, he cried out in relief, and I rode him, slowly, slowly, bending to kiss his chest, his eyes. But we were both too hot, we couldn't wait, and before we wanted to, we exploded, hot liquid spouting out of us, we both screamed in pained ecstasy, I kept crying out, kept going and going, and he kept going for me, until I was completely spent and fell on his chest, he with his arms around me, my cheek on his breast, our bodies still together.

Oooohhhh.

4

$\mathcal{M}$ost weekends, I drive out to the country, to my Sag Harbor house. I leave early Friday morning, hitting the L I E long before the endless line of cars queues up for the Hamptons. But this Friday, my women's group was holding a birthday dinner for a dear friend, Mary Smith, so I agreed to have lunch with George.

He called around eleven to say he was running late. Could I come up to Columbia and have lunch there? At noon?

Of course I could, I said without thinking. But afterward I shivered: another cancellation, and after we'd had such a nice time the night before!

I had to race to dress: I didn't want to go in my jeans and T-shirt. It was a long trip to Morningside Heights, and despite my rushing, I was late. I didn't reach the coffee shop he'd described until almost twelve-thirty. George was sitting with four other people, three men and a woman. He introduced them to me as editors attending the conference. They were halfway through their sandwiches, so I just ordered coffee and a muffin. I listened as they happily dissected the conference. I didn't feel too left out, because every once in a while George would lean toward me and whisper some explanation of what was being discussed. He made me feel cherished, despite the awkwardness of the meeting.

A little before one, they all pushed back their chairs and rose.

"Today's the last day of the seminar," George explained. "They're giving us a cocktail party at five, so we have a short lunch break, one hour instead of two. That's why I asked you to come up here."

Inside, I froze, but I tried to control my facial expression. I stood, tossing some bills on the table for my half-eaten muffin.

"Oh, hey, I'll get that!" he cried.

"It's nothing." I shrugged.

He walked with me out to the curb. "How will you get back?"

"I'll take a cab."

"I'll flag one for you," he said, stepping into the street.

"It's all right. I can do it. Your friends are leaving," I said, nodding at their receding backs.

"Okay, then. Well, I'll call you!" he cried, striding off. He didn't look back.

During the nearly fifteen minutes it took to get a cab, it began to rain. When, finally, a gypsy cab stopped, I took it eagerly. I slid onto the seat, soaking wet, and leaned back, my head numb.

I was shaking with anger and hurt. I wanted to hurt him back. I wanted to leave him in the lurch, let him know what it felt like. I wanted to drive out to Sag Harbor this afternoon, strip off my clothes, and dive into the bay, letting New York—and George—roll off my body like a coat of sweat. He must have known earlier that today was the last day of the seminar, but he hadn't mentioned it. He must have known about the short lunch hour: why had he made me travel so far for so little? If the seminar was over, would he be leaving now? He said he'd call me.

When? From where? Louisville? What was I doing with this man? What was I doing with myself?

I decided to spend the afternoon working. But I couldn't concentrate. I kept jumping up to rearrange a file, water a plant, deadhead another, get a cup of tea. I wandered through my apartment blindly; my magnificent rooms could have been one long subway stop, for all the pleasure they gave me. Around four, I lay down on the chaise in my study and fell into a deep, disturbed sleep.

I woke feeling logy, reluctant to get up. Could I be depressed? That is extremely rare for me. I determined, as a matter of will, when I had my first child under rather trying circumstances, that no matter how unhappy I felt, I would not, like my mother, lay a black cloud over my children's lives. Whatever my problems, I would remain cheerful or at least stoical. To do this, you have to emphasize the hopeful elements in any situation or even, in some cases, invent some. In other words, you have to be able to lie, to others and to yourself. I had grown quite adept at this over the years.

My depression arose because my self-deceit was wearing thin: I was losing faith in George's attraction to me. His seesaw motions were starting to feel like a pattern, in which resided something deep and negative that would never be resolved but would simply continue. I was urgently fighting off an awareness of this. I felt, in regard to him, as if I were carrying a vial of nitroglycerin: if I dropped it, all of what I had planted in him, in our relationship, would blow up in my face. And I wanted to avoid that above all. I'd rather let him treat me shabbily than accept that failure. After all, I had only two choices: I could let myself love him and hope he would return it, thus risking disappointment or even serious hurt in the future; or I could retreat behind my prickly wariness and end this right now.

If I had been thirty or forty, I would have ended it then. Before my mid-fifties, I met attractive men with some regularity. I could count on meeting at least one every few months, and there were periods in my life when the world seemed to be populated mainly by amusing sexy men. There simply wasn't time for all of them, alas, but a light regularly went on in me, indicating that I was sexually alive. I relished the feeling.

This was no longer the case. Nowadays, not just months but years went by without my meeting a man who shimmered for me, who made the night brilliant. Partly this was because I had erected a new barrier to love—age. I created it out of cowardice, nothing else. It wasn't that twenty-odd-year-old boys no longer appealed to me (although, in truth, they no longer did). But mainly I dreaded being perceived as acting flirtatious or seductive toward anyone who might find my no longer young person repulsive. So afraid was I of finding my physical being a source of repugnance that I simply *erased* the young from my sexual vision, I deleted their existence from my sexual consciousness as completely as if they had been some other form of life, robots or chimpanzees, say. But of course, to expunge any class of people from consideration greatly reduces one's possibilities. Moreover, as I aged further, the ban silently spread from people in their twenties to those in their thirties; I was eliminating the most gorgeous people in the world, so of course I faced greatly diminished prospects.

I gave this matter considerable thought, but I always ended up making the same choice. Even if it meant feeling less than alive sexually and possibly even sacrificing some possible felicity, I would censor my vision, limit it to people within a decade or two of my own age rather than find myself reflected in the eyes of some beautiful young person as a ludicrous grasping old lecher.

Perhaps as a result of this policy and the generally uninspiring appearance of most (but by no means all—consider George!) people in their fifties, sixties, and seventies; or perhaps because desire does wane as one grows older; or because older people who remain vivid and interesting tend to be deeply committed to long-term relationships—the last decade of my life had been far less populated with sexual partners than earlier ones. The truth is, there had been none. And while I missed the frequent passionate raids, forays, and pincers movements from near strangers that I used to enjoy—missing, no doubt, because of signs of age on my own person—I was even more disturbed at the fact that I myself rarely felt drawn to anyone, rarely found anyone desirable. I missed feeling desirable, but even more, I missed feeling desire.

Yet I had felt drawn to George from the first moment I laid eyes on him, and felt desire for him the moment he looked at me with excitement. This feeling was too rare, too precious nowadays for me to let it go, even if grasping it meant I would eventually suffer—indeed, was suffering already. With this man, I was sexually reborn, reawakened, returned to youth and vitality. How could I not submerge myself in the feeling, clasp it to me like a dram of eau-de-vie, the water of the fountain of eternal youth?

I thought about all this as I dressed for dinner. I wondered if I would bring it up that evening.

I love my women's group. Women's groups are the most wonderful thing about living in New York or Boston. They do not exist in many parts of the world—although they would if women dared to form them. It just isn't customary in some places. I don't know how things are in Detroit or Cleveland, but if a French or German or Italian woman has no husband, she is likely to have almost no social life either. And most older women don't have husbands, so many lead very lonely lives. I have two communities: one in the city and one in Sag Harbor. I'm lucky enough to have groups of women friends in other cities and abroad too.

Just about all my friends are self-made women, but some of us are more so than others: Mary Smith and I have reinvented ourselves right down to our names. Thirteen years ago, Mary left her husband and academia and took up a new career as a photographer and bisexual. She purposely chose an anonymous name and won't reveal her original one, but ironically, she's made her anonymous name famous. As Mary Smith, she photographs scenes and people in such a way that the violence or hatred underlying them is just perceptible. She'll photograph a parent with a child at a moment when one of them is just breaking into rage, or the sky the moment before a storm breaks. So her name has become part of the language—"Mary Smithing" something means capturing emerging violence when it is barely perceptible.

Mary was turning forty, and her agent, Naomi Gold, wanted to throw a big party for her most important client. But Mary said it was bad enough to be forty without advertising it. I told her if she thought forty was bad, just wait. But she was immovable. So Naomi arranged this dinner instead.

There were to be eight of us—Mary, Naomi, Enid, Dotty, Babette, Hazel, Leni, and me. Mary, Babette, and Dotty are good friends of mine; the others are pals, people I enjoy seeing once in a while.

Babette Goodman is in her sixties. She's in the House of Representatives, a Democrat, ardent and mouthy and tough and effective. You can count on her to support every humane piece of legislation that breaks through the Washington fog and to fight everything that tends to make the rich richer. My friends and I are among the many people rooting for her to run for the Senate. So is her husband, Bob, who, she says, makes it possible for her to function. Bob raised their two boys, Bob oversaw the house, even though he has a law practice. They've been married for almost forty years, but they still adore each other. They are the kind of couple everybody else points to and envies. They are the kind of couple we all believe we are supposed to be but few of us are.

Dotty Dunn, the actor, is in her late thirties, the youngest member of our group. She has to go where the parts are, and since there are few parts for black women on Broadway, no matter how brilliant and beautiful, she's often away, in Hollywood or Europe or on location in some exotic place. She lives in a sinking gloom grace-noted by hope: it's wonderful how actors can sustain themselves by believing year after year that the next part will make all the difference, will make them a star. We all try to sustain Dotty in this hope, which may not be unrealistic, after all. She's a terrific actor. Anyway, she needs it. Dotty lives alone; she's been divorced three or four times but seems to live in the same kind of hope about the next husband as about the next part. I guess she's an incorrigible optimist.

Enid deMaille is closing in on fifty. A professor of French at Hunter, she's written several books on French feminism. She's successful in her field, even famous, but her life is permeated by bitterness. She and her husband used to translate French philosophy together; they did brilliant work, but Julian believed the brilliance came only from him, that Enid dragged him down. In time, he left Enid for a very young woman, a student of his who also worked on translations with him but didn't demand credit on the title page. The quality of his work with the younger woman was much poorer. It was a pity: Enid and Julian both still do translations, but neither is as good alone as with the other. What Enid can't get over, though, is not the lost gift but Julian's abandonment. Her face is sunk in permanent shock and disappointment, which is echoed in her voice.

Enid's best friend is Hazel Heron. Hazel became famous during the Vietnam War, when she won several prizes for her incisive journalism. Her war reportage was collected in a book that became a best-seller and made her rich for a while. She's fallen on harder times in recent years. Maybe nothing has inspired her as the war did. But she also has been involved with several men who lived off her, contributing nothing. She's in her fifties now and worried: her work doesn't command a high price anymore, she's lonely, and she's bitter toward men—and even more so toward women. It's sad.

I had never met Naomi Gold before. She turned out to be a pleasant-faced woman in her fifties, wearing a tight-fitting velvet vest and a leather skirt that just covered her crotch. She's very thin and has good legs, but good as they are, her body and legs are still fifty-odd years old. She is a photographers' agent and Mary's good friend. She was married for thirty years to a great photographer, Parris Gompers. His brilliant photographs and her brilliant promotion made them both rich and famous, and they lived the life of a dream couple, traveling everywhere, knowing everyone, invited to White House dinners, awarded prizes by foreign governments, that sort of thing. But he had left her a few years before for a very young woman, and all the prestige and acknowledgment went with him. Since she had always concentrated mainly on him, signing few other clients, she almost lost her business too. She built the agency back up—Mary's recent fame helped—but she remained hurt and betrayed, in a state of shock. She had long brown hair that hung around her long, thin face, and she radiated kindness. I thought I'd like to know her better.

Then there was Leni Hauser, a playwright, an effervescent woman with curly red-blond hair. Leni is the happiest person I know. She's full of laughter and amusing anecdotes; she has a warm outgoing interested manner toward everyone she meets, from street panhandler to Broadway producer. I've decided her happiness arises from having a lucky life: she has a wonderful supportive husband and three gorgeous feminist sons, and she knows everyone in the New York theater. If she's had a few problems getting her plays mounted, well, who hasn't? And as dramatists go, she's considered a success—she's had a play mounted at the Lucille Lortel!

We were meeting at Jezebel's, a West Side restaurant that serves soul food and southern cooking. Jezebel has draped antique laces and linens everywhere in her restaurant—over the piano, over standing screens and sofas, on the walls. When you enter the room, you feel you are entering the boudoir of a grande dame who lives in some extraordinary nineteenth-century Spanish-moss-hung mansion in a place like Sea Island, where everyone is lolling about, leisurely sipping mint juleps and listening to jazz piano.

Everyone but Mary was already there when I arrived, sitting at a round table in the back, and several of them waved as I walked in. Like all women's groups, it was voluble and explosive with laughter, and hearing them, I smiled. I was just seated when Mary came in. Mary is tall and slender, with extraordinary hair:

it is stark white, and has been since she was in her early twenties. With her young face and white hair, she is a striking-looking woman, and men stop her in the streets, or in stores or restaurants, just to tell her how beautiful she is. I once asked her how she expected to achieve anonymity, given the way she looks.

As she neared our table, everyone cried, "Happy birthday!" and Mary paused and preened, showing off a new satin patchwork-quilt jacket with black lapels. She looked gorgeous as she took her place at the head—well, of course it was a round table—at the symbolic head of our table.

There was busy conversation, ordering, sipping of drinks, and much laughter. Flanked by my friends, I caught up on Babette's news, then turned to Mary and got hers, then talked past Mary (who was talking past me to Babette) to Naomi. Socially practiced as I am, I was able to smile and laugh, despite my raw heart, which I tried to ease by ordering southern fried chicken with collard greens and mashed potatoes—the kind of food that is Jezebel's specialty. Mary ordered pork chops, another southern specialty, but most of the women stuck with fish and vegetables. I declare, it is no fun to go out to dinner with healthful eaters.

Dotty had a part in a new play that she felt had some chance of surviving for a few months on Broadway, a good part, she said, one that gave her a chance to show off.

"I play a real bitch, a seductress with a heart of lead." She laughed.

"Have you ever met anybody like that?" Babette asked. "In real life?"

"A seductress. You mean a whore?" Hazel interrupted.

Dotty admitted she would indeed play a prostitute.

"Are there any other parts for women these days?" Hazel asked the table at large.

"No, I want her to answer Babette's question," Mary urged.

Dotty thought. "Actually, no. Come to think of it."

"So how can you play it? What do you use for a model?"

Dotty shrugged. "All the other cold bitches you've ever seen in the movies, the theater..."

"I know a few you could use," Hazel said bitterly.

"Speaking of unbelievable characters"—Dotty laughed again—"what about all Hermione's heroines? Have you ever met women like them in real life?"

The table roared, "Oh, God! Oh, yes!"

"We're *all* Hermione's heroines," Mary cried. "Tender-hearted, innocent, trusting..."

"Easy prey for the passionate, gorgeous, aggressive, masculine hero..."

"Or villain..."

"Who wants only to get us in bed!"

"Nonsense," Enid said. "Once he's past thirty, he doesn't give a fig for bed. Or if he does, he just wants you to give him head. He doesn't want to fuck you! He may not even be able to! What he wants is for you to take care of him. Fix his dinner and do his laundry and tell him he's a good boy. Just like mommy did. The sex is secondary."

"Do his translating for him..." Hazel grinned at Enid.

"But don't ask to have your name on the title page," Naomi said grimly.

Enid's eyes welled with tears.

I did not want to sit through the latest Julian story, and Enid always had one. They could not seem to get divorced, those two: year after year they were in the courts, still fighting about one thing or another. Enid was in a constant state of outrage. I decided to change the subject. But the conversation was too thick and the laughter too loud for me to get everyone's attention, so I just spoke in a normal voice to whoever could hear me. "I met a man."

The entire table stopped dead. Seven pairs of eyes stared at me. "You did?" Mary asked sweetly.

"Does he have a job?" Hazel muttered.

"How is he in bed?" Naomi wanted to know.

"Is he married?" Enid said anxiously.

"Yes. Yes, I don't know, and no," I answered.

"You don't know?"

"We haven't made it to bed. It's a new relationship."

"How new?" asked Leni.

"How's five days?"

"That's new."

"And you still haven't gotten to bed? What's wrong?" Babette barked.

"Well, that's the problem. He acts eager to see me, he's asked to see me every day this week, but then he runs off after an hour. Or he invites other people along! Or he cancels!"

At this, the table exploded with talk. Everyone had had a similar experience and was recounting it to whomever she could get to listen. I put my head in my hands. Mary stroked my back.

"Patience, sweetie," she said. "So what's his name?"

In relief, I turned to her and poured out every detail of the sorry romance, including its effect on my bodily processes. She listened intently, laughing ruefully, stroking me, lavishing affectionate phrases on me. "Poor baby," she concluded.

Dotty had been listening too. "Yes. Poor baby," she said caressingly.

"And now," I moaned, "his conference is over, and he's going to go back to Louisville, probably, and I don't know if he'll come back north or if he'll ever call me again or not, and I don't know what this week was all about! I don't know what to expect, I'm sick with it, my stomach's in a knot, my heart feels like it's in a vise ..."

"Ambivalence, ambivalence," Hazel said angrily. "I'm sick to death of ambivalent men. All the while we lived together, Terry insisted he couldn't commit, said he didn't want to disappoint me the way he had his wife. Of course, that didn't keep him from mooching, living on me like a parasite. Jesus, I even bought his beer! Five years he spends writing the Great American Novel! I'm subsidizing him, he says; when it's published he'll pay me back. So what does he do? How does he shaft me? He doesn't finish it! Abandons the great American crock of shit and gets a job. And as soon as he gets a job, he walks out on me! So I say get rid of this creep, fast, *f-a-s-t*, ASAP! That's my advice."

There was a smattering of applause, and Babette opened her mouth. When Babette spoke, there was no possibility that anyone else could get a word in, so everyone fell silent.

"I don't agree. You really have it for this guy, don't you, Hermione?"

I nodded.

"Well, how often does that happen? I mean, there's sex as fun and games, and then there's passion, and passion is rare. It's certainly been rare in *my* life."

"What's rare?" Mary asked. "Once every five years? Ten?"

"Once. That's it. Once. But it was forever."

Every head turned to her in silence. Everyone gazed at her in awe.

"Well, that's you, Babette. That's Bob. You think that's not what we all want?"

"Yeah. How many times have I told myself, This is it! I'm in love and it's forever, like Babette and Bob."

"Come on! It can't be that unusual. You have to work at it."

"And how do you work at it, Babette? By going off to campaign, by spending half your life in airplanes, by spending the rest reading legislation, drafting legislation ..."

Babette did them the honor of considering their argument.

Dotty giggled. "Well, I don't know about anybody else, but I've felt real passion at least half a dozen times."

Mary groaned, echoing her: "Half a dozen."

"Passion, shmassion—give me a guy who's good company, buys his own beer, and helps support the household, and I'll be content," Hazel muttered.

"You and most other women," said Enid.

"Speaking of other women ..." Naomi held up her hand. "I want to tell you a true story. It happened to my friend Roz." She turned to me. "You know her, don't you, Hermione? Roz Walker, an editor at Saint Swithin's?"

"Yes," I said, and Enid piped up, "Oh yes, very slender dark woman? Didn't she have cancer?"

"Yes. She had breast cancer. The whole time she was sick, her husband treated her horribly—he blamed her for getting cancer, and he expected her to do everything in the house even during her chemotherapy, although she was sick as a dog. So she left him and stayed in a little sublet on Sullivan Street, just one room So then he said they were separated, and he refused to have his health insurance pay for her treatment. Anyway, she was in bad shape, financially, psychologically, physically, you name it, even after the cancer went into remission. So to help her recover, she went to a cancer therapy group. And she met this guy Allan Luykens, who was recovering from prostate cancer and whose wife had been treating *him* horribly during his sickness—well, I guess she'd always treated him horribly. They started by being sympathetic to each other and ended by falling in love. They decided to get married.

"So they initiate divorce proceedings, and Roz goes apartment hunting. They need a bigger apartment because Allan is staying with his mother on Staten Island and Roz is living in one room. She finds a real estate agent who knows the whole market, East Side, West Side, downtown, and who takes her all over. She asks Roz why she needs a new apartment. So Roz says she's getting married. So this woman is surprised, thrilled—you know: 'Oh, you're getting married again, how wonderful! How lucky!' Stuff like that. 'Cause she knows Roz has two grown children, knows she's been married before. The real estate agent has grown kids too, she's also divorced. It's one of their grounds of connection.

"But she keeps asking Roz about the guy she's marrying. How did she meet him, where did she meet him, what's he like? Of course, Roz parries the question. She doesn't feel like telling a complete stranger that both she and Allan had cancer. But the woman refuses to let up, so Roz finally confesses she met him at group therapy.

" 'Oh!' says the woman, standing stock-still. 'Group therapy! What kind of therapy?'

" 'Well,' Roz says slowly, 'cancer therapy.'

" 'Really!' says the woman. 'Where does it meet? What day? What time?' " Naomi looked around at the silent table. Mary had her head in her hands; Enid was staring at a teaspoon.

"So," Hazel challenged her.

"Women are really desperate. I think if Hermione has strong feelings for this guy, she should hang in there."

" 'A good man nowadays is hard to find,' " Dotty sang. "Or, as the immortal Mae West put it, 'A hard man nowadays is good to find!' "

Naomi was not amused. "Hell, I'm not talking about *good. Any* man is hard to find."

"You think the good ones are all dead?" Mary asked sadly.

"Or never born," Enid said.

"Or gay," Hazel snapped.

Aha, I thought. So that was the story with the last guy, Thomas. I'd guessed as much.

"Or married, I suppose," Dotty said. We all knew her last lover had been married and had promised to leave his wife for the whole six years they were together. He did, too, finally. For a twenty-two-year-old dancer.

"Who's married? Hardly anybody's married," Naomi said.

"The only married couples I know are gay," said Dotty.

"Well, you're in the theater," Hazel explained.

Mary stretched languidly. "I think Hermione should stick it out for a while too, but not because she's desperate. You're not desperate, are you, sweetie?"

I considered. "I thought I had a happy life until I met him. I thought I had a great life, the life I'd always wanted. It's just that meeting him triggered something. You know—the happily-ever-after button? And what is so upsetting is discovering how powerful it is. After all these years. After all those husbands and even more lovers...I never had this fantasy before. I don't recall having it before...."

Moans arose from various spots at the table.

"I thought I wasn't subject to such an absurdity. I thought that if I ever *had* been, I was past it now. If I did have it in the past, I didn't know it. I've certainly never had these feelings so powerfully, so irresistibly. I tell myself it's because I'm old. You know, when you're twenty or thirty or forty, it's really hard to imagine you can love someone for the rest of your life. But at sixty, you can, because when you're sixty, 'as long as you both shall live' doesn't seem all that long. It's thinkable! 'As long as you live' may be only five years—"

Shouts of "No, not you!" and "Twenty-five at least!" rose in the air.

I laughed and held up my hand. "Thank you, my friends, but you know what I mean. At this point in my life, I can conceive of loving just one person for the rest of my life. And I find myself fitting George into the rest of my life as comfortably as a bunioned foot in a nice broken-in running shoe. I have day-dreams about us puttering around together like a couple of old folks, sitting in front of the TV or on the swing on my porch at Sag Harbor...." I dropped my head in my hands, mock-weeping.

Laughter fragmented the group.

"I wonder if I still have that fantasy," Leni said softly.

"You have Grant."

"Oh, I know. But you never have these fantasies about the man you have a relationship with, the one you live with. They're always about someone new and unattainable, don't you think? The man sitting at the table across the room. Once you attain it, the fantasy gives way to something else, something far less romantic. Contentment, maybe, but not romance. Maybe just habit. There has to be a reason why I'm on Prozac."

I swung my head to look at her. Prozac? The happiest woman I know? I didn't feel I could ask about it just then....

"I mean, maybe the fairy tale is intended just to help us get through the days," Leni concluded sadly.

"You're supposed to be my friends," I protested. "You're supposed to help me!"

"Yes, but you're giving us all nightmares," Dotty argued. "If it could happen to you, the Sophisticated Lady of this group, if you could fall into this... what is it?—myth? fantasy? delusion?—then what hope have we? Maybe one of these days we'll all discover that deep down we are waiting for Prince Charming and believing that when we find him, he'll make us happy forever after."

Several groans and confessions: "Discover? We already know."

"I know I believe in it. Not with my brain, but with my heart . . ."

"No, it's with your imagination."

"Well, *I* don't believe in it anymore. Not at all!"

"Maybe it's just our generation." Enid sighed. "Maybe it was the period when we were brought up."

"We're not all the same age," I argued.

"Well, those of us over forty-five. We were raised to believe that all we should want and all we'd ever have was a husband, kids, and a house. And that if we got it, we'd live happily ever after."

"But Leni and Dotty have it too, and they're in their thirties and forties. What about you, Mary?"

"I like to think I'm immune"—she smiled—"but after listening to you, I won't count on it."

"What about younger women, women in their twenties?" Babette glanced around the table.

Heads shook with questions, murmurs of doubt.

I considered. "The only young women I know are my daughters and their friends. And heaven knows Lettice is still waiting for Prince Charming, without a doubt. She really believes some man is going to make her happy forever after. Despite having had two husbands and two kids. So is Stephanie. And Lettice's best friend, Sally. Oh! And there's Liz Margolis, out at Sag Harbor. She's searching desperately for Princess Charming."

"You mean it's universal?" Mary screeched.

"Hell, I don't know," I grouched.

"What about men? Do men have it?" Hazel asked.

"I was talking to James the other night on the phone," I offered. "I was telling him about George——"

"You tell your son your private business?" She was shocked.

"I do. And he tells me his. Up to a point. Anyway, I asked him if he had this fantasy. And he said, 'No, no. I don't.' Then he paused. 'But maybe I imagine that I can make someone happy for the rest of *her* life.' "

Female expressions of affection, oohs and ahs.

"Oh, that's just your son! That's just because James is such a sweetie pie. I don't believe most men feel that way," Dotty argued.

"Do a survey!" Hazel ordered Babette. "Have the government mount an investigation."

"Wonderful," Babette said nastily. "I can see the look on the face of the chairman of the Appropriations Committee when I tell him I want funding to do a survey to find out how many men believe that someday they'll meet a princess with whom they'll live happily for the rest of their lives. How many men do you suppose would admit to it?"

Catcalls and guffaws erupted, and the evening ended in hilarity.

That night, between 1:00 and 4:00 a.m., I sold my Fifth Avenue apartment. George had sold his big old colonial in Louisville, realizing enough on it to buy a three-room apartment on Central Park West. We decided to buy two apartments, one above the other, and build a connecting staircase. That way we'd both have privacy, but we could be together every night if we chose. Much of my night was spent in imaginatively enjoying what we did on the nights we spent together, but there was a limit to those activities, and practical matters surged into my brain.

First I decorated my seven-room apartment, then I decorated George's place. I wanted him to do it himself, but he claimed he wasn't good at it, that he needed help. I insisted he go with me, so I wouldn't pick out anything he disliked. His living room I did in shades of blue, the turquoise blue of his eyes, toning it down with grays and black. The walls were blue, the carpet was a blue gray (he didn't want Orientals), the couch was charcoal, the side chairs were different shades of grayish blue. I didn't use drapes but chose shoji screens and palms, which gave the whole room an airy Eastern feel. It was beautiful. For his bedroom, I reversed that scheme, painting the walls a grayish blue—it took me a while to find the perfect color—that matched the rug exactly. The bedspread was charcoal, and I sprinkled electric blue throughout the room—in the side chair, the throw pillows, and a few glass ornaments. I put shoji screens on those windows too.

When it was all finished, we wandered through it hand in hand. He was happy. He said he'd never had such nice rooms. We decided to cook dinner in his apartment that night. He said he loved lamb stew, so we took the subway downtown to Jefferson Market, where I could buy a breast of lamb, and I made lamb stew with carrots, onions, and dumplings with parsley—the lightest, fluffiest dumplings I'd ever made. They were delicious.

Still, after I finally fell asleep, I dreamed that I was walking to Zabar's to buy coffee and butter and cheese to take out to the country. On the grassy median strip on Broadway, two broken-down, ancient-looking bag ladies sat on a bench. One had no teeth; the other had only some tufts of hair. They were talking volubly, laughing wildly, with glittery eyes and blushing cheeks. As I passed them, one punched the other's arm and said, "You know what? Harry said I was good-lookin'! How do you like that! Good-lookin'."

"Wow!" the other cried. "Maybe he wants to marry you."

5

*G*eorge called early Saturday morning. "Hey. Wanna have lunch?"

"Today?" I could hear querulousness in my voice.

"Yeah. Come on! It's great out!" Eagerly.

"Okay," I said, not very enthusiastically.

"How about a picnic in the park?"

Oh! My heart tumbled a bit: such a romantic idea. I hadn't picnicked in the park since…since Mark. When I bought the Fifth Avenue apartment, I hired the architect Mark Goldman to modernize it, and during the planning phase, we saw each other regularly. We had to discuss the design and work out the details; later, we had to shop for bathroom and kitchen fixtures. But we spent much more time together than was strictly necessary, because we were both feeling that terrific edge of excitement that comes from desire. Often we went into the park to have lunch under a tree. Mark would arrive at my door with a wicker basket filled with pâté, cheeses, fruit, and French bread, or a salade niçoise or a chicken-and-potato salad he'd bought at Bon Marché over on Lexington. I'd pack my own wicker basket with chilled white wine, crystal stemware wrapped in linen napkins, and a large soft blanket. We'd walk across the street and into the park, leaving the paved walkways to wander until we found an idyllic isolated spot. That was in June too, 1971. Twenty years ago! Memories of those days, those feelings, flooded over me as I spoke to George from my desk facing the park.

"I'd love that."

"I'll get the lunch."

"Lovely," I gushed.

"What kind of sandwich do you want?"

Oh.

"Uh. Ham and cheese?"

"Whatever you want. What do you want to drink?"

"I'll bring some wine."

"I can't drink wine at lunchtime. I fall asleep."

"Okay. What do you want?"

"I'll pick up a Diet Coke. You want one? No? Okay. I'll pick you up at twelve. See ya."

He hung up. No lingering for him. Unlike Mark, who, during our courting days, could not bring himself to hang up the phone. And he remained that way even after we were married. Certainly we went on having picnics in the park. We had one two weeks before he died, even though he was terribly weak. He loved the park. And he was always romantic. At least, that's how I remember him.

George's idea of a picnic might be unimaginative and skimpy, but he looked fresh and bright when he appeared at my door. His eyes were brilliant and greenish, reflecting his green-blue shirt.

"God, this place is fantastic!" he exclaimed as if he had never seen it before. "Can I go look at your bedroom again? Do you mind?" He strode off down the hall toward my room, which was large and bright and overlooked the park. After Mark died, I found it too painful to enter the bedroom, and I slept in my study for a few months. Then I redecorated the bedroom in a style that erased Mark, that would not make me think of him, with English prints in lavenders, purples, and greens, a canopied bed and flounced slipper chair. It was obviously a woman's room. I wasn't sure just what George found exciting about it. I felt it couldn't be the view: after all, it shared the same view as the living room and study. I hoped his interest had something to do with me. But I wasn't at all sure of that.

"God, that's a gorgeous room. What a view! It's got the best view of the whole apartment," he announced, returning, smiling at me with those speaking eyes. I stood there and, letting them wash over me, smiled back, hoping my eyes spoke too.

"Ready?" he said.

It was a beautiful June day, perfect for a picnic, warm without being humid. Within minutes, we found a shaded grassy plot away from the walks and drives that meander through Central Park, and settled ourselves on the blanket I had brought, still in its old wicker basket. I poured myself a glass of wine from the chilled half-bottle I'd brought, while George cracked open his cola. I wanted to lie back on the blanket but very carefully did not. Instead, I leaned against a tree.

George seemed excited. His eyes were very bright, and his mouth kept curving into almost a smile. He drank deeply, wiped his mouth with the back of his hand, and leaned against his tree. "So. How would you like it if I moved up here for a while?"

I gasped.

"This guy, Warren Holt, he's an editor at *Newsday*. He was in the seminar, and he asked if I'd like to spend the summer as a guest editor there. What do you think?"

My heart really tumbled then. The whole summer! "That's great!" I cried.

"So what do you think?" he persisted, staring at me with those turquoise eyes. "You think I should do it?"

What was he asking me? Did he want objective advice or my feelings? I remembered an old friend, Oscar Deile, a political scientist who'd come up north to teach at Columbia for nine months and been miserable the whole time. Partly this was because his self-image was terrifically important to him, and he thought of himself as a liberal. But he was a liberal only as long as he stayed below the Mason-Dixon line. When he hit New York, he dwindled into a moderate, even a conservative on some issues. But it was also because he and his wife came from a small community that was warm and close-knit, despite its many vendettas, and they could not adjust to the rootless separateness of life in New York.

I decided to take an impersonal line. "Well, you have to think about whether you can stand it up here. In the North, I mean. I've known some southerners who couldn't, who missed the friendliness and close ties they enjoyed in the South. It's very different here. People are nasty—you know, bus drivers, supermarket checkout clerks, subway token salespeople. We don't meet each other's eyes on the streets; it's too dangerous. You have to consider what you would miss."

He shrugged. "Liddy's in Africa, anyway. I'd probably see Edgar more than I do now. But I want to know what *you* think. How do you feel about it?"

Was he serious? Was this a statement? Could I reveal myself now? I could feel my face softening, turning into an intimate face. He was staring at me as if my answer mattered to him, as if he was hanging on it.

"Well, I'd love it," I said softly, and smiled into his eyes.

He smiled in satisfaction and seemed to relax. He handed me

a sandwich and unwrapped his own. We were both having ham and cheese. He bit into his sandwich.

My mind was riding on a plane above the earth, like a blue line in the sky, above the lowest clouds but not quite soaring. It couldn't soar until he said something more concrete, but it was high, elated, ready to soar. He was considering staying in New York for a while, and he had intimated that my attitude might determine whether he did it or not. That was as close to a declaration of affection as a person could come without making one, wasn't it?

So what now? It seemed to me that having extracted an admission of—well, of something: interest at least, sympathy, affection—he owed it to me to offer an equivalent profession. Of interest or sympathy at least, if not affection. I hung on his words....

He turned and looked off toward the footpath. "Yeah, it might be interesting. *Newsday*'s an interesting newspaper, if you know its history...." He launched into it.

I listened. He finished talking when he finished eating. He wiped his fingers together, dropping crumbs; he dabbed his mouth with his napkin and swallowed the last of his soda. I recognized the signs. I glanced at my watch. It was one o'clock. He had picked me up at noon. An hour. Exactly. Again. "Well, gotta get going," he announced. "I've got a plane to catch."

"A plane!"

"Sure. Gotta go back to Louisville this afternoon." He stood and reached his hand out to help me up.

"What about the *Newsday* job?"

"Well, I've gotta work that out with the *Herald*. If I take it, I'll be back in a couple of weeks. I'll call you."

I felt as if every cell in my body were bouncing, not in the heat of rage, not seething, but shuddering with nervousness. I felt like someone who'd been kissed, slapped, hugged, then hurled against a wall. Curled up on the floor against the wall, bruised and bloody, I gazed, dazed, up at a man who was smiling at me with love. When I reached my apartment, I sat down on the cushioned bench in my foyer. I laid the wicker basket on the floor beside me and just sat there, my hands hanging down beside me. Lou and Ko Chao don't come in on Saturday, so the apartment was, thank heavens, empty. I could not have borne to speak to anyone.

After a time, I got up and went into the kitchen and poured a tall glass of water. I drank it like someone parched, someone who'd been lost in the desert for days. I stood there, looking at the kitchen cabinets, seeing nothing. I poured more water and carried it back to my study. I sat at my desk. My head was shaking back and forth, back and forth, as if I was saying no, no, no.

After a long time, my disciplined self stood up. It went to the foyer and opened the basket, shook out the blanket and folded it neatly and packed it away for another twenty years. I washed my wineglass and left it to drip dry. I rinsed out the wine bottle and put it in the recycling bin.

Then I went to bed.

I lay there unmoving, staring at the ceiling, my hands crossed on my chest like the hands of a corpse.

I tried to remember a conversation George and I had had at dinner a few nights before. I had asked him about his parents. . . .

"You know, I know nothing about you, really. Tell me about your past—your childhood."

"Why do you want to know that?" he barked.

"I'm interested in people's childhoods," I apologized. "Aren't you?"

"Nah. Childhood! Hah! I didn't have a childhood! I had a pair of alcoholic parents who once in a while came out of their daze and remembered they had a kid. I was brought up by my mammy; she was a servant, but she treated me better than my real mother ever did. We lived in South Carolina and were rich as hell—not that they earned it; it was all inherited. My uncle ran the business, a liquor business; my great-granddaddy or somebody back there had started out with a still and, after a while, made it legal. It kept our family and my uncle's afloat, but they ran it into the ground; you can't keep taking out and not putting back in. My uncle, he put it away pretty good too, the whole family did, and when he died, the distillery was swallowed up by a conglomerate. Years ago. By that time I'd been expelled from half a dozen schools and joined the air force. The air force straightened me out. Saved my life. Came out and went to college, journalism school. Stayed straight. Pretty straight. Drank too much. Got crazy. Don't do that anymore. I've been all right since then, except I have trouble with women."

"What was your mother like?"

"My mother was nice when she remembered me, but she didn't remember me very often."

I wanted to ask: Did she hold you, touch you? Did she put you on her lap?

"And your father?"

He shrugged. "He was a lush."

I knew that his brusque foreclosure of the subject had nothing to do with me, but still I felt slapped, shut out. I guess I had lived among women for too long. I was used to their ways and expected them of men as well. And a woman, if anyone shows any interest at all in her childhood, will open up and talk for hours, recalling major events, analyzing the tiny details that impinge upon a psyche, musing on the damage done, the benefits received, and the ambivalence that remains, poisoning her days. Women—all the women I know, anyway—*love* to talk about their parents, their childhoods, and their consequent psychic state.

So perhaps it didn't mean anything—anything personal about George, that is, or me—that he didn't want to discuss his childhood. Maybe men just weren't interested in such things. But it was tempting to begin analyzing him, to hypothesize that he'd been severely damaged by a father who ignored him completely and a mother who remembered him occasionally and gave him a hug, then thrust him back into the icebox. He might not know how he felt. I remembered how the Andersen fairy tale of the Ice Queen haunted me when I was a child, although until I was in my fifties, and having a conversation with my friend Molly, I didn't realize that the reason was she reminded me of my own mother. Yet I wasn't severely damaged. Was I?

But if George could not rest in love, had not ever in his life been able to trust it, he would never love me.

I dismissed this thought.

I tried to remember whether any of my husbands had enjoyed talking about their childhood. Charles had. Of course, he was Italian. I'd known a number of Italian men who were honorary women. But none of the others had, that I could remember. So maybe George's reluctance had no profound meaning.

But then, how to explain him?

I couldn't think. I couldn't feel. I held myself apart from myself. It occurred to me that I needed help.

I sat up and dialed Molly.

"You're there!"

"I'm here. I had an auction yesterday that spilled over till today, and I couldn't get away. I've been on the phone all morning. It was just settled ten minutes ago, and I'm sitting here wondering whether it's too late to go up to the country. So I'm here. How come *you're* here?"

"Mary Smith's birthday party was last night. And I had a lunch date today," I said.

"Oh. How was the birthday?"

"Fine. Stay here, okay? In New York. Don't go to the country. Have dinner with me tonight."

"What's the matter?"

"I'm upset. I need to talk to you."

"Of course I'll stay. What is it? What's wrong?"

"I'll tell you later. Where shall we eat?"

"Alison on Dominick?"

"Great."

"What time?"

"Seven-thirty."

"I'll make the res. See you."

Molly Baum is my agent, but she is also one of my best friends and has been for over twenty years. I started out with a male agent, forty years ago, but in 1968, dear old Harry Horn had a coronary and died. Molly is a quick, decisive woman who nevertheless thinks about things, questions them. She doesn't settle for surfaces. Molly claimed she knew what was good for me even when I didn't, and there was considerable evidence that she was right. She had warned me against marrying Andrew, she said he would abandon me, and she was right. Of course, she warned me against marrying Mark on the same grounds. Well, I suppose she was right again, but even if in the end they do both abandon you, there is a difference between a man who leaves you for a younger woman, after stealing your money and your house on Twelfth Street, and one who dies of pancreatic cancer.

Like me and my friend Mary Smith, Molly is self-created.

Her mother had been pregnant a dozen times and had had seven children when Molly was born. She had more children than she wanted or could feed—she worked in a sweatshop to support them—and Molly had to fend for herself from the beginning. When she was ten, her mother died, and the next year, her father did. The three younger children were tossed from married sister to married sister in the next few years. Molly was miserable. What she wanted above anything else was an education, but she didn't see any way of getting one where she lived.

Molly was smart and determined, though. She saved up money from baby-sitting, and when she had thirty dollars, she left Gary, Indiana, and came to New York. She was fifteen, and beautiful, and she got a job modeling in a wholesale fur house. She was subjected to the harassment young women in such a situation are always subjected to, but she was already tough, and got tougher. She let no man get within a foot of her—and in time won the respect of all the guys in her industry. Earning enough to support herself and go to school at night, she managed to get through college. Then she went to work for a magazine: she'd always wanted to be a writer.

Over the years, she drifted into agenting and into marriage. She's been married—and divorced—three times and has three kids. For twenty-five years, Molly has had her own agency; she sells mainly romance novels, even though she no longer believes in romantic love. After her last divorce, she said she was giving up love, sex, and men forever, and she's stuck to her word for the last decade. She says that women always get shafted in their relations with men, and that once they reach the age of sense (I think she means menopause), they should avoid them. She doesn't object to men falling in love, and she treats her married friends pleasantly, but I know she is more comfortable with women who are alone, like her.

Molly is short and blond, with a wild head of curly hair and a tinkly little voice that can give you a false impression if you don't know her. Men who haven't dealt with her before sometimes treat her like a flake, imagining they can bulldoze her into a deal. But she has no compunctions about putting people down, albeit diplomatically. And she has absolute integrity—something you can't count on finding in an agent.

We embraced and made chitchat, Molly glancing carefully at my face but asking nothing. I know I looked bad, tense and shadowed. I ordered a mâche salad and, my favorite at Alison's, a braised lamb shank with white beans, a dish I could never finish. I always took the remains home with me, to zap in the microwave some other night. We ordered wine. While we drank it, we discussed business matters. I have twenty different publishers worldwide, so there is always a lot to discuss. I waited until we'd finished our main course before I launched into George.

"I've met a man," I said.

"No!" She slammed her cup into its saucer. "I don't believe it! At your age! Don't you know better by now?"

"Come on, Molly, I need help. I really care about him, but he's driving me crazy."

"I can't believe you...." She was shaking her head from side to side, in despair.

"Well, I did, okay?"

I told her the whole story. It carried us through cappuccino and the brandies we ordered afterward. It carried us through the ice water we drank after that. The restaurant was beginning to empty before I finished. After I had recounted this morning's events—his momentous question and his immediate precipitous departure—I stopped, just stopped, my voice dwindling off....

After a silence, Molly asked, "Is that it?"

I nodded. I could barely speak.

"I'm sorry, Hermione," she said quietly, "but I don't understand what you see in him. I mean, he's *mean*. He's thoughtless and inconsiderate, and he doesn't care about you. He toys with you."

"You really think so?" My eyes blurred.

"What *do* you see in him?" she asked.

"Oh ..." I considered. "He's smart," I said. "He doesn't speak well—he's too busy sounding like a good ol' guy—but in fact he has an elegant mind. One day at lunch he discoursed on Clarence Thomas's career; not only did he know all the facts, but he had a perspective on the man, saw his strengths and weaknesses...."

She gave me a look. "Puh-leeze."

"Look." I was embarrassed. "When we first met, he made me feel—I can't believe it was only last Sunday!" I gasped. "It feels as if an eon has passed since then. Anyway, he pursued me so intently... he looked at me with such excitement... he made me feel desirable. I haven't felt desirable since Mark died."

She gave me a look.

"Well, all right. For ten years, though."

She nodded. "You've been alone a long time. As long as I have."

"And don't you feel... a little shrunk? A little dried up, less alive?"

"No! I'm much too busy. Besides," she admitted, "there are always these flirtations going on...."

"Okay. So maybe there have been a few men in the past few years who've acted interested...."

"Lots. Remember Wally Bedell?"

"Oh, please!" I protested. "That's what I mean. They weren't people I could feel desire for. You know, you get to our age...

well, *my* age"—Molly is five years younger than I—"and you feel desire for damn few people. Practically nobody. Who's attractive? They're all old, fat, sloppy, bald, and gray, they're failures wanting to whine or successes wanting to brag! Is there a single man you know that you could feel something for?"

"Not me. And that's fine with me. It's a relief."

"Well, I feel—I can feel—I do feel desire for George. In fact, I'm so hyped up with desire, I can't sleep...."

Molly sagged, both her body and her mouth. "Well, I'm sorry. Because I can't see—well, what do I know? Who knows. Maybe he'll come back, maybe he'll call, maybe you'll live happily ever after, for god's sake."

"Oh, that's the worst part! Never, never in my life...Well, you know, you were there when I married Andrew, when I married Mark.... You remember how tentative I was, how unsure that I was doing the right thing. I said, I remember—I told you just before the judge arrived—that I couldn't picture growing old with Andrew, and you said, 'Don't worry, you won't!' "

We both giggled.

"But this time! I can't sleep, I keep having these fantasies, I see the two of us together, our families together, spending holidays traveling, spending the summers in Sag Harbor together, me spending time in his house in Louisville—"

"He has a house in Louisville?"

I shrugged. "I don't know. He lives there. I put him in a gorgeous modern glass-and-wood ranch, all jutting angles and levels, with views of the forest. I put him in a two-story colonial, white with black shutters. I put him in a grungy apartment that needs immediate redecorating. By me. I put him—"

"Okay, I get it." Molly held up her hand to halt me.

"I put us in an apartment on Central Park West, floor over

floor. I put us across town from each other, me on Fifth, him on CPW. I put us in a house on Twelfth Street, occupying all four stories. Shall I go on?"

She shook her head.

"This has never happened to me before. I never had such fantasies before."

"That's only because before, when you were interested in someone, he was interested in you too. You didn't need to fantasize. You had reality."

"You think?"

"You've probably always had these fantasies. Without knowing it."

I shook my head. "No. No."

"Hermione!" she cried. "Consider how you make your living! How can you write these romances if you don't believe in them? Of *course* you believe in the fantasy of happiness ever after!"

I bristled. "I write them," I said coldly. "I don't believe in them. What do you think I am, an idiot?"

"Oh, come on." She placed her hand over mine, resting on the table. "I've outlawed romantic love from my life, but I sell romances, don't I? We all believe in that fantasy. All women."

"I *don't* believe it."

"It's the way we were raised," she argued, trying to take the sting out. "It's our background. Our socialization."

"Not me."

"What? You were different?"

"Yes. I wasn't raised the way other girls were. I wasn't raised to be dependent on a man. I never imagined living happily ever after; I was never allowed to entertain such a fantasy. Our lives were too hard."

"So where do your novels come from? Nobody could write them as well as you do without believing that stuff...."

"Don't try to butter me up," I muttered.

She gazed at me sympathetically and sighed. "I'm tired," she said, gathering her shawl about her shoulders. "I've been up since five, and it's after midnight."

"Molly, what should I do?

"Forget him," she said.

Sunday morning early, I called the garage and asked one of the doormen to fetch my Porsche. I made it out to Sag Harbor in two and a half hours, with a stop for breakfast; eastbound traffic was light on Sundays. But my body was tense and my driving jerky and distracted. I came close to having a couple of accidents.

George drove out with me. He'd never been to Long Island before and attended to my brief history of the place with interest; he leaned back and relaxed, listening to my tape of the Brahms clarinet quintet. He rested his hand on top of mine, holding the gearshift. We smiled at each other without speaking.

As soon as I drove into the Long Island village with its huge shade trees and quiet streets, my body began to relax. My house, a seven-room cottage, was on an inlet off Gardiners Bay. It had a screened porch along the back; beyond that, the lawn extended to a dock. The house was surrounded by meadows and trees, so that I had no visible neighbors. By then I'd lost George. I unpacked the few things I'd brought out (including the leftover lamb shank from dinner the night before), then stripped off my clothes and threw myself into the water. After my swim, I sprawled naked on a chaise.

I lay there in the warm sun with my eyes closed and tried not to think about George. I tried not to feel the nervousness that had infected my entire body like a virus, the uncertainty and dread and fear that warred with my desire, my sense that he desired me.

My skin throbbed and my breasts ached. My body was clamorous, it tingled all over. I felt like a sick person whose body is crying out for water. Mine was crying out to be pressed against another body. I tried to escape into sleep, but I dreamed about George. Waking, I pulled myself up slowly. I felt like a horny adolescent. It was humiliating.

I sat up and, feeling chilled, pulled the towel around me and ran to the shower behind the garage. I stood there letting warm water pour over me, wondering if Molly could be right, if I had learned a Cinderella view of life as a child. I had always thought of myself as having been forged into steel by my early life. From the day I decided to take the scholarship to Mount Holyoke, I had seen myself as selfish and willful, a woman who succeeded because she refused to sacrifice for others. If I ever made sacrifices for my kids, it was because I preferred the result of the "sacrifice" to the result of not making it. For example, I preferred to work hard and write an extra novel so the kids could go to camp summers rather than hang around New York City, bored and maybe in trouble. That wasn't a sacrifice; it was a choice. Still, I suppose my mother could have said the same about her life. Anyway, being willful and selfish seems to rule out having a soupy romantic view of life and love. Doesn't it?

Maybe not.

Part II

6

*N*ormally, I settle quickly into
the different rhythm of my life in Sag Harbor. In the city, I work
mornings and give my afternoons over to pleasure. After all, why
else live in Manhattan? After lunch at home or out with a business associate or a friend, I go to a gallery, a museum, or an art
exhibition. If I'm with a friend who loves window-shopping, we
might walk down Lex or Madison, gazing in shop windows and
occasionally buying something. Most nights, I meet friends to attend a concert or ballet or play or movie or lecture. I almost always have dinner out. My New York life is exactly as I had
pictured it, dreamed it, back when I was seventeen and imagining a life not dominated by misery. It was packed with social and
cultural stimuli, wonderfully rich if a little exhausting.

On Long Island, too, I spend my mornings writing, but then,
before lunch, I always go for a swim—even in the rain. After
lunch I garden or run errands: I have no assistant in Sag Harbor,
so I do my own marketing, go to the dry cleaner, pick up books
from the bookstore. I do not only my own errands but my own
cooking. I could of course hire someone to do these things for
me, but the whole point of being in the country is to do them

myself and enjoy the luxury of being alone in my house. It's a pleasure to touch the fresh vegetables at the farm stand with my own hands, to feel the firmness of eggplants and tomatoes, to smell the melons and cucumbers and basil. It's lovely to prepare a fine meal and eat it with only a good book for company. I find my country life restful, and there is no problem keeping in touch with affairs in New York. My assistant, Lou, who is a wonder of efficiency and sweetness, is as close as the telephone. When she takes her month's vacation, a friend of hers takes over.

I had instructed Lou to give George my Long Island number if he called while she was there, but I did not expect to hear from him right away—although it would have been nice.

Still, even without high expectations, I couldn't settle down to my usual country routine. I couldn't find a restful place in my mind. After years of experience, I usually could write even when I was upset; after Mark died, I was paralyzed and unable to write for only a month or so. But now I worked on the novel plod-dingly. Though it was nearly finished, I couldn't dredge up the slightest interest in my heroine or her plight. I had to force my-self to sit down at the computer every morning—a far cry from my usual driven writerly self. My mind kept manufacturing scenes for a different narrative, one starring me and George. Un-fortunately, I was still uncertain about the plotline and, above all, the conclusion of this narrative. So much depended on whether George was a hero or a villain: I had no sense of his mo-tivation. And motivation, after all, is the only real difference be-tween a hero and a villain. And here I was, after all these years, still unable to figure it out.

I would get up from my desk, throw myself on the chaise, and stare out at the trees. I'd lie in the warm sun after my swim and gaze out at the water, my body throbbing like a huge metronome.

Desire was constant in my life. I moved and walked in an erotic cloud. When I touched something, my hands tingled with the touching; I was keenly aware of the surfaces of things, the way you are when you are choosing a fabric. I felt the air around me, touching my body, my arms in my sleeveless blouse, my neck, kissing my face. I was a walking throb. This went on day and night. I could not sleep. I bought myself a sleeping mask. I took sleeping pills. I even got up and poured myself a gin and tonic one night. But my mind whirred on with these scenes, and nothing I did could stop it.

I kept seeing George and me, our mouths permanently swollen from kissing, full and soft as overripe plums. Our eyes were electrically connected; they set off sparks when their gaze met. Our short, shallow breathing was fast and uncontrollable. Our bodies were constantly aware of being alive, tingling with knowledge. George smelled musky, dusty, like dried peaches, and his damp skin felt oiled, perfumed. He leaned over and kissed my neck with his open mouth, and I wanted him to devour me.

It was really intolerable.

I sat on the chaise, sat so still I must have looked paralyzed. My hot heart, hotter body, felt familiar. You'd think I'd been in love often. Had I? As far as I could remember, I'd been in love with three of the four men I'd married, and with a few I didn't marry. Yet all my marriages had had bitter endings except the one that wasn't based in love. After all, when a loved man dies, it feels as bitter as his leaving you for someone else. I remember weeping to Molly after Mark died that I would never fall in love again, that I couldn't bear being hurt that way again.

And here I was.

But in love was one thing; full of romantic delusions was another. I had no memory of such things, even from my adolescence. I never lolled in my room as a teenager, modeling new hairstyles in the mirror while the radio played one lovesick song after another. Tina and I didn't even have a radio in our room—although I must admit the radio played constantly in the kitchen where we worked, and it offered strictly romantic music. That's all there was in the forties, and it was enough for us: we loved Peggy Lee and June Christie, Frank Sinatra and Dick Haymes, Tommy Dorsey and Glenn Miller. The popular music of my era was all of unrequited love, lost love, broken hearts. It was steeped in nostalgia, as if, young as we were, we were already doomed to lose whatever love we found—as if loss of love was preordained.

But my first experience of so-called love and marriage was far from romantic. Comparing my actual romantic life with the romantic books I wrote was laughable. A joke.

After Mother's funeral, after Merry and Tina went to New York with Susan, and Jerry went back to Bridgeport, I took a job at the doughnut shop—which was far less demanding than working in Mother's bakery. In fact, the doughnut shop was luxurious by comparison. I worked eight hours a day, five days a week, and when my shift ended, I enjoyed the long walk home, knowing I was free to read or study or listen to the radio, that I didn't still have to knead dough or ice cakes or decorate cookies or scrub down the porch. I was much alone that summer and often lay in bed wide awake, thrilled and terrified by the new sensation of having a room to myself and being alone in a big house. But being alone, being free, opened my mind to think about things I had never considered before.

Mother had had to mortgage the house when Father got sick.

This upset her so much, it changed her posture: she never stood quite straight again. Like people in former ages, her family had prided itself on never being in debt, and she never stopped worrying about making the mortgage payment every month. It was more important to her even than food, which is why we so often had cake for dinner. And before she died, she had paid the mortgage off. It came to me that, sick as she was, she delayed her death until she could burn that note. I hated thinking this. I wished she'd kept herself alive to be with us and see us grow and enjoy us, not to pay off a mortgage—even though I know she did it for us.

This kind of thinking reinforced my already bad character: contrary to everything I'd been taught by my schooling or by the culture around me, I came to believe that self-sacrifice was worthless and oppressive, and selfishness a positive good. No matter how I turned our history over in my mind, I could not reach any other conclusion.

I kept such ideas to myself. I felt my sisters would have found them—and me—monstrous. Jerry would probably have stopped speaking to me. They all worshiped Mother and spoke of her as a saint. They would have pointed out, as Susan did, teary-eyed, that Mother's worry and conscientiousness was responsible for our each getting $2,500 when the house was sold, that she had provided a head start for us, to set out in life. I wanted to tell them that I'd rather have had Momma. But I didn't. Depressed as she was, Momma had been the only solid thing in my life. I missed her more than my sisters did, because I had had less anger at her than they (not that they admitted, or maybe even realized, it). I could love her because I'd gotten out of the bakery.

Jerry had used some of his inheritance to buy a car, and he returned several times over the summer, to clean out the house and the piled-up junk in the basement and garage. He took the few decent pieces of furniture back with him, saying he'd keep them until we had our own places and could claim what we wanted.

After the house was sold, I wrote the teachers at Millington High and told them about my inheritance, offering, in all gratitude, to repay them and relinquish future help. But they wrote back that I was now an orphan and in a most vulnerable position. So they would continue the monthly allowance, suggesting I put what they called my "tiny nest egg" in the bank. I was a little insulted at their calling a sum purchased by my mother's lifeblood a tiny nest egg; it didn't seem tiny to me. But I was also relieved. I thanked them and justified the situation by reminding myself that even with their help I had to work. I had to supplement their generous allowance in a time when textbooks cost as much as twelve dollars and a pair of shoes twenty dollars!

At the end of August, the family gathered again, at Jerry's wedding to Delia Urtnowski. The house had been sold and almost emptied, and my sisters had rid Susan's apartment of its last roommate and were happily lodged together in New York, all with secretarial jobs. In the middle of September, I packed my bags. Jerry came back to Millington to see me off—he was such a sweetheart! After taking me to the train station, he would put the last bits of furniture out for the trash collectors and lock up the house for the final time. Alone, I boarded the train for Boston, where I would get the bus to school. I went back holding myself very still: I felt that moving fast or hard would break something delicate inside me.

At school, I became even more aloof and superior than I had

been. Everyone was used to me that way and ignored it. The truth was, I always felt like a spy—a mole—at Mount Holyoke. I was constantly expecting to be discovered for what I was: a person who knew nothing. Most of my classmates came from well-to-do or even rich families. I had nothing in common with them, and I knew they looked down on my manners and my clothes. I could tell. I felt vulnerable being so much younger than everyone else, such a baby: I had started college at an immature sixteen to everyone else's eighteen. I was still babyish compared to the others. And now I felt utterly alone in the world.

But I wasn't. My family worried about me, and called or wrote regularly. They all invited me for holidays. It was decided that I'd go to Jerry's for Thanksgiving and spend Christmas in New York. Jerry even came to pick me up and drive me to his house.

Jerry and Delia had a five-room apartment on the second floor of a three-story clapboard house, which they entered by an outdoor wooden staircase. Delia called the second bedroom her sewing room; there I slept comfortably on a daybed, sharing the bathroom with only two other people— a luxury for me. Delia and Jerry were sweet and generous, but Bridgeport was boring. So was Delia's family, with whom we spent Thanksgiving. In addition to Delia's parents, there were her two brothers and their wives and kids, her sister and her husband and children. The women cooked all day long. In our family, we never really celebrated Thanksgiving; cooking was what we did on workdays, so on holidays we opened cans of Spam, sweet potatoes, cranberry sauce, and peas to approximate the traditional meal. I was nearly thirty before I learned that some people enjoy cooking. The men sat in the Urtnowskis' little living room—they called it the front room—crowded around a box with a glass front called television. It was boring too; it showed women on skates pushing each other around and fat men wrestling.

During dinner—which I have to admit was delicious, full of things I'd never heard of before, like kielbasa, gołumbki, and jellied pigs feet—the men joined the women in talking about a host of people I didn't know. The entire family was passionately interested in the smallest details about these people—what kind of car the husband drove, where they spent their vacations, where they were going for Thanksgiving dinner, and how many children they had. After dinner, the men stood up and walked straight back into the front room without the slightest shame. They went back to the glass box, leaving the mess for the women to clean up, as if the women were their servants. I had never seen this kind of behavior before, except at Jerry's house last night. It never happened in our family: we all helped, Jerry along with the rest of us. But not here. Jerry went into the living room with the men, and Delia into the kitchen with the women. The pressure was on me to go into the kitchen too, and for once I did the right thing—and spent the next hour simmering in outrage, listening in furious silence to the stupid conversation as I dried dish after dish.

Finally, the women went into the sunroom to gossip some more about some more people I didn't know. I would have given anything for a book. There were no books downstairs, so I sneaked upstairs to look around. I found a bookcase in a narrow hall leading to two small bedrooms and pulled out one strange title after another, until I found one whose cover claimed it was a best-seller. It was by a man called James Branch Cabell, unknown to me. I went into the bathroom and locked the door. But soon enough, someone had to use the toilet. Hiding the book under my sweater, I darted out and into one of the tiny bedrooms. There I happily remained until Delia came up and found me. She was shocked and angry. She said this was a rude way to repay her parents' hospitality. She was very hurt and I felt terrible because she'd been so kind to me. She seemed to have forgiven me by the time I went back to school, but I vowed not to spend another Thanksgiving that way. Little did I know.

I looked forward to Christmas and being with my sisters, who, unlike Delia, shared some of my badness. After all, they had not scrupled to drive Audrey out of the apartment. Their rooms were small, but each of them had her own, unlike at home. We had our old problem—four young women sharing a single bathroom—but remained good natured, making jokes. Having been in Manhattan for almost six months, Merry and Tina acted like sophisticates, showing their greenhorn sister the great city, but it was soon obvious that they didn't know the famous sites any better than I did. How could they? Their New York was a place where you took the bus or subway to work, walked down the block to the supermarket for food for dinner, cleaned up after dinner, straightened up the apartment, washed your clothes, set your hair, and did your nails. There was no glamour in their lives. So they too were awed by the huge Christmas tree and the skating rink and the fancy restaurant at Rockefeller Center. I determined—I took a silent vow—that someday I would eat there. We rode the Staten Island ferry and went to the Empire State Building and walked down Fifth Avenue (in those days a great fashion street), passing Saint Patrick's Cathedral and the grand, forbidding public library at Forty-second Street.

On the weekend, we went to Radio City Music Hall for the Christmas show, featuring the Rockettes; just standing in line for two hours on a street broader and busier than any I'd ever seen before this week was enough to thrill me. We went to Chinatown for dinner, and I found the food, which I had never had before, odd but delicious; and to Little Italy, where I was introduced to pizza and saw many kinds of what we used to call spaghetti (my mother's came from a can) but they called pasta. Along with the Urtnowskis' Thanksgiving dinner, these meals were my first encounter with real food, which I had never known could be so delicious.

I knew I was supposed to admire Saint Patrick's Cathedral and Saint John the Divine and Grant's Tomb, but I didn't. What I loved was wandering through Greenwich Village. We stopped in a little Italian café to have some very strong coffee served in tiny cups. And one night my sisters and their friends took me to a place called Nick's, where they drank beer and I drank Coke and we listened to Dixieland jazz. We heard Pee Wee Russell, Bud Freeman, and Bobby Hackett playing "At Sundown" and "California, Here I Come," in ways I could hardly recognize. The music was full of joy and humor, yet profoundly sad at the same time. I fell in love with it. That was the best night of my entire life.

I went back to school inspired: I had seen a brave new world, and now I knew what I wanted in life. That visit was the start of my New York dream, my first vision of how I wanted to live— not a life you settle for and endure, like poor Momma's, but a desirable life. When I finished college, I would go to Manhattan. I would get a wonderful, interesting job and my own apartment and eat every night in Little Italy or Chinatown. I didn't yet know what kind of job, but I figured I was smart enough (I held my own at Mount Holyoke); I was used to hard work; and I was determined. Everything in my culture assured me that these were the prerequisites for success.

It was strange seeing all my sisters with boyfriends. Merry

and Tina had never had boyfriends before. I was seventeen and a sophomore in college, but I'd never been out on a date. My sisters' boyfriends, who had accompanied us to the Village and taken us to our Chinese and Italian dinners, were fun. These boys—well, I guess they were really men—seemed lighter-hearted, easier and jokier than girls...or, at least, than my sisters and me. There were no boys at Mount Holyoke, but the school held teas and parties, inviting boys from Harvard, Brown, and Yale. I didn't go to them. I said boys bored me, but the truth was, I was frightened and shy. I knew my clothes were not right; I didn't know how to dance. But after New York, I began to think it might be fun to meet boys, and I decided to attend a tea.

Before risking it, I broke into my bank account and took out a hundred dollars. Early one Saturday, I took the bus to Boston and went to Filene's Basement and bought a turquoise dress that looked like silk but wasn't, a black wool coat, and black ballet slippers. The dress was in the current style, the New Look, which was wildly popular—long and slim, with a peplum. But my shoes were not stylish: the New Look required platform heels, which made me teeter like a drunk on ice, and I couldn't walk in them.

The first tea of the season was for Harvard boys. I entered the room with my roommate, Irmgard. The girls all wore dresses like mine (thank heavens!) and heels, with white gloves. I was mortified: not only were my shoes wrong, but I didn't have white gloves. I wanted to turn around and leave, but Irmgard tugged on my arm. There really was tea, served from huge silver pots by two ladies with blue hair, sitting on couches at opposite sides of the room. You had to stand in line and wait, and then they asked you, Sugar? One lump or two? Cream or lemon?—things like that. I didn't know what to ask for, so I got what Irmgard had, tea with cream and sugar, and I hated it. But of course, no one would know if you didn't drink it.

The boys were all at one end of the room, wearing suits and ties. The two camps looked each other over and tentatively began negotiations—a process eased by a few people who knew each other already. In time, everyone was coupled, talking volubly. I ended up with a boy whose father manufactured automobiles. Buicks, I think. When he told me his father made cars, I thought he meant he worked on an assembly line, and I was surprised. I didn't think men who worked on assembly lines could afford Harvard. I thought maybe this boy was a scholarship student, like me, which made me feel easier with him. But I must have said something wrong, because the boy—I recall to this day that his name was Darnton (which didn't seem the name an assembly line worker would have chosen)—gave me an angry, supercilious look and said, what did I think, that his father was a mechanic or something? On the contrary, he said, his father was the head of it. The company that made the cars. The boy seemed to think this made him irresistible and almost divine, as if he was literally a prince. I was mortified at my faux pas and also by his manner. I hadn't encountered arrogance like this before. I started to feel dizzy and needed to go back to my room and lie down. But the boy was right about his irresistibility: the moment I left him, three girls moved in on him.

I don't know if such social events still occur. I doubt it; I think there are almost no single-sex schools now. Young people are much easier with each other and freer about—well, the word no one uttered in those days: sex. But my dizziness, which recurred at every coed social event I attended, arose from the tension induced in me by the ambient conflict between two different agendas, neither of which I understood or shared. I say this with the benefit of hindsight; I didn't understand it then. My agenda was fairly simple—to find a boy to have fun with the way my sisters seemed to have fun with their boyfriends. But that was not the dominant agenda of the room.

As I now know, the girls were looking for love, marriage, and happiness ever after—i.e., Prince Charming. The boys were looking for nooky. Moreover, as I also now know, this doesn't really change over the years. Some women may have periods in their lives when they, too, seek nooky, but the chances are they are hoping the nooky turns out to be attached to a Prince Charming who can become or replace a worn-out Prince husband or lover. And some men do reach a point where they allow themselves to acknowledge their yearning for happiness ever after and consider finding it in someone who is less than a perfect ten, maybe even less than a seven. But that's rare in heterosexual men.

At school, really rich girls and boys acted as if they had absolute rights. Girls seemed to expect lots of spending money; cashmere sweaters, pearls, and at least one fur jacket; to be picked up and driven around; and to feel taken care of—luxuriously if possible. Boys seemed to expect to own things, and every boy I met at Mount Holyoke transformed his experience into possession. Whether it was something he had done, like skiing or visits to England; or somebody or something he knew, like an author or mathematics; or something he really *did* own, like a car, everything was entered into some mysterious budget, in which a certain score denoted a winner.

In fact, the boys *had* done things—they had skied, sailed, played tennis or golf, traveled abroad. But so had the girls—my roommate had even ridden in steeplechases—who didn't treat the things they had done as possessions, items in a great scorekeeping, the way the boys did. Boys bragged about everything—their skiing, their sailing, their tennis, even their drinking. All of this overwhelmed me. Between my ignorance of the manners expected at such events and the paucity of my wardrobe and my pocketbook, I was uncomfortable enough to make excuses on the few occasions when a boy invited me to his school to a dance or to a football weekend.

The upshot was, I didn't learn anything about romance in college.

As the summer of my sophomore year approached, my siblings spent considerable time on the telephone, discussing my future. I, happily immersed in physics and French and Renaissance literature, was unaware of this until Susan called me one evening and told me it had been decided that I would spend the summer with Jerry.

I balked. I had not found Bridgeport even faintly interesting. Why couldn't I stay with my sisters in Manhattan? Or get a job as a waitress in a summer resort? Susan said there was no room for me in the Manhattan apartment, I could certainly see that: it was one thing to bunk in for ten days, but three months would strain things. And sure I could get a job at a resort, but it was already May. You had to have a job like that sewed up by spring: had I done that? I had to confess I had passively done nothing, leaving worries about my future to others. I liked Delia, didn't I? Susan argued. And Jerry wanted me to come. Jerry really loved me. Well, that silenced me. Because I loved Jerry too. So I packed my things and Jerry came and got me, and when he hugged me hello, I thought again how sweet he was. But he never talked, so spending time with him was difficult.

Delia worked in an insurance company. She didn't seem to mind my living with them. I suspected she was actually grateful for a little conversation, but she said she was grateful for my help with the cooking and the marketing and the dishes and the cleaning. Jerry left all the housework to her, just as if she didn't have a job. I couldn't believe this man was my sweet-natured brother, who had been so obliging to my mother. Not that he wasn't sweet to Delia; he was. He just never lifted a finger to help in the house.

Beyond that, he never wanted to go anywhere or do anything. He had bought a television set, and like Delia's brothers and father, all he liked to do at night was sit in front of it. It's true he was always tired: the poor guy went to work at four in the morning and didn't get home until afternoon. He'd take a nap, then flop in his new reclining chair and eat his dinner from a tray table in front of that blasted box. Apparently, he didn't love his work: his skin had turned gray, and he acted distracted. But he was mesmerized by television.

Delia never complained about this, never got angry at him. I felt sorry for Delia, who was a truly good person. Of course, I also had a little contempt for her, because of my bad character. But I scrupulously followed their house rules. I never discussed Jerry with her beyond his preferences for dinner or sports shirts. I never brought up anything more serious about her than her weight or her hairdo or the new lamp she'd bought. I pretended to be a good person. I behaved as good people were supposed to in 1949.

One afternoon, though, I slipped. It was a beautiful Sunday, and Delia, who never got out, begged Jerry to take her for a drive to Westport or some other lovely place—she couldn't drive. He was sullen and grudging; he didn't say no, but he didn't move. He hadn't shaved and he looked like a bum. Seeing Delia's crushed expression, I exploded. After all, he was my brother.

"Jesus, Jerry, what's the matter with you? You look and act

like a lazy bum!" I cried in exasperation. "You don't want to do anything or go anyplace! You barely carry on a conversation! You're a zombie! Delia works all week too, you know. She'd like to get out of the house on a Sunday!"

Jerry looked up and fixed his brown eyes on me like bullets. "Oh, that's easy for you to say, isn't it!" he yelled.

"What's easy for me to say?"

"You, you've always had everything! You don't know what it is to be tired, to work and slave for other people and never even see them! You all got to stay home with Momma all those years, while I lived in a shitty rented room and supported you all! You all got to stay home and be together and have fun, while I was all alone! You got to go to college!"

By this time, he was near tears, and Delia was edging toward him, sending me anxious looks. I didn't know what to do: I was flabbergasted.

"I didn't know you felt that way," I said finally. "I'm really sorry, Jer. But I have to tell you, we weren't having so much fun."

His eyes flared, but then he dropped his gaze and a tear appeared on his cheek. Delia put her arm around him, but he pulled away. I couldn't keep silent.

"But if that's how you felt, all the more reason to have some fun now that you're not alone anymore, now that you have someone who loves you, someone who wants to enjoy herself with you. Instead, you hold on to your sadness as if you loved it, Jerry. You act as if you love your sadness more than you love Delia!"

At that, he put his hands over his face and began to sob loudly. Delia was now sending me violent looks and waving her hand, urging me out of the room. I left, but I peered behind me. I saw her crouch down next to him, stroking his back and murmuring, and after a while he put an arm out and embraced her. Then I went outside.

I spread a towel on the back lawn and lay down with Blake's *Songs of Experience,* but I couldn't concentrate. I kept thinking about Jerry and love and sadness. I remembered how Jerry acted around Mother, and how she looked at him differently from the way she looked at us girls. Jerry was always lighted up inside when he was near Mother, and she had a special tenderness for him. With us, she was hard, almost tough, as if she was preparing us for ... war, really. For hardship. Delia looked at Jerry with the same kind of tenderness Momma showed; I wondered if that was what brought them together. But he didn't seem to return it. Not anymore, at least: he used to. I remembered how he'd looked at Delia during the wedding, with soft, flaming eyes. What had happened?

I closed my eyes, raising my face to the sun. Suddenly, I heard Delia whispering.

"Elsa! Elsa!"

She was standing over me.

"So sorry! Were you asleep? I'm sorry to wake you, but I didn't want to go out without telling you."

I sat up.

"Jerry and I are going for a drive," she said, smiling broadly. "Thanks!" she mouthed, not even saying it out loud. She bent quickly and kissed my forehead, then ran toward the house, turning back once to smile at me with mischievous complicity. Jerry had backed the car out of the garage; he had shaved. Delia hopped into the passenger seat, and they both waved goodbye. I sat there smiling, really pleased with myself. I think that was the first time I had the sense that I had done something good for someone else. But I did it by being bad, by breaking the rules. So much for goodness.

Jerry's apartment was on a bus route, which was convenient for me. I took the bus to town to find work, and in a couple of days

I found a job waitressing in a popular restaurant right on the bus line. I worked 4:00 p.m. to midnight, five days a week, thirty-five cents an hour plus tips. On a good night, I could earn five to six dollars, which Jerry said was the best money a girl could make short of going on the streets.

"Jerry!" Delia protested, blushing. My brother had certainly changed.

The restaurant, Mario's, served what in those days passed for Italian food in most of the United States: heaping plates of thick, soft spaghetti drowned in a sugary red sauce, with iceberg-lettuce salads piled high with Russian dressing (mayonnaise and chili sauce) or an "Italian" dressing Mario bought in huge bottles that contained not an iota of olive oil but lots of sugar. The waiters and waitresses got a spaghetti dinner as part of their pay, but the food took my appetite away. I lost a lot of weight that summer.

I started work in June, right after my eighteenth birthday. Jerry had brought a decorated cake home from the bakery, and Delia served it after a special dinner of my favorite foods—rib lamb chops, mashed potatoes, peas and carrots. She also bought me a beautiful new slip, pink satin with lace on the bodice. My practical sisters sent me five dollars in a card. Since all of this was considerably more than I was used to, I was content. I look back at my simple old self with affection. Nowadays, my birthdays are usually celebrated grandly, with parties for two hundred thrown by the Altshulers or small elegant dinner parties at the Four Seasons or Chanterelle hosted by my publisher Heartbreak House, or intimate dinners at charming out-of-the way places organized by Molly. Charles, my second husband, used to take me to Martinique or Venice for my birthday, and Andrew, my third husband, used to give me diamonds—well, of course, he took them all back. But in 1949, I was thrilled to get a slip—an item of clothing women do not even wear today. Or if they do, they wear it as a dress.

I found waitressing very difficult. The hardest part was being nice to insulting, contemptuous customers, but at first, I was also overwhelmed by having to remember and carry massive orders of baked stuffed clams and fried zucchini and eight or ten different pastas for a family group. The chef frightened me with his bad temper and violence: once, when I returned a dish a customer had complained about, he threatened me with his cleaver. The waiters frightened me too. They acted as if I was supposed to behave in some way that I didn't. I didn't know what they expected (looking back, I suspect I was supposed to defer to them because they were male), but I certainly felt their fury with me for not obliging. They made nasty comments about my character even as they surveyed my body in what seemed to me an extremely rude way. The other waitresses, much tougher than I, told me to ignore them, and sometimes one of them would yell at the guys to lay off. After a few weeks, I could yell that myself.

In time, I made friends with the other waitresses, one of whom, Meg, had a driver's license and a brother with a car. On an occasional Monday (when the restaurant was closed) she'd borrow it and drive a bunch of us to the beach.

But my best friend on the job was Bert Shiefendorfer. He was a waiter, but he wasn't like the others. A student at Bridgeport University, he went to school by day, waited tables at night. He was majoring in physical education and was on the college track team; he wanted to be a track coach. Bert was scrawny, very white and freckled, with reddish-blond hair and blue eyes.

In the early days, when I was inexperienced, Bert helped me carry the heaviest trays, and he'd shut the other waiters up when they started in on me. But the nicest thing he did was walk me to the bus stop after work and wait with me until my bus arrived. The restaurant closed when our shift ended, and the street was dark and deserted. Downtown Bridgeport was barren at night, dangerous even in those relatively innocent days. Bert wasn't attractive, but he was very kind.

One Saturday night, as Bert and I waited at the bus stop in our usual silence—conversation was not easy for us—Bert blurted out abruptly, "Say, you wanna go to the show on Monday?"

I was puzzled. "What show?"

"The *show*," he insisted, looking at me as if I were demented. When I continued to stare dumbly at him, he added, "The movie show."

"Oh! The movies!" I hesitated. I didn't want to reject him. I didn't want him to get angry with me and stop helping me at work or waiting with me at the bus stop. On the other hand, on Monday nights—Monday was a day off—I always went to a movie with Delia. She looked forward to it, the only time all week she got out for fun. But I knew Delia would feel that any invitation from a boy superseded anything girls did together—anything at all. I quickly slipped Delia into second place, figuring I could go to a movie with her on my night off and stay in Bert's good graces. So I said yes.

Delia felt precisely as I'd thought she would. Bert and I had an okay time. He *was* sweet, if a little slow. Soon it was a regular thing, the Monday-night movie with Bert. The only problem was finding two decent movies in the Bridgeport area in one week.

I felt comfortable with Bert in a way I never did with the boys at college. He came from the same class I did: his father ran a gas station, his mother worked at Woolworth's. He didn't try to impress me. He just sat and smiled at me with his sweet open face, and sometimes he held my hand. I figured he was fine for a summer flirtation. I could make a wry anecdote of it when I went back to school—my summer with Bert. No one at Mount Holyoke would guess that the egghead snob I appeared to be would date a boy whose English wasn't up to par, who was just plain dumb. So things went along peacefully through July and into early August.

But then, one Tuesday in the middle of August as we waited for the bus, he said, "You got tomorrow off, doncha?"

I nodded.

"Me too," he said. "Wanna go to the beach? I can loan a car off my pop."

"Sure," I said, glad for any chance to tan. "But I have to be back by six." Tomorrow was my movie night with Delia.

"No problem," he said. "I'll pick you up at ten. Where exactly do you live?"

I was happy the next morning, piling into his old wreck of a car with my beach bag, everything in it smelling of suntan lotion—a smell that still raises my spirits. We drove not to the public beach where I went with the other waitresses, but to a private beach in Greenwich. A friend of Bert's worked as a guard in the parking lot, and he let us in. No one could tell we didn't belong there, since we were white, Bert said, adding in a knowing tone that it would have been different if we were jigs. I asked him what that word meant, and he acted as though I was being snotty or snobbish or something. He explained it finally, as if he were talking to someone mentally defective, and was outraged when I said I didn't like the word and wished he wouldn't use it: it was disrespectful. He looked at me as if I had asked him to undress in public. Things were not going well with us, but the truth was, I didn't care.

The knowledge that we were trespassing made us both nervous, and that made us giggly. Entering an enchanted paradise forbidden us in the normal course of life, we looked at each other and smiled in an oily, wary way. Our nervousness bound us together, and the bad patch passed.

The beach was pebbly, like all the beaches on Long Island Sound, but it spread beyond us for miles and had hardly any people on it. The public beach was smaller than this, and it was always jammed; it was hard to find a spot to light where you wouldn't be pelted by sand thrown up by the hundreds of kids running around, or hear the roar of portable radios, the screams of mothers, or comments on your body from passing males.

Here, on this weekday, there was a small cluster of women—no more than a half dozen—with babies and small children, settled together on the sand near the snack bar. Some young men and women were playing volleyball farther down the beach, and a couple of isolated blankets lay scattered beyond them. We trudged past them, clambered over some rocks, and found a tiny island of dry sand, lapped by gentle water. We spread our blanket and settled down. Bert lavished suntan oil over my back and the backs of my legs. His hands were warm and gentle: very nice, that was. I did the same to him. That was nice too; I felt all tingly afterward. Then we lay down in the sun and just drank it in, barely talking.

When we were burning up with heat, Bert said, "Hey, let's do it," and got up and reached his hand to me and pulled me up, and we dashed into the Sound and splashed in its coolness. Heavenly, just heavenly. Then we walked to the snack bar, and he bought us hot dogs and beers, and we walked back with them and ate and drank and lay in the sun some more and swam some more, and Bert went for more beers. I wasn't sure I liked the taste of beer, but the hot sun made me so thirsty, I drank two bottles. I felt a little woozy; it must have been the sun. When we lay down again, his arm lay across me and his body was pressing against mine. Soon after that, it lay partly on top of me, and he was kissing me, and I was kissing him back. And we kept kissing, and then his hands started to move around my body. I wanted his hands to do what they were doing, I wanted to do that to him with my hands, and I did. After a while, he pulled a towel over his back and took off his bathing trunks and slid down the bottom of my two-piece suit and put his penis inside me. I wanted it there, I felt a desire for it, but I wanted something else too. Somehow the penis wasn't enough, but I didn't know what would be. I was excited but also let down when he gasped hard and rolled off me. I felt wet inside. He lay on his back and threw his arms out, exhausted. I waited for some ceremony more. None came.

He slept for a while; I lay there confused. When he woke, he looked at his watch, said, "I'd better get you home!" and jumped up, full of energy. I tried to catch his eye, but he wouldn't look at me. We packed up our gear and trudged back to the car. He dropped me off at the house with a peck on the cheek. "See ya," he said, then drove off.

I did not know what to make of this. Of course, I didn't tell Delia, who had already told me how important it was for a girl to be a virgin when she married. I sat through the movie that night in a daze, like a frozen person. Delia, dear as she was, didn't even notice.

I went in to work the next night with trepidation, wondering how Bert would act when we met. He was pleasant and helpful, exactly as always, except he never looked straight at me. This continued all week. I felt shattered. So when, Sunday, as we stood at the bus stop, he said, "Show tomorrow night?" I shook my head no.

He stopped short. "You busy?"

"No," I said. "I don't want to go out with a person who doesn't look at me."

"Whatdya mean? I look at you plenty." But even then he wouldn't meet my gaze.

"You *used* to look at me," I said. "Before... the beach. Then you stopped."

He studied the sidewalk, considering. But the bus arrived before he said anything, and I got on without saying good night. I spent Monday hanging around the house, wondering if he'd come by to discuss it, or at least call, but he didn't. Tuesday was his day off that week, and Wednesday was mine, so I didn't see him again until Thursday.

He acted like a stranger. His sweetness had vanished into a distant regard. He used a thin, formal voice when he had to say anything to me. He didn't walk me to the bus stop. Friday, I confronted him. I waited until he went into the storeroom behind the kitchen for some salad dressing, then followed him in.

"Bert. Don't you think we ought to talk? I don't understand what happened."

"What do you mean, you don't understand what happened?"

"Just what I said. We were friends. And we had a nice time at the beach. Then you suddenly turn cold on me. Why?"

"*I* didn't turn cold; you did!" he yelled. "We always go to the show on Mondays and all a sudden you say no!"

"I said no because you weren't looking at me!"

"That's crazy! That's crazy! Of course I looked at you!"

"You didn't! You averted your gaze! You wouldn't meet my eyes! You still won't! Look at me! See, you can't!"

"I *averted my gaze?*" he mocked. "What kind of fancy talk is that?"

I stared at him. I didn't know who he was. I didn't know what he was feeling, what he was saying, or why. I turned and walked out of the storeroom. The hell with him.

7

*I*n the few weeks remaining be-
fore school resumed, I took one more jaunt to the public beach
with the girls from the restaurant, went to the movies with Delia,
and shopped for clothes with her. Though I bought only what I
absolutely needed, at cheap stores, it took all but ten dollars of
what I'd saved of my summer wages.

Jerry drove me back to school, and this time, Delia came
along. She'd never seen the college, and she was impressed by
the beautiful campus. She kept remarking: "Oh! how lovely!
How beautiful!" Delia had never been out of Bridgeport except
for a trip to Washington, D.C., with her eighth grade class and
one to Manhattan when she was fifteen, to see Rockefeller Center and Radio City Music Hall. Her enthusiasm made me aware
that I felt different about the college now: I was eager to get back
to where (I now knew) I belonged, to people of my own sort
(even if they hadn't seemed so when I was there). That year I
would drop my snobbish act, begin to socialize, make some
friends. So what if I didn't have the right clothes. Some people
would like me anyway. I would *make* these people my people,
even if they weren't. I was pleased with myself for my new resolution: I felt I was growing up.

But I had been at school only two weeks when I realized my period was very late.

I waited. I took hot baths.

After two more weeks, I confided in Irmgard. "Take a rabbit test," she said.

In those days, colleges like Mount Holyoke expelled girls for marrying or for pregnancy; abortion was illegal and dangerous and expensive, and many people had never even heard of it. Also, boys, as a rule, when told that the results of the rabbit test were positive, felt guilty and responsible—unlike young men of today, who feel noble if they put themselves out to accompany their lovers to the abortion clinic—and actually married the girl. I do not hold this up as a model; far from it: marriages that began as a match between a desperate girl and a boy who was reluctantly doing her a favor out of fear of her family or societal disapproval did not generally become the "happily ever after" sort we all wanted.

I got the Shiefendorfer number from information and called Bert.

"Pregnant! How could you be pregnant?"

"We must have a poor connection," I said.

"How do you know it was me?"

"You had to notice I was a virgin. And that is the only time I ever...did that."

Long silence.

"What are we going to do?" I asked finally.

"We? Do?"

I had an inspiration. "I can't keep it from my family forever. My brother will find out...."

"Brother?"

"You know. My brother in Bridgeport. The one I was staying with."

Another long silence. Then: "I have to think." I assumed he meant he had to consult his mother. "I'll get back to you."

"Okay. Call me before Friday. I'm nervous."

I myself had no notion of what to do. Irmgard told me about a friend who had gone to a woman in a filthy apartment on the Lower East Side in Manhattan, paid $150, and been freed of her burden. It was a horrible experience, but she was rid of the thing. Irmgard's friend was at Smith. She could call her. She could get the name.

This terrified me. I'd heard my mother whisper to Susan about a woman we knew who had died after an abortion. She was an older woman, married, she was Italian and already had ten children, and she did something with a coat hanger. I wasn't ready to die. On the other hand, I wasn't ready to get married, especially to Bert. But I was dying either way: I was going to lose everything—my scholarship, my dreams. My apartment in New York!

I had to talk to somebody. I called my sisters. When Susan answered, I burst into tears. She immediately knew.

"Don't tell me," she said.

"Yes." I sniffled.

"Shit. You blew it. You blew your life. You stupid little fool. You were the only one of us who had a chance, and you blew it."

Sobbing now, I could hear her talking to the others. She was holding her hand over the mouthpiece, so I couldn't hear her words, just a rumble of voices. Susan came back.

"Who's the father?"

"Bert Shiefendorfer. A waiter at the restaurant I worked at this summer."

"In Bridgeport? Not some snotty Harvard kid?"

"Yes. No."

Susan sighed. "Well, that's a little better. All right. You'll have to marry him. If there's a problem, Jerry will deal with it. You hear?"

"Yes."

"Does he know? Have you told Jerry?"

"No."

"What about the boy? The father."

"I told him."

"And?"

"I don't know."

"How far along are you?"

"I...I missed one period. Three weeks ago. I had a rabbit test."

"Okay. Go to Bridgeport this weekend. Take the bus. Tell Jerry what time you're coming; he'll meet you at the bus station. I'll call him. I'll deal with him. Okay?"

"Okay."

Bert didn't call by Friday. I was a sniveling mess, led by my runny nose. Throwing a change of underwear and some books into a bag, I left the campus Friday after Advanced French. I took a bus to Springfield and caught the late-afternoon bus for Bridgeport. It was dark when I got there. I'd cried myself to sleep on the bus, and my face was hot and swollen when I arrived. I dreaded seeing Jerry; I was sure he'd feel contempt for me, just like Susan but more so, since he already thought that my sisters and I, especially me, had had things so much easier than he had. But I knew I just had to take whatever they handed me: I needed their help.

My crying on the telephone had been like a rifle shot or a bomb blast triggering a military campaign. Susan mustered the entire family into action, and everybody fell into line as if we'd been practicing for this all our lives. Jerry was standing there when I got off the bus, and he walked over and put his arm around me and led me to the car. The minute he touched me, I began to cry. He didn't say a word, just opened the car door for me and got in himself and started off.

I managed to calm down after a while, and we drove in silence, but when we got to his house, he turned off the motor and sat there for a minute. I looked at him. He turned a little in the seat.

"Listen, kid. Delia's shocked. I mean ... just ignore her, okay? Don't pay any attention to her; don't let her hurt your feelings. She'll get over it. She's very ... proper, you know? It's how she was brought up. They're very Catholic, the Urtnowskis. Well, you know; you've seen their house."

I hadn't noticed any signs of their religion in their house.

"She really likes you, and she'll get over it, okay?"

I nodded. My stomach was numb with dread: Delia was angry with me.

"And one other thing. I'm not gonna mention this upstairs, I'm not gonna mention it to the sisters, either, see. But there are things you can do. I can help you out. I know some names; I got cash. You don't have to have this baby if you don't want to. Okay?"

Again I nodded mutely, but his words hardly penetrated. I could only think about Delia, angry with me.

We went upstairs. Delia was sitting in front of the television set, but she jumped up when we came in. She turned it off and swung around to me. Her face was white.

"Elsa! How could you!" She looked furious.

I burst into tears again. Jerry put his arm around me. "Come on, Del. Give her a break," he said, rubbing my arm. "How about making us some tea, kid," he pleaded. She turned, tight-lipped, and went into the kitchen. Jerry sat me down in the easy chair and plopped himself on the ottoman, legs spread around it, leaning toward me.

"Now I wanna hear how this happened."

"Wait!" Delia cried from the kitchen. "Wait for me!"

Jerry took my hands and stroked them. He had strong hands from years of kneading dough for our mother. Delia came in carrying a tray with a teapot, cups, and several different cakes. They got them all free, of course. Suddenly ravenous, I ate half a butter cake all by myself. Delia was sitting on the couch across from me, gazing at me coldly. Every time I looked at her, I felt like crying, so I stopped looking at her. When I finished eating, I told them how it had happened. I told them a faltering story because I didn't understand it myself, really. I couldn't remember, couldn't bring back or describe the way I'd felt that day at the beach. So I couldn't explain why I had done what I did. Obviously, Delia didn't understand, either. But oddly, Jerry seemed to.

"So you're all warm and mushy, and he gets you drunk," he said in a low, bitter voice.

"Drunk!" Delia gasped.

"I only had two beers," I responded indignantly.

"You ever have a beer before that?" Jerry asked.

"No."

"Drunk," he repeated.

"Drunk!" Delia echoed.

I began to cry again. I wasn't sure which was worse, getting pregnant or getting drunk.

Jerry patted my hand. "Don't cry, kid. It wasn't your fault. That guy took advantage of you; you're just an innocent kid."

Delia burst out sobbing. "He took advantage of a poor innocent girl," she cried, and ran over to my chair and hugged me. "Poor baby! Poor little Elsa!"

I was so happy that Delia was forgiving me that I didn't argue, but this line of reasoning made me very uncomfortable. I didn't like feeling like a dupe, especially the dupe of a dope like Bert. I had, after all, known what I was doing, sort of, and I did want to do it at the time—heaven knows why. And I didn't have the sense that Bert knew a whole lot more about this business than I did. But clearly this was the approach my family had decided to take with regard to the matter, and whatever my reservations, I felt it was better than Susan's damning me for a fool or Delia's damning me as immoral. So I sat silently, complicit in their indictment of Albert Shiefendorfer, corrupter of innocence.

As I sat on the dock at my Sag Harbor house, remembering my sad past, I had to stop occasionally, look around, and draw a deep breath. Those days were over, and although they would in some sense always live in my consciousness, I was out of that trap now. I looked down at my body, still firm and fit despite my years, and wondered at it and at myself. That I had made it from there to here was miraculous. What was even more amazing was that I had somehow managed to cease my constant self-castigation and learned to be happy over the years. I wasn't sure how I had done that, moved from there to here. But I let myself feel a little pride that I'd done it, no matter how.

I thought again, as I often had before, that I had created my life, created myself, Hermione Beldame. And so had most of my family and friends. And we could do that only because we lived in the period we lived in; we couldn't have done what we'd done a generation earlier. Something had happened in the world, something that lifted people like us up and let us breathe freely, let us move around in the world, let us choose our own lives. That was the difference between then and now. It wasn't anything *I'd* done; it was something the world had done. It was a blessing. I could only wish it had happened twenty years earlier, in time to save my mother from the miserable trap that caught her.

I had determined to live like a hermit this summer, figuring that was the only way I could avoid talking about the subject that was driving me crazy, but after only a few days, I was starving for company. So I was delighted when Tess called and asked me to have dinner with her on Wednesday.

Tess runs a boutique here in Sag Harbor. Summer and fall, she sells figurines, paintings, dishes, small sculptures, and other things she finds during the winters, which she spends in Mexico, Guatemala, Belize, and other Central American countries. Her lover, Ellen, is a secretary in a UN department that handles Central American affairs, which is how they met. Ellen works in the city during the week and comes out only over weekends and for her month of summer vacation.

Tess is striking, tall and full-bodied, olive-skinned and black-haired, with a white stripe down her part. She always wears long gowns and capes made of gorgeous Central American fabrics, with huge earrings and lots of bracelets. During our Wednesday dinner, she often seemed distracted. I was a bit annoyed watching her run her eyes over the other patrons of the American Hotel, where we were dining. She was surveying the women.

I tried to get her attention. "So, Tess..."

"Umm." She leaned her head on her hand and stared at me with huge gray eyes. "What, sweetie?"

"Do you believe in True Love? I mean, do you think there's

one person out there for everyone, the perfect mate, who, if you could just meet her, would make you happy for the rest of your life?"

"But of course! What do you think I've been searching for all my life!"

"And you have never found it?"

"I keep thinking I have, but then ... I don't know."

"What about Ellen?"

"Ellen's sweet. But ..."

"But ... ?"

"Oh, I don't know. What about you?"

"Well, I've just gotten that feeling ... I've met this guy ..."

"Really!" She put down her fork. For the first time during our meal, she kept her eyes on my face and did not look around the room. She listened with wide, intense eyes.

"And ..."

"Well, he keeps sending out contradictory signals."

"Umm. Ellen says I do that."

"Really! And do you feel you do?"

"No. Not consciously."

"Is it unconscious? But you love Ellen, don't you?"

"Of course!"

"So ..."

"Well, she's a little dull, you know. Her mind isn't ... really of the first rank."

"She's *so* beautiful!" I argued.

"Yes. I know. It's true, she is beautiful. But ... she's a *secretary,* my dear."

I was shocked into silence. After a moment, I found my voice. "So are the two of you breaking up?"

"Oh, no!" she cried. "She comes out every weekend. We have

a sweet time. It just isn't *enough*, you know. There's just a little something missing. A *je ne sais quoi*, you know." She shrugged. "We get along fine; it's not that. I suppose I'm quickly bored. But that's just *entre nous*, my dear. Of course."

"Ummm." I was gazing hard at her.

"But you, you have to think about your feelings. I mean, the question isn't how he feels about you but how you feel about him!"

"I'm crazy about him," I admitted miserably. "I'm obsessed, really. I wish I weren't...."

"You can't worry about how other people feel or act. You know what *you're* feeling; you're sure of that. You have to trust that, darling. Trust that." She laid her hand on her heart. "It's all you have. All you can depend on. And you're madly in love. I must say I envy you, sweetie."

"Envy me?"

"Certainly! Isn't that what we're all looking for? All the time? All our fucking lives? To be madly in love with someone we know will make us happy for the rest of our lives?"

"Is that what we all want?"

"Certainly! All women, and all men too, although they rarely admit it!"

"So do you have anyone in mind?" I asked slyly.

Tess dropped her voice, leaned her head forward. "Don't turn around. But do you see that woman over there in the corner, sitting with the man with the bushy beard? The woman with the gray-blond streaked hair? Isn't she handsome? Isn't she distinguished? Isn't she someone famous?"

"How can I see her if I don't turn around?"

"Well, don't turn around while I'm talking about her."

I laughed. "So talk about something else."

Tess pointed to the little sconces that lined the walls. "You see those sconces over there? I found them for the restaurant—well, for Nicky, the owner. I found the first one in Mexico and had the rest made to order, copied. You like them?"

I turned then.

"That's Emily Shoemaker," I said, turning back. "She lives in East Hampton. She's a millionaire art collector. She supports all the arts."

Tess's eyes gaped. "Really? Do you know her? Can you introduce me to her? Do you think she might be gay?"

Thursdays, Liz Margolis comes to clean my house. She's young, just thirty, the daughter of my good friend Betty Margolis, a painter who lives in Sag Harbor. Liz is also an artist, a sculptor, but she has to earn money to live, and has found she can earn most, with the least investment of time and energy, by cleaning houses. Jobs that pay more require expensive clothes or commutation, or leave you no spare time. Cleaning houses locally doesn't take that long and pays fifteen dollars an hour. So Liz cleans six houses a week in three ten-hour days and spends one six-hour day at my house, cleaning and doing the laundry and ironing. This enables her to survive out here if she lives frugally. She rents a little cottage behind Betty's house for a minimal rent. She wears nothing but jeans and T-shirts, or, in cold weather, sweatshirts and men's woolen shirts, and she eats mainly vegetables and brown rice. Most of her earnings go to buy her materials, which are terribly expensive—she works in wood, beautiful varieties, or steel, or sometimes in marble. She's a lovely artist, and I've bought several of her smaller pieces, but most of her work is so huge it won't fit into a house. She's uncompromising, Liz: museums or nothing.

She's uncompromising in other ways too, and so is constantly unhappy either with her current lover or with her lack of a lover. One of them complained that Liz was so uncompromising, she could not drive on Long Island parkways because she was paralyzed by the sight of the word *merge* on a road sign. Over the past few years, I've listened to Liz's laments about Lotte, who was lively but perhaps too lively and, besides, lived in Germany and was never available; and Emma, who was sweet but maybe too sweet, who wanted to be with her all the time and hung on her, which drove Liz crazy, given the size of her house. Before that, there was Nora, who was moody and unpredictable and kept Liz on edge; and Dorian, who was cold and aloof and had a hard time touching another person. But for the past six months, Liz had been complaining about loneliness, the silence of her little house when she goes home at night, the paucity of opportunities for cruising out here in the boonies, and the general unfairness of life.

"What do you think about a poetry reading? Is that a good place to meet women?" she asked as she emptied the dishwasher. "God knows I can't afford to join the yacht club." She snorted. "Poetry readings are free."

"I don't think you'd meet anybody you'd be interested in at a yacht club, Lizzie," I said from my chaise, where I was sipping a midmorning coffee. I always reserved an hour for conversation with Liz on Thursday mornings. I knew it made all the difference to her feelings about her work, so I treated it as part of her salary. "Poetry readings sound good. The right kind of venue."

"The right kind of venue! Oh, Hermione! What a nice way to put it! Makes it sound so...respectable!" She wiped down the stove. "So how's *your* love life?"

She always asked this, although in all the years I'd known her, I had never had any answer for it except "What love life?" I figured she felt she had to ask me: it was quid pro quo; she was a feminist and wanted to be sure she didn't dominate the conversation. But this time, I shocked her.

"Terrible," I moaned.

Her head shot up. "Really! What! Woman or man?"

"Man."

"Oh, well, what do you expect?"

I forbore from pointing out that she had been less than successful with women.

"Umm. I'm just having trouble reading his signals."

"Oh, one of those ambivalent creeps who give out double signals? Nora did that all the time! Drives you crazy! 'Spend the weekend with me.' So you cancel all your plans. Then she says she wants to be alone. Jeez, Greta, give me a break!" Liz started to mop the kitchen floor. "So what's this guy do?"

"Well, like that. Asked me to have lunch with him every day last week, but never stayed longer than an hour. Asked me— with great intensity—how I'd feel if he worked in New York, then not only drops the subject, but leaves town. Goes running in to examine my bedroom every time he visits my apartment, says he'd love to spend time with me, but never puts a finger on me, doesn't even kiss me hello or goodbye. And he always has to run off."

Liz was leaning on the mop, staring at me sympathetically. "Umm. Weird. Sounds weird. Are you in love with him?"

"Well ..." I looked away. It was too embarrassing. Liz was so much younger than I; she was from a different generation.

"Oh, poor Hermione. Poor thing."

"Sounds bad to you, does it?" I asked tentatively.

"Umm. Yeah. Especially for a man. You know, they always want to get in your pants right away. But sounds to me as if you haven't ..."

"No," I said quietly.

"So it's weird."

"Maybe he can't," I said.

"Yeah. How old is he?"

"Fifties."

"Maybe he's gay," she offered.

"You think everybody's gay."

"That's true. Still, you'd be better off if you'd get involved with a woman, Hermione."

"I probably would." I started to rise. Our hour was nearly up. She was still leaning on the mop, gazing at me. I put my cup and saucer in the sink. "At least there's work," I said, with as much cheer as I could muster. "What's wrong?" I asked, looking at her face.

"I just can't believe it keeps on like this. Does it keep on like this forever? Forgive me, Hermione, but how old are you? You must be close to my mom's age. She has Jack, of course, for whatever he's worth. But you're still going through stuff like this?"

I have to confess she was making me cross. "I don't tell my age," I snapped.

"I'm really sorry. Really!" She slapped her forehead with the palm of her hand. "It's just that . . . all these years, no matter what happened, even when someone really broke my heart, I had this idea, this *dream*—I was *positive* that someday I'd meet the woman of my dreams and we'd live happily ever after. It never occurred to me that this stuff could keep going on, right into your sixties, your seventies—my god! It's a nightmare! I don't think I can stand it!" Bursting into tears, she dropped the mop, which clattered to the floor. She snatched some tissues from a box on the counter and ran out to the dock.

That night, after dinner, I sat on my screened porch in the darkness, staring out at the water, visible only in streaks of reflected moonlight. When the moon vanished, I decided to sleep on the porch, and fetched linens to make up the daybed. It was sweltering in my bedroom, even with all the windows raised, but on the porch, I needed a blanket. I lay snuggled in and warm, breathing the wonderful clean night air, feeling safe and comfortable enough to return to memories of my early years.

I sat unmoving while Jerry and Delia embraced me tearfully. Though I welcomed the embrace and the apparent forgiveness, I was uncomfortable with what I felt were slightly false grounds and with the way Jerry swung into action. His firm chin and lips, his beetled brow, the rigid set of his head on his neck as he nodded it up and down, told me that no interference from me was desired. He was a man with a mission. The only thing I had that he wanted was Bert's telephone number. With a strange certainty, I knew that it gave him pleasure to be so outraged, that in fighting for me, he was drawing on emotions that had nothing to do with me at all. I sat, swollen-faced and drained, watching what seemed to me like an overacted performance, the making of an Alp out of a little mound of dirt. I felt like a small soiled thing, about to be laundered; a corpse, grateful that other people were buying the coffin and arranging my body in it, planning the rites needed to move me into my future, such as it was. But I said nothing. It was also true that once Jerry took over, I relaxed; I felt cared for, protected. That night I slept until morning for the first time in weeks.

Saturday, after the three of us had finished breakfast, we went into the living room, where we sat in silence until ten o'clock. On the dot of ten, Jerry, looking at his watch, stood portentously, walked into the tiny entry hall of the apartment, and picked up the phone. Delia and I rose and followed him, hovering in the archway. Jerry took an extremely casual posture, leaning against the wall with his legs crossed at the ankles like Fred Astaire. But the knuckles of his hand holding the receiver were white.

"Mrs. Shiefendorfer? The mother of Bert Shiefendorfer? Yes. My name is Jerry Schutz. I'm Elsa's older brother. Elsa Schutz, yes. Well, I would think that name would be familiar to you. Is that so. Well, we have a matter to discuss, and I'd like to come over and see you and your husband. Bert should probably be present."

A long silence on Jerry's end.

"You know, Mrs. Shiefendorfer, it would be better if we could handle this matter in a calm and friendly way. You have to think ahead, Mrs. Shiefendorfer. A grandmother shouldn't alienate the mother of her grandchild and her family. I feel sure that Bert must have discussed this with you, Mrs. Shiefendorfer. You know I manage a million-dollar corporation, Mrs. Shiefendorfer. Yes, the Homey Honey Bread Company."

Actually he was the assistant manager.

"So I have some resources, Mrs. Shiefendorfer. But I would hate to have to hire a lawyer and go to court and expose your son in the newspapers, especially since the boy got my sister drunk, fed her beer, which she'd never had before in her entire life, a college girl, an innocent girl who never even had a boy-friend. . . .

"Right. Right. Sure thing. I can be there in an hour. You wanna give me directions?"

Jerry scrawled on a pad, hung up, and turned to face us with a big smile. He held up his hand, making a circle with his thumb and middle finger. "Success! She's scared to death," he announced. "Her precious boy's future's threatened. There's not gonna be a problem," he assured us.

Delia hugged me and kissed Jerry. I smiled at him, but it was a tense smile. I couldn't tell him that I hated what he was doing, that I couldn't stand it, that I didn't want any of it, that I just wanted to be dead. I said I didn't feel well and went back to my room and lay down and tried to will myself to die, just the way I had when I was little and Mother scolded me.

Jerry was right. When confronted, Bert collapsed and cried, admitting his guilt—the beer, the sex. Then the Shiefendorfers too collapsed, grudgingly accepting that he was responsible, although they spoke my name with sour mouths. But they didn't criticize me to Jerry: they were afraid of him. He was an executive, a man who knew about lawyers and newspapers. (They never guessed that the "manager" of a bakery actually walks around in shirtsleeves, nagging slow workers, arranging for rat extermination, ordering machinery repairs—or making them himself—and overseeing deliveries of things like sugar and flour.) They agreed that Bert would have to quit school and get a job that paid more than waiting table. His two years of college and being on the track team could maybe help him get on the cops, Bert's father suggested. Bert's father was in with the cops; they hung out at his gas station, and he played poker with a sergeant on the Bridgeport force. And the idea seemed to appeal to Bert, Jerry reported.

Jerry became my liaison with the Shiefendorfers. He and they planned our future: neither Bert nor I was consulted. I was too stunned to care; no doubt Bert was too. I suspected that except for Jerry, who was enjoying his centrality, his sense of power, everybody was as numb as I was. The thing was a shock, a sudden dramatic end to everybody's plans and hopes, like being told you have a terminal disease.

Bert didn't call or ask to see me. I didn't really care. Most of the time I lay on the daybed in Delia's sewing room and stared at the ceiling. I knew it was my own fault, my own doing, but still I blamed my sisters. Why didn't they warn me? Why didn't Susan or Merry or Tina—or Delia or my mother—why didn't they sit me down and have a long talk and say, *This one thing you must not do or you will ruin your life forever, you will lose everything you have,* which was little enough as it was! Why had nobody impressed this on me? Yet I had to admit I knew it anyway, knew it somehow without being told. Every girl knew it: it was universal knowledge. Still, at least ten girls in my high school class had been pregnant at graduation. But they didn't have as much to lose, I thought: who else had a full scholarship to college? To a wonderful college? You'd think a person smart enough to win such a scholarship would be smart enough not to wreck her life, and for what? What Bert and I had done on the beach hadn't even felt good. Well, it felt nice at first, the kissing and the touching, but then, when he put his thing on me, on my leg with just a little tiny bit of it in me, that had not felt good; it felt like nothing at all, and it got me all wet and sticky. For that I had ruined my life?

The hardest thing I had to do was write the Millington High School teachers. I kept picturing them sitting together in the coffee room reading my letter, shaking their heads, their hopes in me smashed. "These girls," they'd sigh, and lay the letter aside, their disappointment palpable in the room. It took years before I could think about that without feeling a pang, sharp as a heart attack.

It was almost as hard to quit school formally: I wrote the dean that I was getting married. Everyone knew what that meant; I was glad I could do it by mail, so no one would see my face. But

I had to go back for my things. Jerry drove me up on a weekend, when, I hoped, few people would be around. I didn't want to meet anyone I knew, to have them look at me, to have to explain anything. I dreaded bursting into tears, humiliating myself utterly. Amazingly, I didn't bump into anyone, not even Irmgard, who must have been away for the weekend. I packed my clothes, my precious books, my portable typewriter, and sneaked out of there feeling déclassé, a little shopgirl who'd slipped in like a stowaway but was found out before she had done any real damage.

Jerry and I barely spoke on the drive to South Hadley. He kept the radio on to pop music until we reached the hills and got only static. Then we drove in silence until Jerry cleared his throat, and I knew, I knew exactly what he was about to say.

"You think at all about what I said to you, kid?"

"Umm, well, I don't know, Jer."

"It don't have to be this way, you know."

I couldn't think how to tell him what I felt, that I was appalled my own brother would urge me to do something illegal, something I could go to jail for, if I didn't die of it first! I knew there were people who'd had abortions, but it was a terrible thing, it was against the law; no decent girl, no respectable girl, would even think about it! I knew Jerry loved me and wanted the best for me, but I couldn't understand how he could imagine that I would do such a terrible thing. . . .

My eyes overflowed. "I just can't, Jer," I wept.

He reached over and patted my hand. "Okay, kid, okay. Don't cry. Listen, it was only an idea. Forget it, I'm just an oaf. I been hangin' out with the guys at the bakery too long, you know. . . ."

I took his hand and smiled at him. I did love my brother. I'd adored him when I was little; I used to follow him around the way a baby duck follows its mother, Momma used to say. At the thought of my mother, a fresh batch of tears poured out of me. Thank god she wasn't alive to see this, to be shamed by me....

"Come on, kid. It'll be all right, wait and see. You'll have the kid and you'll love it and you'll forget this stuff—in a couple of years it'll be just as if you were madly in love with this guy. You know, love doesn't last, anyway." He stopped suddenly.

This was an alarming new idea.

"Don't you love Delia anymore, Jerry?"

Jerry had a tannish complexion, but he blushed right through his tan skin. Still, I didn't stop. I had to know.

"Don't you, Jer?"

"Sure, sure I do, of course! Just maybe in a different way than I did before, you know? You don't know a lotta stuff about people when you marry them, you know?"

"But Delia's so sweet and good and nice," I whined. I couldn't bear hearing that two people I loved so much were less than happy, and I knew that if Jerry was unhappy, so must Delia be.

"Yeah, yeah. She is. I know that. But you know, she's so Catholic."

"I thought you converted. Aren't you Catholic too?"

"Sure, I had to; she wouldn't have married me otherwise. But you know I don't care about religion; we weren't religious in our family."

"No. But why do you care if Delia is?"

"Well, the Catholics have all these rules about birth control and stuff, and Delia doesn't want to have a family until we've saved up enough to buy a house, and she won't use birth control, so ... there's very few days in the month that are safe...." He hit the steering wheel with the palm of his left hand. "Listen to me, will you? Running off at the mouth. Just pay no attention, okay, kid? Delia's a sweetheart. She is. Just sometimes we don't agree. That's inevitable, right? Happens to everybody."

I was still holding Jerry's other hand, and I squeezed it. I wanted to tell him that whatever he did or felt, I loved him, but that I wanted him to stop talking. I wanted him to stop talking *now*! Once I realized they had one, I didn't want to know their problem, Delia's and his.

But Jerry's problem with Delia became mine before too long.

We were in Goodman's, a local department store. Delia had insisted I buy a wedding dress. I said I didn't want a wedding dress—we weren't going to have a formal wedding. But she looked over my clothes and pronounced them unsuitable for any kind of wedding.

"We won't spend much," she argued, "seein' as how it won't fit you in another month or two and probably not afterwards, either."

She found a beige rayon shirtwaist dress with a wide belt. "If you do lose weight later, this is a dress you can get some wear out of," she urged, always practical. I didn't care. I bought it, and a wide-brimmed beige felt hat, and low-heeled shoes to match. Delia was pleased and offered to treat me to coffee and cake in the store restaurant. I loved the store restaurant: the white table-cloths and the neat waitresses in black with little white lace-trimmed aprons and caps. I was happy to be there, and Delia was happy with my outfit. She saw me smiling and that made her even happier, and she rested her hand on mine and said, "I'm glad you have that navy suit you're wearing. It looks great on you; it isn't too tight yet. You ought to wear it when you meet Father O'Neill. I want you to look nice for him."

"Father O'Neill?"

"Yes. I've made an appointment for you, for tomorrow evening. Jerry'll drive you; I already asked him. You'll have to

take religious instruction with Father before he'll marry you."
She was still smiling.

"Why would I do that? I'm not Catholic."

"No, but Bert is. You'll have to convert."

"How do you know he is?"

"I had Jerry ask them. You have a right to know, after all."

I digested this for a while.

"I'm not converting, Delia," I said. I wasn't smiling, and now
she wasn't, either.

"You have to!"

"Who says?"

Her voice rose. "Your brother converted to marry me."

"My brother loved you."

"You can't marry a Catholic without converting. It's wrong.
It's a sin!"

"It seems to me that's up to Bert and me, and he hasn't said a
word about my converting." Of course, he hadn't said a word
about anything.

"Don't you want to be the same religion as me?" She was near
tears now.

"Delia, I love you, but I don't even believe in a god, much less
in a religion. I'm not going to do it, and there's nothing you can
say that will persuade me, so please don't let us fight about this.
I have the right to be whatever religion I want, or none at all."

Delia turned white. "You mean you're an . . . *atheist?*"

"Of course. We all are in my family," I said blithely, then I
saw her face.

"Jerry isn't. He's Catholic."

"Yeah. Except Jerry," I amended quickly.

"You're an atheist," she repeated, looking at me as if I'd grown
horns.

"Oh, Dell . . ." I put my hand on her arm, but she pulled away.

"No wonder you got pregnant," she said harshly. She pulled her bag open, removed her compact and lipstick, and redid her lips. Then she opened her wallet and laid a dollar on the table. "Ready?" she asked coldly.

Delia never forgave me. I had tried her too hard, pushed her morality further than her affection for me could bear. And it seemed her morality was more important to her than her affection. Maybe that's true for all of us. I don't know, because I have a bad character.

Delia was good and she went on being good, despite the worst I could do. She said she and Jerry would give me a wedding reception—champagne and cake in their apartment. Jerry could get a case of New York State champagne real cheap—a friend of his owned a liquor store—and the guys in his plant would make a wedding cake for me for free, she said. Delia borrowed glasses and dishes from her mother and wrote invitations to my sisters and Bert's parents and brothers and sister. Of course, she would have to do all the work. And she spoke to me—she didn't stop speaking to me—but she was cool and made an effort not to spend time with me alone. She stopped going to the movies with me. I knew this had to hurt her as much as it hurt me: she didn't have any friends, just her family, who rarely went to movies. So she lost one of her few pleasures. I kept believing she'd get over it, just as Susan had kept believing Mother would someday forgive her. But just like my mother, she never did. Good people were strange that way.

8

*G*eorge and I commuted be-
tween Louisville and New York to stay with each other on long
weekends or short vacations. On my visits to his house in
Louisville, I redecorated it. The color schemes in particular took
detailed planning: for his living room, I used a deep velvety
brown accented with muted rose and blue; in another version, I
used shades of the palest blues and greens.

George would come up to New York for three- or four-day
weekends, and I would get tickets for the theater or a concert. I'd
take him to the best restaurants in town. I had a suspicion he
didn't care for really good food, but if that was the case, he'd
have to improve his palate, because I couldn't live on a steady
diet of the sort of food served in that coffee shop near Columbia
where I met him for lunch.

No. Toss that scenario. Let's say he got a permanent job at
Newsday and moved to New York. At that point, I could choose
one of the many lifestyles I'd already invented. Wherever we
lived, he'd come to my apartment for dinner one night a week, and
we'd cook together. Another night, we'd go to the theater or a film,
a concert or a reading, and have late-night supper at the Algon-

quin or the Brasserie or some other ancient sentimental spot that
would make him nostalgic or give him a kick. Weekends, we'd
have a lazy brunch, often entertaining. Ko Chao would come and
help serve and do the cleaning up. We'd serve scrambled eggs and
smoked salmon, caviar omelets, fettuccine Alfredo (which everyone would groan about and then devour), or a mushroom risotto,
hot popovers and biscuits, a huge fruit salad filled with melon and
berries that I would have prepared the day before, and a tray of
sweet breads and pastries. I pictured my friends meeting him,
heard their conversations, saw them charmed by him.

We'd take long walks in the park and spend holidays out at Sag
Harbor. We'd invite all our children—whenever his daughter
and my four kids could manage to get to New York at the same
time. The whole family would cook. We'd make vitello tonnato,
or stuffed veal breast, or roast loin of pork with crackling skin, or
some other delicious politically incorrect food. We'd have luscious pastas, rich soups, simple desserts. I spent hours planning
the pastas and soups, making them in my mind, revising old
recipes and trying out new ones. I invented a wonderful mushroom soup thickened with the stems instead of cream.

In the summer, we'd drive out to Sag Harbor every weekend
and throw ourselves into the water, then lie naked on mattresses
on the dock, just our fingertips touching. We'd lie close together
at night, making love only when desire overwhelmed us. But the
rest of the time we'd be warm together, cuddling, soft, tender,
filling that hurt empty spot that never goes away, that has been
hurting since you were born, it seems. It would be wonderful.
Paradise. I'd be happy for the rest of my life.

Friday morning, Lou called me in Sag Harbor with what she said
were a ton of messages. Utterly beyond my control and contrary

to my will, my heart began to beat jaggedly. But as she droned on and on, reciting them, the magic word did not appear. Crash and burn.

I was having lunch with Ilona Markovich that day. I gave up my resolve not to discuss George. The situation was clearly beyond my control. I had to talk to someone. Only it seemed that no matter how many people I talked to, I didn't feel better.

Ilona can meet her friends only at lunchtime, because Guy Kislik, the man she lives with, is jealous of her evening hours. At night, she goes only to professional meetings, events mandatory or at least important to her job as a professor of biology at Stony Brook. Guy is also a professor—of political science, I think; I know so little about him. He doesn't want Ilona to go out at night, and he himself almost never does, rarely accompanying her even to parties or concerts. I've met him only once or twice in all the years I've known Ilona, and she never talks about him at all. It's almost as if he doesn't exist. Except every year, she'll show me photographs of the two of them on their most recent trip—mounted on camels or elephants, mountain climbing in Nepal, standing near a giant turtle on the Galápagos, snorkling in the Great Barrier Reef. It's very strange to see her with a thin, bearded man with his arm around her as if he knew her. He seemed a puppet who came alive when they went abroad but whom she kept in a box the rest of the year.

This day, she had no photographs: it was too early in the year. She was planning a trip to Tasmania in late July—I assumed with Guy, not that she mentioned him. Ilona was an enthusiastic teacher, though, and her conversation was full of news of end-of-term problems, brilliant student papers, brilliant student failures. We were eating at Citron, and were into the dessert course (Ilona loves dessert but refuses to order it unless you agree to share it), enjoying a luscious profiterole, before I ventured to bring up George. I used my usual line: "I've met a man."

Ilona put her spoon down. "You have!"

"Well, sort of." I described the situation. By now I had it down pat, could tell the story in about six paragraphs, ten minutes flat.

"Wow. How exciting!" She gazed at me with large warm brown eyes. "How wonderful for you!"

I frowned. Had she been listening? "Well, it isn't, really, Ilona. He's so indecipherable. And I feel so ... so full of longing, you know? It makes me feel a fool, like some Cinderella waiting for her prince."

She nodded sagely. "Yes, but it's worth it. Waiting. He'll come. And you will live happily ever after. I know. I was past thirty-five when I met Guy. I'd been married, and I'd had a couple of long-term affairs, but they weren't right, they just didn't work out. But the minute I met him, I knew. The way you know with George. You just know." Her eyes were wide and candid and soft. "We've been together for twenty years now, and I've never regretted anything, not for a minute. He really is my Prince Charming."

Saturday night, Ann and William Stevens were having a dinner party. The Stevenses were charming and interesting and, amazingly, they worked together: Will was a furniture designer (people called him the only straight furniture designer in the Hamptons), and she owned—she'd inherited—a furniture-making business. They were an argument for old-fashioned marriage, marriage as an economic arrangement, because their connection was economic and solid, and in addition, they seemed really happy. Ann benefited because she got exclusive access to Will's popular designs, and Will benefited because he was assured that anything he designed would be made. He worked in their gorgeous house in East Hampton, she worked at her office in New York or down at the factory, in some little South Carolina town they both loved. They had a nice mix of togetherness and apartness.

People did not know what to think about the Stevenses. It's very hard on people to see a couple who seem to live in absolute bliss, who seem to have everything. Ann and Will always behaved like the ideal couple and always seemed ecstatically happy. It was a pisser. They also always gave pleasant parties that brought together people who had an edge but also (unlike Liz) knew how to merge. I always felt good in their house; I always had a good time. But afterward, I invariably felt consumed with envy of their relationship, their life. My bad character again.

I got dressed up—well, what passes for dressed up these days—in a long silk skirt in wide stripes of rust, green, and gold, a short-sleeved brown silk top, and a paisley vest that mixed all the colors. Maybe there'd be a new man there tonight, I thought—as I had thought thousands of nights before as I dressed to go out—one I haven't met ten times before, who is straight and not too young and interesting and interested.

Of course, there wasn't, but I had a nice time, anyway. I had so nice a time, in fact, that I stayed late, something I rarely did these days. When I pulled into my driveway, the moon was low on the water, and the sky was so black that the stars seemed as close as a blanket dotted with brilliant flickering lights, which you could reach out for and pull down over you. I was tired, and I happily contemplated my nice cool bed, and being in it alone. Why was I so driven to have someone else in my life? Why did I feel I wasn't fully alive without a lover? Wasn't I really contented as I was?

I got out of the car and walked toward my house, admiring its peaks and gables, its silhouette, low against the night sky, hung about with trees. I went into the house and immediately undressed and brushed my teeth, but instead of sliding naked into bed, as I usually did, I put on a T-shirt and went out onto the screened porch on the back of the house, facing the water. I settled down on the soft long daybed I had been sleeping on and pulled a light afghan over my legs. The moon spangled a path across the water. The night was so dark that the light from the moon and stars was incredibly brilliant.

My mind, exhausted from the weeks of nights without enough sleep, upset with the sticky-sweet sickness that comes from too much daydreaming, could not rest. Why did I want this man so much? Would I really be happier with him in my life? Were people who were with people happier than people who were alone? Everyone believed they were: it was an unspoken law, an absolute if unproven truth.

Consider the people I'd talked to this evening. My sweet friend Betty Margolis, a plump woman with graying dark hair, was voluble and excited about her latest paintings and the show she was having in Southampton next month. Her eyes glistened. She'd waited decades for artistic success and was enjoying it profoundly now that it had come to her. I asked if she'd seen Liz that day—Liz had never come back to my house after running out of it on Thursday, leaving the mop and bucket right in the middle of the kitchen floor. I was a bit annoyed. I was also unsure whether I would ever see her again. But I didn't tell Betty that. No, she said, Liz seemed to be away—her pickup was missing. She hadn't seen Liz since Tuesday, in fact. Even though they lived so close together, they did not live in each other's pockets! She laughed.

Her husband ambled over. Jack O'Reilly was a failed writer,

an unhappy man who was always whining to someone about something and who really seemed to expect his listener to solve his problem. As a child, Liz had learned to retreat from her stepfather, fleeing his emotional demands, and I often suspected that this was part of her problem with lovers today. I have to confess, though, that I, too, ran when I saw him coming. But Betty always smiled at him lovingly and tried to take care of him. She didn't seem to feel he was a burden. Everyone agreed that Betty was a saint.

"Betty... Oh, hello, Hermione, hi. Betty, listen," he whined urgently. "You see that pasta salad on the buffet over there? I ate some of it. You think it's got mushrooms in it? You know how allergic I am to mushrooms. What do you think? I think I have the beginnings of a rash. Here on my neck, look, right there."

As Betty examined him, I said I didn't think the salad contained mushrooms; neither did Betty, who could find nothing on his neck.

"Well, I definitely have a headache coming on. Just like when I get an allergic attack. And I know I saw little bits of brown stuff in the pasta. It could have been mushrooms...."

"Sun-dried tomatoes, I think," I said, looking for ways to escape.

"Umm. I don't feel too good."

"Do you want to go home, dear?" Betty asked with concern. I squeezed her arm and wandered over to Dalton Schwab. He was as handsome and beautifully dressed as ever, if thinner and tighter about the mouth.

"I'm glad to see you," I said.

"And I'm overjoyed to see you, dear heart."

We hugged. "How are you?" I asked.

"As well as I can be, I expect. I've been trying to write about it."

"A memoir? A new play?"

"Memoir, I think. Of Tim. And some of the others." His voice caught; he stopped, then began again in a light, almost mocking tone. "I'm afraid it's getting to be a cliché. So many plays, books. People are sick of it. And what more is there to say?"

"No one ever has anything new to say about anything, really, you know. It isn't important to say something new, but to say it in a new way," I said piously, then added, laughing, "speaking of clichés. But seriously, Dalton, you always have your own brilliant, eccentric take on things."

We flattered each other for a bit, then I got serious. "Dalton, are you lonely?"

"Can't say that. When I had him—when he was there— when he was alive... it was bad this last year, horrible the last months. Well, you know, you saw him. It was agony just looking at him, remembering how beautiful he'd been. Just watching him try to do things for himself... And of course, I had to take care of him. He needed a lot of care. I loved him, I would have died for him, but that part was agony. And he was so unhappy and got so bad-tempered! Nothing one did for him was good enough.... I wasn't sorry when he died. For him or for me. I can't say I'm lonely for the Tim of the past months. The Tim I miss left long before that. All of them, all—they died long before they died."

Well, of course. Wrong person to ask.

Ann Stevens joined us, hugging us both, asking gracious questions, sweetening the conversation. She was full of new plans for their South Carolina house, a thing of some grandeur, I'd heard, although I'd never seen it. It was designed by Sidney Farber, a house of wood and glass perched on a cliff in a forest. She was bubbling over with well-being, with high spirits. High spirits usually attract people, but this evening, neither Dalton nor I had access to high spirits. She must have sensed this and glanced around her, searching for someone she could cheer up, but her eye caught Will's, and he immediately came over to us and put his arm around her. Dalton flinched; I bit the inside of my cheek. I was especially pleased to see that Dalton's character was as bad as mine, because I liked him a great deal and respected him too. If his character was as bad as mine, bad character could not be a seal of doom. I stood there listening to the happy couple make happy talk for as long as I could stand it. But as soon as I saw Perry Pears, an old pal from years ago on Twelfth Street, I edged away from the Stevenses. Perry was a good friend, although we met infrequently. How was he?

"The most incredible thing, Hermi. I'm walking around bedazed, bedazzled, bedight—"

"Bewitched, bothered, and bewildered?"

"Them too."

"*What?*"

"This woman—a girl, really: well, she's a married woman with children, but so much younger than I, and gorgeous, and so-o-o nice—well, she's announced that she's in love with me! Can you imagine? Out of the blue, the azure, the plain where the clouds roam, wandering buffalo, this just happens! Just happened." He gave me a dazed, sheepish grin.

Perry is a good-looking man, but he is also, after all, closing in on seventy.

"How old?" I snapped.

"Thirty-eight. Gorgeous. Elaine is her name. 'Elaine the fair, Elaine the lovable, Elaine, the lily maid of Astolat.'" Perry taught Victorian literature at Brooklyn College before he retired. "She lives down the block from me, we have clandestine meetings at the supermarket and the gym, we pass in the street, we chat about her dog, her kids, her husband, my need for a good home-cooked meal...."

I tsk-tsked. Perry had always looked sunken-cheeked, in need of nourishment, but I had thought the days when women believed men incapable of feeding themselves were gone. My character was getting a workout tonight. Still, consumed with envy though I was, I couldn't help being happy for Perry. He deserved to be loved, I thought.

"That's wonderful, Perry," I said sincerely. "How did you meet?"

Not everyone was blissfully happy. The Parkers sniped at each other across their martinis, and the Steiners—well, Jim Steiner never let his wife, Diane, get more than a phrase out of her mouth before he interrupted her. Then I ran into Eric Stoller, another old friend, who had a house in Hampton Bays. I had dinner with Eric a couple of times a year, so we kept up with each other. Eric made documentary movies, mainly in Asia and Africa, and over the years had slept with every beautiful or intelligent woman he encountered—including me, years ago. For Eric, sleeping with interesting women was simply an essential part of everyday life, like eating breakfast, bathing, or combing his hair. But when he reached fifty-five, he began to have trouble finding women to sleep with: it was not that he didn't find *any* but that he couldn't find one every night. This was a terrible shock, a comedown, his first sexual failure. He had a very interesting woman as a lover, but she was living in Germany at the moment. Alone, he was irritated and bewildered. He could not understand what had happened.

"Essie isn't coming over this summer?"

"She's coming, but not until July. Then I'll go back with her in August. But I have to return here in September to start shoot-ing a new film. Out west, in the redwood forests."

"Well, that isn't too bad."

He grimaced. "You don't understand. Women don't under-stand. You think if there's someone in your life, that's enough. You don't see."

"What am I missing, Eric?" I smiled.

"It's lonely. I want company, someone to do things with, travel with, go to the movies with. . . ."

"Well, of course! We all do. That's why we have friends."

"No. Not friends! I need a woman for that, a woman I can sleep with afterwards; it's the only way I feel comfortable, the way life feels right."

I considered. "Maybe you should have married again."

"Ugh!" He gestured in disgust. "Although I tell you, Hermione, sometimes I even think it might be worth it. The worst thing happened to me last month! So humiliating! I was in Nairobi; it was spring. I was just back from Tanzania, the Serengeti—I was doing a film on endangered species. . . . So I'm staying in the Nairobi Hilton, there's a bunch of us there, all in-volved in the film in one way or another. And this one woman who works for the executive producer, a nice woman, acts really friendly to me, and I think, Well, this is more like it, this is like the old days. She's really zaftig, you know, not young but still juicy, in her late forties, semi-interesting, not a genius but smart enough. . . ." He sipped his wine.

"So one day, she calls me up and invites me to go to the the-ater with her. And I am cheered up; I think this sojourn may turn out to be fairly pleasant, after all. But the night we go out, she never stops talking; she chatters incessantly. I am relieved to say good night—I don't make a single move.

"And what happens! She calls again. I take her to dinner. She does it again. But this time I stop her. I ask her why she is calling me, why she talks so much, what is going on. And she stops dead. 'Oh,' she says, 'it shows.' 'What shows?' I want to know. 'Well,' she says, 'you see, I had my forty-fifth birthday eight months ago. And it did something to me. Because after my birthday, I started screwing without stop, screwing every man I meet, any man I meet, every night someone, and my shrink tells me I have to stop, I can't keep doing this. So I thought, well, I'd call you! Someone old, who doesn't do it anymore. . . .'

"So that's what I am now!" Eric cried. "A safe older man, helpless, impotent! Ye gods!" He laughed but squeezed his glass so tightly I feared for his hand. I patted his back gently. "You don't look old," I say. And he doesn't—to me.

Toward the end of the evening, Nina Brumbach, the poet, headed for me. I was fond of her, found her a restful, consoling person to be with when she was in a good frame of mind. She wore her graying black hair long, hanging in her face, and she was terribly thin, too thin by my standards, but then my standards are not the world's, and my friends all agree with the Duchess of Windsor that there is no such thing as *too* thin. Because she was so thin, clothes clung to her as if they were enamored of her body. She was wearing a sea-green chiffon thingy, belted at the waist with huge gold metal links. She seemed to have no trouble at all in walking in her high, high gold heels. I bit my other cheek.

"Nina! How great you look! Fantastic!"

"Oh, thanks, Hermione," she said listlessly.

"And congratulations on your poem in *The New Yorker* last week! I loved it—so allusive, so sad. I hope that's not how you feel."

She shrugged. "You know how it is."

Nina regularly said that since her husband, Garson, died she felt only half alive. But Garson died seven years ago.

"I was just talking to Dalton," she explained.

"Oh."

"Tim was so great." Her eyes grew damp. "And he had such promise."

"Yes," I said piously. It isn't that I didn't agree; but there's something ghoulish about lingering over a young person's death. And Tim had been dead for four months.

"Duncan has tested positive, you know."

"No!" I cried.

She nodded. "Just diagnosed. Last week. He's fine. For now."

"Uhh," I moaned, holding my head.

"Such a talented boy, too. And he's only in his twenties."

I wanted to run out the door right then.

"He was supposed to be here tonight; he's with Armand these days, you know. Well, he was.... But Armand says he's horribly depressed. Well, I know all about that...." Nina's eyes teared again.

It was not one of Nina's good nights, but I felt I could not decently walk out on this conversation.

"Has something happened, Nina?"

"No. Not really. It's just.... I was cleaning out a closet today and found Garson's high school and college stuff—yearbooks, awards, some of his early writing from the *Crimson*. Boxes of this stuff. I don't know what to do with it. Do you think it should go into an archive?"

Garson Brumbach had written brilliant hard-boiled political essays. I had loved his early work, but by the time I met him, in the late sixties, I couldn't read him anymore. He'd started out a socialist and ended up a reactionary—antifeminist and arrogantly elitist. Nina, who had a great heart, never seemed to notice his politics. It seemed to me she was always remembering the old Garson, the professor twenty-odd years older than she and married, with whom she'd fallen in love while she was at Vassar. Garson divorced his wife to marry Nina. Of course, once Nina married him, Vassar expelled her. She never finished college. She said it didn't matter: a poet was educated in a different way, she said.

Garson was seventy-seven when he died. No one could say he didn't have a great life and a long one. But Nina kept mourning him. I wondered if the Garson she mourned hadn't died long before he died, like Tim.

"I just sat there on the floor, reading and weeping," she concluded. "God, I still miss him so much. The conversations we had..."

I tried to remember conversations I'd had with Charles, or even with Mark, who was more recent. I know we had them. I remember laughing and being happy, and I also remember some heated political discussions and lots of arguments. I wondered what Nina's conversations with Garson could have been like, that she still remembered them with such keenness.

"It must have been a wonderful marriage," I said piously, wondering if my inner cheek could stand another bite. It was pretty sore. "But you have a great life now, don't you? You're writing so much more, publishing so widely. You give readings all across the country. You didn't do that when Garson was alive."

"No. He didn't like me to.... I didn't like to leave him. And I'm glad I didn't. I'm glad I treasured every moment of our forty-six years together."

I remembered Garson going off on lecture tours and leaving

her alone for months every fall. There were plenty of rumors about him and young women too. My smile was getting stiff.

"But what am I going on like this for?" she said suddenly. "God knows you've done your share of suffering; you've lost a husband too."

"Two," I said in a little voice, feeling fairly sure that being widowed *twice* (not to mention divorced twice) somehow invalidated any claim I might have to martyrdom. I was right: Nina blinked and started. But she's a good soul. She tried to recover.

"So of course you know!" she exclaimed. "How wonderful it is to have a close relationship! How lonely life is without one! Who should know better than you? So. Tell me. Is there anyone in your life at the moment?"

I looked around furtively. "Actually..." I looked around again. "Actually, yes. Or sort of yes."

Her whole face lighted up. "Really!"

"Nina," I whispered, "would you like to have lunch?"

I huddled under the afghan as cool air blew in from the water. My eyes felt heavy. Perhaps this was a solution to my sleeplessness—a party, then meditation out on the porch. I leaned my head back against the couch pillows. Had I really been happier when I was married or in a love affair? I seemed to remember considerable anxiety attached to the love affairs and considerable irritation attached to the marriages, although I could not say why, could not recall actual instances. Well, come to think of it, there was Charles's habit of throwing his socks on the floor at night. He had particularly smelly feet, and his soiled socks stank up the entire bedroom. He liked his own smells, including that one, so I had to nag to get him to throw them into the bathroom hamper; he often forgot. He'd be snoring away, and I'd be lying there sleepless, with that smell in my nose. But that was such a small thing; wasn't it? And we had such good times together; didn't we? Together was certainly better than alone, but not of course with a Jack O'Reilly, or a dying Tim, or that weird Guy Kislik, or Jack Parker or Jim Steiner.... Actually, I could think of lots of friends I pitied for their husbands.

That night I slept.

9

*A*fter a relaxed Sunday, and an-
other good night's sleep, I was wakened early Monday by the
sun, a huge orange egg yolk hanging just over the water, looking
as if it were about to spill into the bay. I had neglected to lower
the blinds the night before, and light poured into the porch very
early. The birds were intensely talkative, far more than usual, it
seemed to me. I imagined they were gossiping about my presence on the porch. I lay there for a while—it was too early to get
up—gazing out through the screens at the cool greenness that
surrounded me, luxuriating in the sweetness and comfort of my
life, the life I had been fortunate enough to end up with. I remembered rising in the morning to the smells of baking bread
and the knowledge that downstairs waited my mother and
her sorrowful silence. I remembered waking in a dark little
dormered room, locked in pennilessness with a hostile husband
and a screaming baby. I remembered waking to the knowledge
of misery, day after day after day.

I lost Delia and gained Bert. We finally had to see each other, because we had to go together for a Wassermann test and to apply

for a marriage license. I was home alone when he came to pick me up in his father's twenty-year-old Packard. He stood in the doorway, pale and bitter-mouthed. He didn't say hello.

"Ready?"

I nodded. I didn't invite him in, just went for my coat and bag and left, slamming the door behind me. We walked down the wooden staircase in silence, our steps like out-of-sync mechanical taps. He opened the car door for me. We drove to the doctor's office and had our blood taken. Then he drove me back home. We didn't say one word to each other; we never even met each other's eyes. If the blood test showed we didn't have syphilis, we could get a marriage license. Then, in three days, we could marry.

Marry. How could we get married if we weren't even on speaking terms? I determined to be nice to him the next time. A few days later, our Wassermanns having shown negative, he called to say he'd come and pick me up to get the license.

"Sure. How about we go out for lunch?"

"What for?"

"I don't know. I thought it would be nice."

"Nice to spend my money?"

"I wasn't suggesting anything fancy. A sandwich and a beer," I said, remembering his preferences. "Dutch."

"Oh, and then get accused of getting you drunk again?"

"If you don't want to, forget it. I thought we should get to know each other a little. We're going to be married."

"Don't remind me."

So I was cool and unspeaking when he arrived. But after we filled out the forms, he said, "You wanna get some coffee?"

I just looked at him. A number of cutting responses crowded into my mouth, but I shut my teeth on them and shrugged okay.

We went to a smoky, greasy coffee shop near the courthouse and sat in a booth.

"My mother says you're right," he began, staring at his coffee and stirring it round and round.

"About what?"

"We should talk."

His face was pale and hurt. He'd been thin before, but he was skinny now; he looked as if the wind would blow right through him, and his face was pinched. My heart moved over a little for him.

"Look, Bert, I know this has disrupted your life, ruined your plans, put you in a miserable situation. But it's done the same to me. Even more so. I had a full scholarship to a wonderful college! I even had an allowance from my high school! I've lost it all."

"You're a girl. It doesn't matter."

"What?" I was confused. "Look"—I returned to my prepared speech—"we did something without thinking and now we have to pay for it. There's no point in your being angry with me or my being angry with you. We both did it, and we're both suffering now."

"We're not both pregnant," he said.

"*What?*"

"You're the one who's pregnant!"

"And who made me pregnant?" I shouted.

"Shut up! Shut up! You want everyone in the place to hear?"

I glared at him and sipped my Coke.

"You could have had an abortion," he muttered.

"No I couldn't!" I screamed. I couldn't get over the way men were about this. It was easy for him to want me to do something like that. I'd be the one to die, not him. Or I'd be in jail. He'd be rid of me.

He flushed and looked away. I suspected his mother would have been horrified at the thought of an abortion and that he knew it.

We sat in silence for a while, then I stood up. I laid a quarter on the table, for my Coke and a dime tip, and walked out. He leaped up and ran after me.

"Where're you going?"

"I'll take the bus home."

"Don't be stupid."

I didn't answer, just kept walking toward the bus stop. He followed me, his hands in his pockets, his head hangdog, misery spread across his face. "Okay, okay," he said, "I apologize. What do you want from me? I'm sorry, okay?"

I stopped. "Sorry for what?"

"I don't know. For everything. All of it. For the beer, for . . . the beach. For blaming you."

I looked at him. He was pitiful, I thought, wondering if I looked the same way.

"We're both in the same boat," I said.

"I didn't even go inside you!" he cried.

"You didn't?"

"Of course not! Couldn't you tell? Don't you know . . . ?" He looked at me incredulously, then dropped his gaze.

"I don't know anything except that I'm pregnant. And that I have to get married. To someone who doesn't even like me!" I burst into tears.

He faltered, looked teary himself, then patted me lightly. "I don't not like you; it's not that. I liked you! I like you! It's just kind of a shock, you know. It was all so long ago, and then out of nowhere . . ."

"I know," I said nasally, wiping my face.

"And I really wanted to be a gym teacher; I wanted to coach track."

"I know." I hadn't known what I wanted to be. "How's it going, you getting on the cops?"

"I have to take the test. I'm studying. It's really hard. I'm working days in my pop's garage and nights at Mario's. I study when I have time. I have to get some money. We have to get a place to live. My mom doesn't have room for us. I share a room with my two brothers."

I was deeply grateful for this fact. The idea that we might be forced to live with the Shiefendorfers was enough to engender thoughts of suicide. But I cursed myself for apathy: I'd been doing nothing but lying in bed and reading Delia's old movie magazines. "I should get a job."

"You're pregnant."

"Just for a few months. To save up some money."

His forehead wrinkled. "You wouldn't go back to Mario's, would you?"

I stared at him. "Why?"

"I just wondered."

"I might," I said.

He looked alarmed. "It's not a good idea. It's hard work, waiting table, it's too heavy for a pregnant girl, you shouldn't do it."

"What, have you been bad-mouthing me all over the restaurant?"

He flushed a deep pink. One thing, I thought, he'd never be able to lie to me.

"What a prince you are," I said, turning away. I continued toward the bus stop. He followed me. I turned back. "Just go back to your rock, toad, okay?"

"Look, I'm sorry."

"Yeah. Me too."

We stood together in silence, waiting for the bus. When it came, I mounted the steps and got on it, and he stood on the sidewalk, watching me—just like the old days. "See ya," he said.

He called me a week later. "My mother found this apartment—well, it's one room, really, but it's big and it's only thirty dollars a month. You want to look at it?"

The apartment was the gabled attic of a neat brick house on a nice street, two blocks from the bus line. This was important, because we would not have a car. It had a decent bathroom ("Great! That's something you don't always get in New York City, Elsa!" Susan gushed over the phone, sending me nearly into sobs) and an alcove with a stove and a sink and a little refrigerator. With ingenuity, you could block off areas for sleeping, eating, and sitting. And we could just about afford it. After taxes, Bert averaged thirty-two dollars a week at the restaurant. (It turned out that Mario paid the waiters fifty cents an hour, fifteen cents more than the waitresses. When I heard this, I was outraged.) His father paid him ten dollars a week for working part time. I had found a job as a clerk-receptionist in a roofing-tile company and took home twenty dollars a week. As long as I lived with Jerry and Delia, I could save almost half my wages. Bert was able to save most of his—his mother didn't charge him rent. But of course, I wouldn't be able to work once I began to show. Women had to leave office jobs after the third or fourth month of pregnancy; they were considered obscene.

On Saturday, the twenty-ninth of October, 1949, Bert and I went downtown and were married by a justice of the peace. Jerry and Bert's brother Hans went with us as witnesses; Delia refused to go. No one in Bert's family suggested we have a church wedding. I wondered if they felt a secular wedding wasn't real and so could someday be broken. I certainly thought so. When we got back to Jerry's apartment, my sisters and Bert's family were there. Delia's eyes were red, and every once in a while she'd get tears in her eyes. But no one thought anything of it; women were expected to cry at weddings. Everyone drank a little too much champagne and acted happy. Bert and I had saved up to go to New York for our honeymoon: we would stay at the Hotel Taft for the weekend and see a show. He borrowed Hans's car and drove us down. But being in New York pushed against my heart, reminding me of my dreams, making the present unendurable. We ate at an Automat and walked back to the hotel. I threw up. I threw up the whole wedding night. Bert sat on the double bed, watching me helplessly. It was not an auspicious start to a life of wedded bliss.

Our room was furnished, mostly by Mrs. Shiefendorfer and Delia, with bits and pieces of furniture from the attics of families and friends. It was waiting for us when we returned to Bridgeport Monday afternoon. We stopped at the supermarket to pick up something for dinner. Mario's was closed on Mondays, and Bert would have dinner at home. I kept nudging us toward cold cuts and rolls and canned soup, Bert wanted hamburgers or frankfurters and beans or a steak, things you had to cook. I told him I didn't know how to cook. He couldn't understand that. He seemed to think that girls got the ability to cook automatically, the way they got periods. In the end, we bought frankfurters and a can of beans and some potato salad. I told Bert I didn't know how to cook frankfurters. When we got home, I examined the package; it didn't even have directions!

"I mean it! I don't know what to do with these."

He raised his eyes at me. His face was sunken in. "But the woman is supposed to—" he began again.

"Forget *supposed*," I cried. "I *can't*."

"How hard can it be to make franks and beans?" he sneered. Then, casting a look of contempt at me, he flipped open a newspaper. I had never seen Bert read a newspaper before. He was copying his father, I was sure.

So I was to do the cooking, whether I could or not.

I did try, but somehow I burned the beans and served the frankfurters cold inside. Bert stormed from the table and out of the house. He was gone a long time. I put the frankfurters back in the pan, but this time I burned them. Since by then I was hungry, I ate around the burned parts of the franks and beans, filling up on the gluey supermarket potato salad. Bert walked all the way to his mother's and ate there.

In time, we settled into a routine. I walked to the bus stop at eight-fifteen every morning to catch the eight-thirty bus, which got me to work by nine. After my day's work, I took the bus home, stopping at the grocery store every day or two; I couldn't carry enough food to last more than a couple of days. On Saturdays, I went to the laundromat, dragging a laundry bag on a metal cart, and sat there smelling the clean damp soapy air and reading the movie and true confession magazines that always cluttered the place. On Sundays, I cleaned the apartment, which was small and perpetually messy. Jerry said, "Jesus, kid, you live in a hamper." I worked as long as they'd let me. Fortunately, I didn't protrude until my fifth month. I needed money for the hospital and the gynecologist.

Bert was working nights at Mario's, days at his father's gas station, and was studying for the police exam on his days off. When I was five months pregnant, I began staying home all day, and

Bert studied in his mother's house, where he could sit in the sun-room and no one bothered him. In our little attic, the two of us were on top of each other.

The Shiefendorfers had triumphantly presented us with a double bed as a wedding present. I imagine they reasoned that while we didn't share much, we apparently shared a sexual at-traction. Sex between us was moot on our honeymoon because I was sick the first night and sobbed myself to sleep the second. And we were not even speaking, much less kissing, that first Monday in our "little nest" (as his mother called our apartment). After Bert stalked out, I unpacked my things and washed the dinner dishes, amazed at how many there were for that simple meal, and at how hard it was to remove burn from an aluminum pan. I scrubbed and scrubbed: my hands were raw when I fin-ished, but the pot was still black. Then I washed out some un-derwear and hung it in the bathroom, and threw myself on the bed—the most comfortable article of furniture in the apart-ment—and tried to read Blake.

But the truth is, I never read Blake in that apartment. I never read Blake again. Misery, if it's deep enough, can close the mind, the eyes, the ears, can dull the brain as well as the heart. I closed the book, put on my pajamas, and slid under the cov-ers. I don't know what time Bert came back. When I awoke next morning, the bed was messy on his side, but he was up. He must have been in the bathroom; though I didn't see him, I smelled toast burning. *Burning!* And we had an automatic toaster, a wedding present! I smiled and rolled over and went back to sleep.

Five nights a week, Bert arrived home from Mario's well after midnight, by which time I'd be sound asleep. Only on Monday and his night off, whenever it was, did I have to worry about Bert's presence. So most nights I was left to my soup-and-sandwich dinners. But I have to admit I got tired of them. I began reading the woman's page in the newspaper and decided to try some of the recipes printed there. I actually made a tuna casserole and a Jell-O salad with carrots and celery without disaster. Then I tried a lima bean casserole: that was ghastly, but I had to eat it because I was out of money until Friday, when Bert got paid.

It was as if we weren't married at all: we didn't eat together and rarely slept together. By sleeping together, I don't even mean having sex; I mean just consciously, actively getting into the same bed. The first time we did this, on Friday, Bert's day off from Mario's that week, he had worked for his father and gone home with him for dinner. His mother must have wondered about us, but I think she liked having her boy home with her: he was her favorite child. He watched TV for a while after dinner, and showed up at the attic around ten-thirty. I was still awake.

We had tacitly fashioned a politely formal manner for the rare occasions when we had contact with each other. I was slumped in bed, reading a library book—a trashy novel—when I heard him unlock our front door. I pulled myself up to face him. His face showed shock at actually encountering mine.

"Hi," I said.

"Hi." He shook off his wet shoes on a rug near the door.

"Snowing out?"

"No, it stopped. But there's a foot on the ground, more in the drifts."

He walked into the apartment, toward the kitchen.

"Hungry?"

"Uhn-uhn. I ate at my ma's."

"Want some tea or something?"

"Nah. We got any beer?"

"No." I carefully did not say, You want beer, you pay for it out of *your* allowance and *you* lug it home.

"Coke?"

I shrugged. He stared at me.

"Look and see—you're not blind, are you?"

He sagged over to the fridge and opened the door. I knew perfectly well there were two bottles of Coke in there. And of course he knew that I knew. He pulled one out, removed the cap with his thumb (I hated that!), and threw himself down in our single armchair. He drank deeply, almost emptying the bottle with one draft. I found that revolting. I returned to my book.

"What did you do all day?" he asked.

I was shocked. He never initiated conversation. I felt a rush of gratitude and put down my book. "Nothing much. Went to work, did the ironing. I finished that disgusting lima bean casserole. I hope you got paid today."

"Yeah." He reached in his pocket and pulled out some folded bills. "My dad paid me." He got up and walked over to the bed, laid the money on the nightstand near me. From the first, he simply assumed that I would take care of our money—stretch it to pay the bills, buy the food.

I glanced at the wad and saw that it was his entire pay. "Don't you need some money?"

"Nah. I got bus fare, and I'll get paid at the restaurant tomorrow night."

He was good, I thought. That way, anyway. He could be worse. He could hang out in bars: he loved his beer. Lots of guys like him hung out in bars. He wasn't the worst. That was something to be grateful for.

"Tired?"

He leaned his head back. He was very pale. "Yeah," he sighed.

Suddenly, I understood. He felt shy about getting in bed with me awake.

"Why don't you get in bed?"

"Yeah. I should." But he didn't move.

I let my eyes hit the book again, waited a few minutes. He was still sitting in the armchair, but he seemed asleep.

"Bert?"

He was asleep.

"Bert!"

He shuddered awake. "Yeah! Yeah!" He swung around.

"Come to bed, Bert," I said firmly, sounding more like a mother than a wife. It was the right tone. He got up, went into the bathroom to undress, came out in his pajama bottoms, and slid into the bed without looking at me.

I slipped out of bed, slid the chain lock on the door, turned out the lamp by the easy chair, and got back in bed. Bert was already asleep, his mouth fallen open, his pale eyelashes trembling on his white cheek. He looked like a boy, timid and fragile. I put my hand on his shoulder and stroked it, and he sighed and turned and nestled his head in my side. I went on reading, feeling his warm head against me, and for a moment, it felt all right to be married—it was even comforting. I read a little longer, turned out the light, and slid down in the bed. Bert's head was pressing hard into my shoulder. I gave him a light push, and he turned over and crept, asleep, back to his own side of the bed.

One Monday, Bert came home right after I did, around six o'clock, with a paper bag full of hamburgers.

"Look what I got!"

"Bert! How great! Where did you get it?"

"White Tower. It's new."

Fast food had arrived. It saved my life. We devoured the burgers, french fries, and coleslaw. They tasted delicious to me, better than anything I could ever produce. We ate messily, with our hands; our faces were greasy, and when we looked up at each other, we were smiling. It was the first time since our marriage that Bert and I had enjoyed ourselves together. I praised him for resourcefulness and thoughtfulness as much as I could without becoming absurd. He lapped it up. The praise bore fruit.

"That was good," he concluded, washing his hands and face at the kitchen sink. "How about—you wanna go to the show or something tonight?"

I hadn't been to a movie since August. I hadn't been out of the house at night since we got married.

We went to the seven-thirty show, a double feature that let out a little after ten-thirty. It was past eleven by the time we got home, late for us. We were both tired but quietly contented. On the way from the bus stop, Bert took my hand, and we walked home swinging our arms together. We prepared for bed privately, in the bathroom, as usual, and we both put on pajamas. But tonight we did something we'd never done before—we talked as we moved around. We talked about our favorite characters and scenes, silently cherishing the sexy ones. And we got into bed at the same time, naturally, without strain.

But once we were in bed, tension set in. Bert immediately slid down, turning his back to me; I reached for my book, then thought twice about it and switched off the bed lamp. I slid down, too, but turned to face Bert and put my arms around him. A sigh like a gurgle sobbed from his throat. He turned toward me swiftly and grabbed and kissed me. He was already hard. I knew it was the movie that had aroused him, but it had aroused me too. Inexperienced as I was, I let him take control and do as he wished. This was not necessarily a good idea. He was sexually starved, and for him I was merely a receptacle.

Bert never had a clue about my sexuality. True, I never tried to enlighten him. I was too embarrassed, for one thing: I knew he believed that women were not sexual. It occurred to me that my brother believed the same thing, that that was one of the problems between him and Delia. And maybe Delia thought so too. But even stronger was my sense of the impossibility of explaining myself to Bert. How could I assert my sexuality to a man who never understood that I couldn't cook but who went on believing that I refused to do so out of malice? A man who, no matter how we discussed the subject, really believed I had tried to trap him into marriage, that he was a great catch for me, that I had nothing else to do with my life but have babies.

When I felt an overwhelming need, I masturbated during the day. I'd been doing that for years; it was nothing new. I never impeded Bert's pleasure. I figured I owed him something. He was supporting me, after all, me and the baby I was carrying. I was giving him service in return for money: that's what marriage was, wasn't it? That, certainly, was how everyone saw it in the fifties and even in the sixties and seventies. Probably some people still do. And heaven knows, sex with Bert was over fast enough. Apart from the fact that I ended up wet and slimy, it was painless.

After that, until I got too big for sex, Bert brought home White Tower every Monday night. Every Monday night we went to the movies, and every Monday night we had sex. Like clockwork.

In March, Bert took the civil service exam for the police force and passed, but with a low grade. The Bridgeport force hired him anyway, probably because so many of the older men were friends of his father's. He was to start training school in July.

In the middle of April, though, I gave birth to our baby. It was a girl. My pains began in the late afternoon and became intense by evening. Bert wasn't home, and I couldn't locate him—there was no answer at his mother's (it was her bingo night), and his father said Bert was not at the gas station. It was his night off from Mario's. I called Jerry.

Delia came with him, which made me teary, and I hugged her and held on to her all the way to the hospital. They stayed with me as long as they could before the nurses took me away. Jerry promised to keep trying to locate Bert. I had no idea what I was in for: the enema, the shaving, nurses and orderlies checking between my legs. I didn't cry or even whine or whimper; I had determined I would not. But as I lay there in pain, in a roomful of screaming women, without a friend or relative to hold my hand, only the brusque nurses swishing around, I thought this had to be the worst experience of my life.

The baby wasn't born until one-thirty in the morning, and by then Bert was there. When he saw me being wheeled out of the delivery room, he started babbling guiltily: he'd been playing poker with some cops at a guy's house, he said. As if I cared where he'd been, as if I had a big account book and was going to give him a demerit. He didn't even ask how I felt. I was zoned out from the Demerol and the ether but I looked for Jerry and Delia. I was so happy to see them. They were the only ones who loved me, even if Delia was mad at me, and I reached my arms out to them like a baby and they bent over and held me. Bert was still apologizing.

Over the noisy objections of the entire Shiefendorfer clan, I named the baby Lettice, a name I'd found in a novel. Bert asked nastily if I intended to name the next one kohlrabi. I laughed: this was the first example of wit I'd seen in him. But before long, everyone but me was perfectly happily calling her Letty.

Ironically, in those days of inhumane birthing, they allowed you to stay in the hospital for five days. The bad part was, they didn't let you see the baby except to nurse her. Fathers and grandparents could glimpse the infants only through a glass. It wasn't good for the babies not to be close to their mothers from birth, but it did let you rest up a bit, gain strength for the ordeal ahead.

And an ordeal it was. Baby crying all hours of the day and night, dirty diapers piling up, stinking up the entire room, baths and oilings and powderings to be administered daily, and all that laundry! The whole apartment was given over to the baby, and Bert hated that. Truthfully, I didn't love it myself. But I had no alternative; he did. Once he started training, I hardly saw him: he no longer had to work at Mario's, but he was either at the police academy or out drinking with the boys. I didn't blame him. If I could have escaped from my life in any way short of suicide, I would have.

From the day Bert started training as a cop, he began to change. He'd been a passive, dense, selfish boy with a sweet nature — at least, when he was not unhappy. He became a stubborn stupid man obsessed with displaying control. He swaggered around with his gun on his hip, often touching it like a talisman. He seemed to think of the gun as a means to enforce his will; he stroked it for reassurance. He would make irrational assertions, in a tone of utter conviction, about the proper roles of men and women.

One of the things he was intent on proving his control over was the baby. I told him that the only way to control a baby is to kill it, but he would yell orders at me, demanding I keep her quiet. Lettice was what they used to call a "colicky" baby: she cried a lot and would not be calmed. I would walk her around the room for hours, or put her in the carriage and walk her for miles, but between four in the afternoon and eight in the evening, she wailed unceasingly. When I could not quiet her, Bert would slam out of the house.

He calmed down somewhat once he finished training, though. He'd probably been afraid of failing; maybe he too was shocked by the macho police ethic (of course, we didn't have the word *macho* in 1950; at the time, I didn't know how to describe his behavior).

The first time Bert, white-faced, shrieked at me, "Can't you keep that brat quiet, woman!" in a contemptuous tone of voice, I made an instant decision: I would leave him as soon as possible. After Bert went off to his afternoon shift, I felt cheerful for the first time in almost a year, so I knew that leaving was the right thing for me to do. I knew women were not supposed to leave a marriage, they were supposed to find some way to make their husbands happy, but my determination made me feel—for the first time since I had found myself pregnant—like a human being with a future, instead of a dumb animal caught in a trap.

It was fortunate that I had already accepted that I was not a good person, because if I had had ambitions of goodness, I would have been tormented. As it was, my decision made things considerably easier between Bert and me. I stopped getting upset that he noticed Lettice only when she cried, that he refused to change her diaper, that he never held her. I knew it was just as well he didn't care about her, because he wouldn't miss her and I wouldn't feel guilty taking her away. And while he more and more often treated me with an easy, arrogant contempt, I could keep my temper, reminding myself that it wouldn't be long.

But of course, it was a pipe dream, because how was I going to get away? I took to reading the local paper every day, poring over the want ads. The jobs for women ranged from clerk to typist to stenographer to secretary. Only top-notch secretaries could earn enough to support themselves. And I did not want to leave Bert to move across the street or across town; my goal was New York City! I began to push Lettice's carriage to the public library every day and read the want ads in *The New York Times* and the *Herald Tribune*. But they were the same as the local ads, only somewhat higher paid. There were no interesting or well-paid jobs for women. I thought about my mother creating her own business, without money, with just her skill and energy and drive. But I didn't have any skill at all. I couldn't do anything.

I walked to the laundromat several times a week, piling the bag of laundry on top of Lettice in her carriage. I always took a library book with me; I still entertained notions of improving myself. But the truth was, I could no longer concentrate on serious literature. My mind rejected it. I wanted trash, I wanted escape. So I often picked up one of the tattered "women's" magazines lying around the laundromat—movie magazines and *True Stories, Modern Romances,* and *True Confessions.* Rocking Lettice's carriage with my foot, I would leaf through it idly, adopting an attitude of superior contempt. But the stories caught me, and I began to read them with a growing fascination. I read them the way I watched television (when I was forced), like an anthropologist studying the customs of an alien people. Yet the people in these magazines were not alien; they were women just like me.

One after another story was about women who had "fallen," who had given in to a night of passion and ruined their lives. The question was, what did they do then? Only a few tried to raise the baby themselves. Some of them gave their babies up for adoption and tried to go back to their old lives. But they were forever haunted by their dark secret, which would rise to crush them just when they thought they were safe. Often, a poor girl fell in love with the boy from the big house on the hill, who was a spoiled brat and denied any responsibility for her; sometimes the girl was from the big house on the hill, and she had a mad passion for the dark-haired angry boy who lived near the railroad tracks. But in the end, through sincere repentance and good behavior, some women were redeemed! A redeemed girl learned to speak and dress and act properly, so she could marry a man with a little money and pass into the middle class.

On the back pages of these magazines, there was always a true account, written by an ordinary girl about her sufferings. You wrote your story and sent it in, and if it was chosen, you got a hundred dollars. A hundred dollars! That was a fortune. In a fit of daydreaming, I had checked out the price of a tourist-class ticket on the *Île de France:* it was $165. If I could win two of these contests (and of course, if I did not have Lettice), I could go to Paris. Paris! That was even better than New York!

I began to spend the hours I walked Lettice back and forth in our attic room imagining my own story. Not my real story, of course: it was too bleak. But suppose Bert and I had found after we married that we really *did* love each other. It was possible, wasn't it? He could be a little nicer than he was, a little less stupid, a little more educated; I could be a good person like Delia and a little less educated, not quite so bright. We could learn through suffering.

I decided to try my hand.

It was much harder than I imagined. The hardest thing was to get the tone right, to have it sound like the work of a sweet, honest, well-meaning girl who wasn't too smart—yet without sounding like complete drivel. Day after day, I worked on it, concealing my efforts from Bert. I never threw scratched-out sheets into our garbage but folded them and the good pages and slid both into the Kotex box I kept in my bureau drawer. I knew Bert would never look there. When I went out each day, I took the bad pages and, tearing them up, threw them in a Dumpster near the supermarket. After a month, I had a story I thought was passable. I sent it off to *True Stories*. You had to include a self-addressed, stamped envelope if you wanted your manuscript back—which I did, figuring I could send it to the others—so I used my name and Jerry's home address, and called to warn him that something might come for me in the mail.

I was too nervous to sit around waiting for the results, so I immediately started another story. This one was different: in this one, the girl was in college, had come from a more middle-class background, and so was even more reprehensible. It was harder to write, because the girl was bright and a little privileged and had to be so penitent. In one night of sordid passion with a boy who works in a gas station, she blows her future with handsome, wealthy Clarence Bellows, a Harvard junior who is in love with her. Giving up her baby to a woman who has longed for a child for years, she ends in quiet, patient acceptance of her sin, working in a maternity hospital to help others like herself, hoping for redemption. It was truly sickening.

All I had to do to write these things was to imagine what a good woman would do, or feel, or say about the single most loaded situation women seemed to face. And I knew plenty of good women: my mother had been one. Delia was a good woman, so was my sister Merry, and most of the women in Delia's family and in Bert's were good women. At least, they tried to be. They thought they were. I just had to conjure them up, with sentences out of their own mouths. Now, when Bert and

I had Sunday dinner at his mother's house, I took interest in what was going on, I paid attention; if someone said something especially typical, I dashed into the bathroom to jot it down. Whatever happened with the stories, my new project was making my life a bit more bearable.

I must have done something right, because the third story I sent in won. I wrote more, under different names, and won again later that year. I had two hundred dollars! Enough to go to Paris, but not enough to get me and Lettice out of Bridgeport.

In the spring of 1950, a little bookstore opened in the same strip mall as the supermarket. It offered new and used romances, mysteries, and adventure tales, like the shop Merry used to patronize. In those days, public libraries did not carry romances, on the ground that they were not literature. But books were bound in paper now and could be bought new for twenty-five or fifty cents, returned for a dime, and bought used for twenty or thirty cents. Passing the shop, I remembered how romances had gotten Merry through a hard time of her life. Vaguely wondering if they could do the same for me, I suddenly found myself inside.

I didn't know how to choose from so many books, all bearing similar covers—most often, a young woman with a ripped bodice, and a dashing man in boots, carrying a whip. A glance at the back cover suggested that they all had the same plot too. But certain authors seemed more popular than others—the shelves held tens of books by them. I decided to go with those and chose one by Barbara Cartland. One was all it took to hook me. Feeling alone and unloved, unlovable even, living a life of such tedium that a telephone call was an event, I was sucked into the heroine's passionate adventures as into quicksand.

Having completed only two years of college, I couldn't claim to be an educated person. But I was aware that the book I was reading offered a false vision of reality. Yet there was some kind of reality in it, one I couldn't pinpoint or name, a kind that was somehow tied to what I'd been reading in the magazines. I had a vague sense that women's lives lay untouched, unseen, like tiny violets covered with snow. No one knew they were there, and no one cared, really. No one was interested in depicting them. The closest anyone came were these sweetish teary books that were soaked in fudge or caramel or strawberry sauce, allowed to dry, cut into pages, and sold. I felt I understood both the books and the thinking behind them, understood them with some part of myself, not necessarily my intellect.

I fell into the habit of getting a book each time I went to the market. I could easily have gulped down several of these confections a day, but I couldn't afford to. I had to make the book last a few days or be without one.

In time, I became quite knowledgeable about the genre and knew the names and pen names of the better-known authors. I felt I could tell if the author was male or female (all the authors' names were female), and I was familiar with the plots, basic morality, and taboos that characterize romance fiction. I became aware when an author was stretching convention—by introducing a mixed-color or mixed-religion relationship, for example. It occurred to me that these books could be agents of moral change—although I didn't use such an exalted phrase at the time.

I never confused these books with mundane reality, never expected the glamorous men who inhabited my literary fantasy life to appear in actual life or let myself slide into delusions that I had any glamour myself. Only I did think that someday I would like to travel to the thrilling places in which many of these novels were set, places like Egypt, Rome, Paris, London, Singapore, Macao. (What a disappointment when I finally visited Macao!) I alternated romance with good fiction obtained from the library—that year, I read all of Trollope and Galsworthy—but the pull of romance was irresistible. When I was not reading a romance, I daydreamed one, sitting in the laundromat or ironing to radio music or on my knees, washing the bathroom floor. It's true that during this time, I had a sense that I was wasting my life. I felt sickly sweet, like a child who's eaten too much candy. I felt I was damaging myself.

After reading maybe forty romances and winning my second story contest, I was struck by the idea that *I* might be able to write a romance. My heart began to thump, the way it does when you stumble onto something that is absolutely right. I knew it was something I could do.

Bert and I didn't go to the movies anymore; we would have needed a sitter, and he never suggested it. Neither did I. As a result, we didn't have sex: the one seemed connected to the other in his brain. They were connected in mine too, which was why I didn't suggest a sitter. Of course, for two months before and two months after Lettice was born, we were not supposed to have sex, so maybe he just got out of the habit. I don't know; we never discussed it. But he was almost never home: when he wasn't at work or helping his "pop" at the gas station, he was playing poker and drinking beer with other cops. He obviously didn't miss me. I didn't miss him. I could work seven days a week if I chose.

I determined to start writing immediately after New Year's, but Christmas held me up. Somehow, without a car, a baby sitter, or much money, I was expected to buy gifts for everyone, Bert's family and my own. This led to much quarreling with

Bert, whose help I absolutely needed. It all ended badly in every way; with great effort, I bought paltry gifts, which still nearly bankrupted us, and Bert and I were not speaking when we—or I—celebrated Lettice's first Christmas. It took me some time to recover.

But the winter days were so dismal, so unvaried in their pallor and emptiness, that my mind drifted back to my project as the only cheerful or colorful element in a bleak life. By mid-January, I began to imagine characters and a plot—both severely limited by the genre. The style was another matter. I set myself to write paragraphs of description in different styles. I went to the library with Lettice in her carriage, and pulling a half-dozen novels from the shelves, I copied their opening paragraphs. I studied the styles of the romances I'd read. Finally, I decided on a sharp, edgy style rather than the breathy effusiveness or flowery emotionality of most romance writers.

What was most important, though, was my decision not to make my heroines good girls. Most romance heroines were simperingly good: they were a little sickening and, in my view, by my morality or amorality, whatever it was, a bad lesson for the reader. I would give my heroines the author's imprimatur of moral rightness, but I would make them girls who thought about what *they* wanted, and saw sacrifice as an oppressive form of manipulation. I realized it might be wise to tone down this aspect at first and start with more conventional, less developed heroines. But from the first, I had a long-range plan.

By March, I had decided to set my first novel in a dilapidated antebellum mansion in the Deep South, a place I had never visited. I named the novel after the mansion, *Willowand*. It didn't mean anything; I just liked the sound of it. My heroine, Elsinore (I was shameless, and snobbishly figured my readers would not know *Hamlet*; my fan mail showed that I underestimated them), was nineteen and an orphan, like me. But a great-uncle she has never met agrees to take her in and has her transported from the cold, rational Northeast of her childhood to a steamy, swampy, Spanish-moss-draped overgrown plantation in Mississippi. No, Louisiana. This first quandary—my ignorance of either state—sent me to the library to study the South. I didn't take books out; Bert might just possibly notice them. I liked the library: I sat there, one hand rocking the carriage gently as Lettice slept, the other holding a book, happily reading in the quiet, sweet-smelling room. This was research! It was fun! I was having a glorious time; it was like being back in school.

I finally chose Alabama, which would have more antebellum mansions than either of the other states but was equally steamy and swampy. In an illustrated study of the South, I even found a picture of the exact house I had in mind. I studied it for a long time, jotting down its features in an old notebook purchased for my lamented junior-year English course.

I started writing *Willowand* in April 1951. It began: "The girl woke with a start as the train lurched, and her eyes widened as she saw through the window a soft green land where even the houses lacked hard edges, blurring into the trees." I was tentative and nervous. Though I wrote fast, each day I crossed out much of what I'd written the day before, so my progress was slow. Just as before, I hid my manuscript and crossed-out sheets. I enjoyed plotting this secrecy almost as much as I did the writing, and thought I would write my second novel about a girl who is imprisoned and under surveillance—albeit by superficially friendly forces—and uses such tricks to escape. It would be a romance, but it was also my life.

I finished my first manuscript in July. I was so pleased with myself for completing it, and for doing what I thought was a good job, that days passed before I realized I had no idea what to do next. I decided to consult my sisters, the New York sophisticates. As always when we called each other, they got on separate extensions, and we all talked at once. They squealed approbation when I told them what I had done.

"But I don't know what to do now. I've made a list of the companies that publish romances, but they're all in New York, and I don't know how to get an entrée into them...."

"Arlene Scott," Susan said. "She's a secretary at a publishing house. I met her through Ginger, an old roommate, who worked at Stratford Books before she got married. She'll know what to do. I'll call her tomorrow and call you back."

"Umm. One other thing.... I haven't told Bert about this."

There was a long silence on the other end as this got digested.

"Okay," Susan said finally. "So if he's home, I'm just calling to see how my one and only niece is. How is she, by the way?"

I waited in tantalized agony, pins and needles in my fingers and toes. But several weeks elapsed before Susan called with instructions to mail the manuscript to a friend of Arlene's called Nadine, who was a secretary at Swan Books, which specialized in romances. "Nadine's friendly with a couple of editors there, and she'll ask them to read it," Susan concluded.

It was my turn to squeal.

My brother's and sisters' lives had changed over the past two years. Tina had gone off to Hollywood to make her fortune, and we rarely heard from her. A few months after Lettice was born, a crumpled package arrived in the mail, containing a tiny outfit, already too small for her, with a card from Tina, but no news. Susan was now secretary to the vice president of her agency and made very good money for a woman. And she was engaged to a designer in the agency's art department, Eldon Willis. Eldon owned a car and had driven Susan and Merry up to Bridgeport to welcome Lettice into the world. Merry was still the same, as she lamented. And she still read romances.

After Lettice was born, Jerry and Delia bought a house in the country, just outside Bridgeport, a wonderful big old place like our house in Millington. Delia had learned to drive and had her own car now, and Jerry, sounding cheerful, told me they were trying to start a family. I rarely spoke to Delia, but Jerry stopped over a couple of times a month and took me and Lettice out for a little drive, for ice cream or a trip to a park. He was a godsend. He knew I never went anywhere but the supermarket. Maybe he wasn't a good person in the way Delia was, but in my book he was better.

The family had split apart in some ways. Living in New York, my sisters were exposed to things Jerry and Delia never thought about. They went to art museums once in a while, and to plays; they saw movies that didn't come to Bridgeport; and their speech had improved. They acted and sounded like educated middle-class women, whereas Jerry's speech had deteriorated from his working in a factory with uneducated people, and since he never went anywhere to speak of, he seemed sort of—I hate to say this—provincial. When they were all together, my sisters and Jerry, they seemed like members of two different classes. Yet Jerry and Delia were probably better off financially than Susan and Eldon and, certainly, than Merry, who was still just a secretary in a pool. Someday, though, Eldon might make more money than Jerry. Class was a subtle thing.

Listening to my siblings, I realized that my own speech was decaying swiftly from constant exposure to Bert and his family, with whom we frequently had Sunday dinner. I thought about

Shaw's *Pygmalion* and realized that my Millington teachers had hoped I'd improve myself at Mount Holyoke. Maybe I could still get educated—not by college but by the women's magazines. They, after all, were the only honest and direct source of truth about women in the world. They and only they openly admitted that for women, class and money were everything. Oh, they mentioned virtue, touted as the highest good: women had to be virtuous. But if you considered what they really meant by virtuous, it had to do with appearance and manners. The virtuous girl was rewarded with marriage to a prosperous, faithful, well-spoken man. For a girl like me, a girl who had fallen, redemption was the only hope. And redemption was marriage to a man with some money, a man who wore a suit to work. And the only way to get him was to speak well, dress well, be humble and chaste. I sadly realized I was already unredeemable.

---

10

*F*rom the quality of the light, I guessed it was time to get up. Yawning, stretching, and listening to bird chatter (which had dwindled a bit since daybreak), I thought about the day ahead. Tuesday. A croissant and coffee for breakfast, work until noon, a swim. Then I'd have lunch and rest, sitting in the sun reading my *New York Times*. Afterward, I might do a little weeding. A gardener took care of the grounds, but I liked to put my hands in the soil once in a while. Later in the afternoon, Alma Nutley, the publisher, was holding a tea for the British writer Edith, Lady Haswell, who was staying on the Island with her for a few weeks. It should be an elegant affair, everyone in high gear. I would probably end up going out for dinner with someone there. If not, I could nuke my leftover blanquette de veau from dinner at Citron the other night. It would be a pleasant day.

After my swim, I sat outside on a chaise, drying out, a notebook on my lap, a sandwich and a pitcher of iced tea, the portable phone, and my Rolodex on the table beside me. I called the plumber to look at the outdoor shower, which was dripping; I made a dentist appointment. Then I lay back in the lovely warm sun and sipped iced tea. I was sleepy, and didn't feel like reading the *Times*. I baked in the sun, remembering my first acceptance. . . .

It took nearly two months for an editor to read and approve my manuscript, but eventually someone did and called Susan—I couldn't leave my own number—to say her company would publish it and pay me five hundred dollars. Susan called me at home. "Can you talk?" she screamed, and gave me the news.

Of course, they wanted a few changes, and needed to set up a meeting. I was going to have to go to New York. For a while, that seemed impossible. I considered telling Bert the whole thing, but the mere thought of getting him to understand what I had been doing—and why—was overwhelming. Besides, I intended to leave him without any warning. I knew he'd try to stop me, not because he loved me or even enjoyed my company, but because I was his property, I belonged to him. I didn't want to fight with him or listen to him yell and threaten. It would be a waste of time.

But I could tell Jerry now: I'd hesitated to confide in him, afraid he might discourage me. Jerry couldn't take Lettice for me, but Delia could, and Jerry could talk her into doing it. She had finally become pregnant and, forced to leave her job in her fourth month, was sitting at home, bored and miserable. And indeed, it all worked out.

So in October 1951, just before my first wedding anniversary, I took the bus to New York. There, I met with Eda Doyle, an editor at Swan Books. She was a well-dressed, hard-looking woman in her late forties, a little portly, a dyed blonde with a thick, hard mouth and skin toughened by years of foundation makeup. But she would show herself over time to be a woman of great kindness. She suggested some changes and said they'd like the finished manuscript in a month. I signed a contract without even reading it. She asked if I had an idea for another book. I told her my idea about a paranoiac heroine, and she liked it. It was not all that original, even I knew that, but given the conditions of my life, I'd probably recounted it with some fervor. I said I'd like more money for it—$750. Her eyebrows rose, but she agreed. "If we like it, if we accept it, okay.

"One more thing," she added tentatively. "We feel—well, the authors of romances usually use pen names. They like to take somewhat romantic names...."

"Yes, I know. And Elsa Schutz isn't romantic." I'd written the book under my maiden name. In fact, I never in my life called myself Elsa Shiefendorfer. "I've picked out a name."

"Yes?"

I felt my face grow hot. I was as embarrassed as if I were laying my sexual fantasies on the desk for her perusal. "Hermione Beldame," I offered shyly.

She looked as if she were going to choke. After a moment, she repeated, "Hermione Beldame?"

I watched her face.

She finally met my eyes. Was her complexion a little pink? "Let me think about it. You like it, huh? You think it's beautiful?"

My eyes were somewhat damp, and I made my lips thin and mean to keep them from trembling. I could tell she didn't think it was beautiful. She thought it was ludicrous. I wanted to sink under the desk and disappear, but I held my head up stiffly.

"It's a name I think women will like. Trust me."

My authoritative tone made her head snap up. "Really." She looked at me sharply. Was I an idiot hick twenty-year-old or a smart cookie who had figured the angles? I could see her mulling this over. I decided to play it tough.

"Yes. I'm sure of it."

In fact, I was. I had tried it out on Delia, Susan, Merry, even Jerry. All of them felt it had solidity and trustworthiness, but also a fluttery, lacy feminity. I left Eda's office buoyant. I was launched on my secret career, on my way out of Bridgeport and away from Bert, on the freedom road.

The sun was hot. The ice in my tea had all melted. I stirred, thinking I should get a move on, do something. I could hardly avoid finishing the present novel within a day or two, no matter how much I continued to procrastinate. I should start thinking about the next one. Maybe I should give myself a change of scene to get the imaginative juices flowing, go someplace that would inspire a romantic story: Venice, Bombay, Suzhou, Paris. I could simply pull out old guidebooks and recall these places, but cities change, even Paris, and it's better if one's impression is fresh. Perhaps I'd go in August, when it emptied out. Of course, all the decent restaurants in Paris were closed in August. Maybe better to wait until September. But I'd like to go soon—next week, or the week after. The hell with George. If I went to Paris next week, I'd beat the August exodus. I could stay three or four weeks, come home at the end of July. But then, Paris was full of tourists in July. Ugh. Perhaps I should go to Africa. I hadn't been there in a few years, and the weather was fine there in July: skies clear as ether, broad as the sea, a world of sky. I could visit West Africa, countries I hadn't visited—Ghana, Côte d'Ivoire, Benin, say. Yes, that was what I should do! I was searching my Rolodex for the phone number of Marlene, my travel agent, when the phone rang. I answered it absentmindedly.

It was George.

Heart-stop.

"Hi!" Hearty as ever, never know he'd been away. "What the hell are you doing way out there, wherever you are?"

"Hi! Where are you?"

"I'm in New York," he said, as if it were self-evident. "In a really snazzy apartment Warren got for me, midtown, walking distance to the office. It's really neat."

"When did you get back?" Did my voice sound cool? Why was that?

"Last night. Called you but just got your machine. Called again this morning and got somebody called Lou. What a great girl! Really nice! Terrific! She said you were out in Bag Bar, or whatever you call it. So when're you coming back?"

I'm not coming back, I wanted to say, I'm here for the summer. Or: I'm on my way to Paris. Or Harare. Or Ouagadougou.

But what came out of my mouth? "Oh, probably tomorrow. Why?"

"Want to do something?"

"Sure." I considered. "Why don't I get us tickets for a play?"

"We-ell... don't get anything too highbrow, okay? Remember I'm just a country boy."

I decided to take some control. "Why don't you give me your number there, so I can call and let you know where to meet me?"

"No, I'll come and pick you up. Plays start around eight, don't they? So I'll be there about seven-fifteen. See ya tomorrow!"

And he was gone.

I did not allow the thought that he had outmaneuvered me to perch even briefly in my mind. Swinging into action, I called Lou and asked her to get tickets for *The Good Times Are Killing Me,* and make a hair appointment with Antoine for tomorrow afternoon. And buy fresh milk and oranges and croissants for my breakfast. I ran indoors and tossed soiled towels in the hamper and dishes in the dishwasher, preparing to leave the house for an unlimited time. Accra would have to wait.

I did not pause to say to myself, Hermione, what are you

doing? I did not question how it was I was abandoning all my resolve, all my plans, to fly back to New York, dropping everything at the mere sound of George's voice. In my soul, in some
deep part of me, I felt I was fighting for my life, struggling, like a
drowning person trying to keep her head above the waterline.
Perhaps my brain knew I was fighting not for my life but for the
life of the dream, the fantasy, the yearning, the need. But so en-
meshed with, so identical to my own life had it become that I
knew I could not live unless the dream came true. Anything at
all was warranted; I would do whatever I had to to preserve it.

I can't say I was happy. My excitement was nervous, penetrated with anxiety; my head and heart pounded. I longed for
some resolution. Tomorrow, perhaps.

So there we were Wednesday night, in a cab heading crosstown
to the theater to see the off-Broadway production of *The Good
Times Are Killing Me,* when George, sitting half-assed on the taxi
seat, facing me and leaning toward me as if he wanted to press
against me, said: "The reason I don't want to get involved with
you, Hermione, is that I don't want to end up a character in one
of your novels."

I did not want to discover what he was *really* telling me, because I suspected that he really meant what he *said* and the different signal his body was sending out came from his body alone,
an entity with which he was not in close or regular contact. For
a moment, I searched my mind to find a way to make him feel
happy or pleased or at least comfortable, but I could discern no
way to do that, so I just sat back and let him take control. I
wanted to ask him: If you don't want to get involved with me,
why do you keep calling me? But I said nothing. He relaxed. As
we stood in line to enter the theater, I slipped my hand through

his arm, and he smiled down at me, his eyes bright with pleasure. Maybe, finally, I'd done something right.

And he liked the play, was amused and moved by it, and was pleased I had chosen it. He had himself picked out a restaurant near the theater and made reservations. This pleased me, and I avoided thinking about his need to stay in control. We had a fine dinner at a steak house: he ate a huge sirloin and I ordered lamb chops I could not finish. We both had the baked potato and excellent creamed spinach that are typical steak house fare. He liked his meal. He seemed to like me. He gazed at me with warm eyes and a sweet smile, listened to me with interest, spoke about himself more easily than usual. I wondered if perhaps he had missed me.

That evening was the best time we had spent together, and he did not seem in any rush to get home. It was a beautiful summer night, and we walked over to Columbus and then uptown for nearly a mile before we decided to take a cab to my apartment. He asked if I wanted to have lunch the next day. I did. I was almost in bliss, I was right outside the door to bliss, the door was ajar. There was just this anxiety....

He said he'd keep the cab to take him back to his place. It was on the West Side, downtown, back where we had come from. Oh, I said. At my building, he stepped from the cab. I slid over and got out, and looked up at him standing there. The light from the canopy shone on his fair hair, and, his head illuminated, he was beautiful and austerely sweet, like an angel in a Van Eyck painting. I gazed up at him, and my heart lurched: I could not bear to let him go. It was breaking my heart, making my body scream, to let him go. I wanted to reach out, to clutch at him, to beg, "Come upstairs with me!" And without thinking, suddenly, I stood up on tiptoe and kissed him. On the lips.

I shocked him. Horribly. His shock was so extreme, waves of it hit Jack, the doorman, who was standing behind me: I could feel him reverberate. Yet he was used to seeing me kiss my friends good night at my door. George must have gasped, jumped back, looked pale, must have done something I didn't see but felt—chill, horror. The goddamned cabdriver was probably shocked! Not only was everyone shocked, but there wasn't even any pleasure in it: he didn't kiss me back, so there was no passage of electricity. He didn't really even accept my kiss, so there was no tenderness. My kiss was like a bird peck on a pole, immobile and inanimate: my head bobbed forward, his bobbed back, like two wooden birds on sticks and strings in an old children's toy. I walked into my building, holding myself erect, and did not look back.

It had been a terrible, maybe fatal, mistake.

I prepared for bed with a sense of dread, sure that my move had damaged things. I considered calling a friend to talk about it, but the situation was really beyond help. And I was tired of talking about it.

My skin moisturized, my teeth flossed, I sat in bed looking out over the park, a large dark space dotted with tiny lights. I wished I smoked. I would have smoked if I'd had a cigarette. I decided to let an idea into my mind that I had heretofore barred the door to, very firmly: I entertained the possibility that George was impotent. I'd had experience with that, in a number of different men, both older and young. I had been able to help those I was willing to take in hand, to speak metaphorically. But all of them—all but one, anyway—were eager for sex, were raging with desire. Whereas George alternated between abrupt propulsion and abrupt revulsion and seemed to be in control of neither.

I remembered Harvey, a lawyer in a publishing firm, who for

three years pursued me with relentless fury. While I was married to Charles, he offered me eloquent conversation, much of it about poetry, over long lunches at La Grenouille and La Caravelle, after morning visits to art galleries and museums. After Charles died, he offered it over dinners at the Four Seasons and Lutèce before or after the theater, a jazz club, a carriage ride through Central Park. I say "fury" because he pursued me ardently but with a cold rage at my intractability. Yet he *never* tried to make love to me, never made any physical contact beyond holding my hand. Pouring out his desire in lacy language, he never asked me how I felt about him. Sometimes I felt like a statue he'd chosen for his delectation, an idol he used to stimulate his poetic impulses. He'd sit and gaze at me, reciting poetry and defining me—at least, that's how it felt. "You're really above it all, aren't you, Hermione?" he'd say. "So brilliant. One of these days you're going to write a real novel, one that shows your true talent. So brilliant and cold, so glittery you are, your eyes cold and beautiful...." Stuff like that. His descriptions varied from time to time, but in all of them, I was beyond his reach. So of course I didn't want to go to bed with him. I would just smile, and he would scrunch up his eyes as if he were dying and order another martini. We drank martinis in those days.

When Andrew began laying siege to me—and he did, oh, he did!—I saw less of Harvey. And once I realized I was in love with Andrew, I told Harvey I couldn't go out with him anymore. He began to cry, great gasping sobs came out of him, tears poured down his face, right there in La Côte Basque. The waiters were shocked. And I felt terrible—after all, I did like him a great deal—so I said that I'd never been beyond his reach, that all he had ever had to do was just that, just reach out to me. He didn't seem to understand what I was talking about, so as a parting gift,

I took him home with me and led him to my bed. But of course, I *was* out of his reach, not because I was the unapproachable lady of the sonneteers but because he had stuck me on top of a pedestal—no, a pyramid—and he knew that if he climbed to the top, I would be standing there waiting to cut his heart out. I wasn't the troubadours' cold lady he'd made me out to be: I was a fucking Aztec priest.

I didn't see him for years after that, but one night around Christmas, when I was with Mark, I ran into Harvey in the Pool Room at the Four Seasons. He smiled and made conversation, while his eyes regarded me with hate.

But George was nothing like Harvey. Was he?

George pursued me with such intensity. So had Harvey.

George had such kindliness in his face. Well, so did Harvey.

George gazed at me with such warmth. So had Harvey.

But George left in a hurry; Harvey had never wanted to let me go. And George spoke a funny male language, full of boyisms and sincerity and enthusiasm, whereas Harvey used a rhetoric of poetry, high-blown and sentimental, often soaring into true eloquence. And George had recently been involved with a young woman he had mentioned to me—sexually involved, I was sure. Whereas Harvey had not been involved with any woman for several years before I met him and (I thought) for several years after. They were nothing alike, I decided. I put out my imaginary cigarette and slid down to sleep.

Thursday morning, George called. He sounded irritable. Bad morning he said: a thousand interruptions, lousy writing by a person who should know better.... Just one of those days.

"We on for lunch?"

"Sure."

"I'll be by at noon, then. See ya."

By the time he arrived, his mood had improved. We wandered over to our usual lunch place on Lexington, in pleasant conversation, his smile as warm as ever, his eyes sexy and intense and focused on me. I was telling him about my novel, and a question I had about the conclusion. I had reached the penultimate point, at which my heroine rejected the villain. She had pushed him away and run, because the man's embrace and kiss overpowered her, made her feel smothered, small and powerless. She did not recognize that his behavior showed he cared only about his own desire, not hers, or that this was a sign of his evil nature. On the contrary, she felt apologetic toward him, because his aggressiveness had also aroused her somewhat, and she suspected that her sense of insignificance was a result of her own weakness, was a flaw in her character. She felt that, having failed him, she owed him something.

Now he, of course, being a villain, was going to take advantage of her apologetic attitude toward him to kidnap and rape her. (You must realize that in romances, as in eighteenth- and early-nineteenth-century novels, a woman's virginity is a great prize, which can be won only once and, once lost, is irrevocable. I know it seems silly, but that's the convention. You just have to accept it, the way you do chess moves.) My question was, how would the hero feel if he thought that the villain had succeeded? (Of course, he would not succeed. He would be thwarted by the heroine herself, a gutsy little thing called Lila.) But the hero would *think*—for a while at least— that the villain had accomplished his dire purpose, and his response was the revelation of *his* character.

Smiling, I asked George, "Do you think that in this day and age, a man of thirty-odd would turn against his fiancée if she was kidnapped and raped? You know, reject her as spoiled, used goods?"

"How old is this fiancée?"

"Twenty-five."

"She's twenty-five and still a virgin?"

I laughed.

"That seems completely unrealistic to me."

"Well, it is nowadays in urban circles. But it's conceivable among some people. And anyway, this is an unrealistic literary genre. What do you think the man would feel?"

"It might just as well turn him on," George said.

"Whoa!" I stopped in my tracks. "That's a new one! You think a guy might get turned on...?"

He shrugged. "Who knows? Why not? It's as possible as anything else."

I laughed again. "I can't use that for my hero, but I'm going to file it away and use it for a villain in some future novel."

"As long as the villain isn't based on me." He smiled.

"It's your idea," I said. "You came up with it."

He stopped then. He looked at me seriously. "You're not going to put me in one of your novels, Hermione, are you? Promise me not!"

I giggled. "You're too old! My cast of characters comes from the nursery! And much as I'd like to cast you as a hero, I'm afraid you aren't one. Nor are you a villain. So what role could I give you?"

"Woman-hater," he muttered darkly, and started walking again.

I ignored that, firmly refusing to ask what he meant. We reached the restaurant, ordered, sat sipping iced tea.

"So, Hermione, what do you want? You want to get married again, or what?"

My heart leaped a little, but only in a Pavlovian reaction. His tone of polite inquiry had no intimacy in it.

"Oh, I don't think so. No."

"So you want to live with someone?"

"No. In the ideal—if I could have my druthers—I'd like to live separately. Maintain separate households but see each other regularly, several times a week. Spend most weekends together. Travel together. But still have separate social lives. I think that's ideal. What about you?"

"Me, I hate women." He bit into his sandwich.

I looked at him, puzzled.

"I mean it, I really do. I don't understand them…it's all beyond me." He stared off into the restaurant, chewing doggedly.

There was nothing to say. I stared off into space too.

He told me about a quarrel at the newspaper among a group of editors, about a split infinitive. He wondered how I felt about split infinitives; he seemed seriously interested. So I, too, treated it seriously, explaining that being of the old school, of course I disapprove of split infinitives; they invariably hit my ear as crude and déclassé. I offered my old-fashioned opinion for what it was worth, and he launched into a series of grammatical questions that plagued the editorial desk at *Newsday*. As he paid the check, I remarked that it was impressive that the editors would argue about such high-flown subjects. I thought grammar was no longer of interest to anyone except a few linguists talking to each other by E-mail, I said. We walked out of the restaurant; it was eight minutes to one.

"Well, it was sure interesting to this woman I met on the plane," he said, as we started back to my apartment.

I cocked an eyebrow at him.

"This woman was sitting next to me on the plane coming back here, and we got talking. She was real nice, I thought—at first, anyway. She'd been a grammar teacher. Years ago. Was all agitated about the grammar in a column in the Louisville *Herald*—*my* paper! I was insulted! Actually"—he laughed—"the columnist is a kind of dumb bunny and he writes this sentimental slop, but he's the most popular writer on staff, so we can't discipline him. I wouldn't be sorry not to have to deal with him again...."

"Why would you not have to deal with him again?"

"If I didn't go back. If I stayed up here. Oh! I didn't tell ya! They've offered me a job here, fabulous money." He peered at me. "Of course, I suppose it wouldn't seem like a lot to you."

My heart stopped, weakly started again, then perked along at a snail's pace. I tried to get my head clear. I said nothing.

"So we were having a nice talk, everything was fine, and then she asks me where I'm staying in New York. And I said I was being put up and didn't have an address, and she said, Well, I can always reach you through *Newsday,* can't I. And I am sitting there frozen. Reach me through *Newsday?* What for? And she says, You know I'd like to see you again, and she puts her hand on my arm, and I'd like to die. I thought we were just having a nice conversation, and here she was...I didn't expect to see her again, I'd just been talking to talk, to make conversation on the trip, the way you do. This happens to me over and over! Over and over! I tell you, it just keeps happening! That's why I hate women! I really hate women!" He glared at me. "You tell me! What was I supposed to do?"

"Oh. I guess we're all sometimes approached by people we don't...have interest in," I said in a thick voice. "You learn, don't you, over the years, how to deal with it...." I examined his face, tried to read it. He looked like a teenage boy in a state of outrage.

"Well, I don't know what to do. I just hate women!"

We had reached my building. I stood there, not knowing what more to say. "Well …"

He glanced up. "Oh! Well, I'll call ya. Bye," he said, and walked off; then, turning back to face me, walking backward, he said, "Take care, Hermione" and "I'll call, okay?"

My body was quite still inside, even as the outside of it went through its motions. Not letting myself feel anything, I brushed my teeth, I sat down at the desk and read the mail, I got up and fetched a glass of cold water, then I sat on the chaise in my study, leaning back my head, letting it rest in its throbbing numbness.

What was this now? What was he telling me? Did he mean me? Then why did he call me at all, why did he keep asking me to lunch, why did he keep promising to call?

The weather had turned hot and humid, and the apartment felt sticky and mildewy. I should turn on the air conditioners, which I hated. But at least their roar would blot out the sounds in my head, the dull *beat beat beat* that seemed to interfere with my vision.

I didn't want to see anyone, which was just as well, since most of my friends had left town for the summer. I would finish the novel tomorrow. I should go back out to Sag Harbor. After I'd recovered a little, I'd think about traveling abroad. I needed something other than Paris. Africa was the thing. Maybe Victoria Falls again, or Great Zimbabwe; I'd never been there. I dragged myself back to the desk, and forty-odd years of discipline kicked in.

George called on Friday. Edgar Allen was in town and wanted to have dinner with us, and George wanted me to meet an editor he worked with at *Newsday*, Darcy Meeks. The plan was for Darcy to meet us at the place where we usually ate lunch. It was an inexpensive bistro, okay for lunch but not for a good dinner. I didn't demur, though, didn't suggest that another restaurant might be better. I wondered what would happen to me if George and I did get together. Would I lose my personality? Would I submerge myself in him? Would I lose the power to say no? Would I go along with whatever he wanted? I realized with a surprising serenity that I didn't care: I didn't care if I had to eat overcooked pasta and dried-out fish at cheap restaurants for the rest of my life; I didn't care if we went only to mainstream movies and plays, and I had to sneak off with one of my friends to see anything interesting. I didn't care if he never went to a museum or an art gallery with me, or to a concert or lecture. I just wanted him to love me. Just that: I asked for no more. I wanted it so ravenously, so fiercely, that nothing else existed. I wondered if that was how Ilona Markovich felt about Guy Kislik, Betty Margolis about Jack O'Reilly, Nina Brumbach about her Garson. It was a sobering thought.

I dressed with special care, wearing clothes that would not stand out in the kind of restaurant we were patronizing yet in some way flattered me. I chose black linen pants and a black-and-white-striped linen shirt, with black sandals—not city evening clothes, but they would pass. Yet compared to George, who picked me up at seven-thirty, I was overdressed; he wore a shabby pair of chinos and a wrinkled summer shirt. The night was balmy, a relief after a terribly humid day, but he was disgruntled.

"Edgar will be late, he's always late," he complained as we walked over to Lex. "I don't know where he is; he doesn't leave a number, he's always running around seeing people—got to be with this one, that one!" He stopped in exasperation, walking with his hands thrust into his pockets.

"And I told Darcy to be there at seven-thirty; he'll be having kittens. Edgar won't be there, and the whole point of this dinner was so Darcy could meet Edgar, he's keen to meet him, he saw him in *The Little Merman*. But Edgar didn't answer the phone when I called, god knows where he is—he may not even show up after all this!"

His eyes were a little wild. He kept sniping at Edgar during our walk to the restaurant and began to mutter, in the same tone in which he had muttered that he hated women, that he hated Edgar. "God, I hate that Edgar—he drives me crazy. I don't know why I hang around him; I *hate* unreliable people! Actors! Always have to stop for one more bit of gossip—doncha know, darling," he finished in a mincing mimicking tone.

Yet I knew from his frequent references to Edgar during earlier conversations that Edgar was really a friend to George, his only friend, that they talked every few nights on the telephone and had for thirty-odd years. It seemed clear to me that George loved Edgar. I held myself taut and silent, refusing to think about who the object of this rage really was.

George was right: Darcy Meeks was at the restaurant, waiting for us, sitting at an outdoor table with a glass of red wine and reading the editorial page of *Newsday*. But he appeared relaxed, not at all annoyed. He seemed to have cultivated composure. He was a warm reddish brown, with close-cropped salt-and-pepper hair and a mustache and eyeglasses. Unlike George, he was well dressed, in a smart lightweight sharkskin suit. George introduced us and immediately lit into Edgar again. Darcy Meeks's eyebrows rose a bit; he glanced at me questioningly, but I was no help and just shrugged. George calmed a bit when the waitress arrived and took our drink order, and Darcy tried to make polite conversation with me.

"George tells me you're a writer," he said.

I knew what he would think of the kind of books I write. I smiled. "Yes, I write romances."

His eyebrows went up again. "You know, my sister reads those, goes through 'em like Kleenex. And she has a Ph.D. in anthropology."

"They should be right up her alley, then." I laughed. "They are studies in American culture." When literate people are trying to be nice about my writing, they always bring up some Ph.D. or nuclear physicist they know who reads romances.

"I guess maybe I ought to try one," he said, graciously.

"Men tend to be wary of romances. My theory is they're afraid they'll get hooked and feel unmanly ever afterward."

He laughed. "Probably true."

George was fuming, fussing, swiveling his head around, paying little attention to our conversation. "Where is that Edgar? God, I hate actors. As much as I hate women."

Darcy gave me another questioning look. I met his gaze but kept my face impassive.

"How long have you been at *Newsday*?" I asked, as if George had not spoken, and we launched into a civil private conversation, talking above George's occasional muted explosions. We talked until Edgar tore up, pink-faced and breathless, full of apologies. George muttered and grumbled at him, exploding, "I hate actors!" which Edgar ignored. He was bubbling over, excited with theater gossip he'd just picked up. He'd met with the producers and director of a new musical in the process of being cast, hoping to get a part, along with others who were reading. "They didn't call it an audition, they couldn't, how insulting—you can't ask Edith Hoppe to *audition*, can you! So they just asked us to *read* together, but we all knew what was really happening, it was all right, it salved our pride, and it was so fun to dish with all of them."

And it was fun to listen to Edgar repeat it for us, to hear about Morrie's divorce and Lee's affair with no less a star than Mark Hosmer, and the terrible squabble between Angela Grigg and Helena Hope, and the fallout from it.... Edgar's relish for gossip and his high style in conveying it carried us through our rather poor meal, George's persistent muttering, and Darcy's and my confusion about just what we were doing there. Edgar's wife, Beenie, a costume designer, worked more regularly than he and so knew even more gossip. So when he had run through all his own, he launched into hers, which took us through cappuccino. Perhaps he sensed the stiffness of the evening; he certainly was aware of George's foul mood. So although it was George's party, it was Edgar who played host, who took control and saw us graciously through an evening that without him could only have been remembered—by both me and Darcy Meeks—as seriously unpleasant. I'd always been fond of Edgar, but that night he went up several notches in my estimation.

After the cappuccino, I wanted to go home, but I felt immobilized. I could not act on my own. I had to wait for George's signal, his command. I was no better than a dog, I thought, thinking about the instruction manual written by that middle-aged Parisian Ménagier for his fifteen-year-old bride, suggesting she model herself on a little dog who fawns on its master no matter how often it is scolded or kicked....

It is much harder to extricate oneself from an unpleasant party than a pleasant one. Everyone is reluctant to break the spell cast by misery, as if to announce that one is leaving would be to admit that the event has been a disaster. We all sat on, tied in knots to the chairs. In the end, Darcy's good manners came

through. Looking at me, he apologized, explaining that he had
work to do that night; looking at Edgar, he said he had to read a
new government report; looking at George, who seemed to
know what he was talking about, he described a thousand-pager
that had to be read by tomorrow. George stood, shook hands,
and was gracious for the first time all night. But after Darcy left,
he collapsed in his chair as if exhausted from carrying the entire
evening alone on his poor shoulders. Darcy's departure liberated
me from my stupor: I was able to stand up, murmuring that I, too,
had to get home. Edgar, sweet and generous as a woman, exclaimed how good it had been to see me, such a long time since
we'd really had a chat, I must come out to the house the next
time I was visiting the Altshulers, Beenie would love to see me,
maybe they could have a dinner party, invite the Altshulers and
the Wallachs or Hume and Jessie—I was fond of them, wasn't I?
Would that be fun?

I assured him it would be fun. We were all standing by now.
Edgar hugged me hard and kissed my cheek (I returned his hug
feelingly). Then he turned to George.

"I'm grabbing the Lex uptown," he said cordially. "Talk to
you later, George," and he set off toward the subway.

I began to walk down the street. George followed. I thought
of telling him not to bother to see me home, but I knew he'd in-
sist, and it seemed martyrish game-playing somehow. He was
subdued, and his body was in its most dejected posture. It did not
even enter my mind to ask him what had been going on with him
that evening. I knew absolutely that I would not get a coherent
answer, that he himself probably had no idea. I wasn't even sure
he understood he'd behaved badly. It seemed likely that he was
feeling miserable, but at the moment, I didn't care.

However he looked, he acted as if nothing untoward had occurred. "Sure is a nice night," he said pleasantly, as we walked

along. "How'd you like Darcy? Nice guy, isn't he? Smart too; we have some good talks. He's one of the better people there. He handles all the edgy stuff—you know, the veiled racism—really well. And that Edgar! He sure knows what's going on with these theater people. Course, I didn't know half of who he was talking about, did you? Well, of course you did. You know all about those things, don't you? Do you like Beenie? I really don't. Oh, she's okay, I guess," he retracted, glancing sidelong at me. "A little pushy, maybe. I hate pushy women."

I looked at him. His face was impassive.

"The park looks really neat at night," he said as we came within sight of it. "I'd really like to take a walk through it at night."

"It's not safe," I said.

"That's what I hear. But it sure looks neat. You want to try it sometime?"

"Not without a Doberman pinscher," I said laughing. But it was a thin laugh, dredged up. I don't know if he noticed. Or cared.

We had reached my building. "Boy, Hermione, you know what I'd really like? There's nothing I'd like better than to go up to your place and sit in that great living room and look down at the park. That would really be nifty. I'd really like that."

"Of course you're welcome," I said blankly.

"Oh, I know, but I can't. Too busy; gotta go—gotta read that report tonight, a thousand pages of bureaucratese. We're having an editorial meeting on it tomorrow, nine a.m. sharp!"

"Right. Thanks for dinner," I said, turning to him and trying to smile. "Good night." I walked toward my building.

"Hey, Hermione!" he cried as I entered the front door.

I turned.

"I'll call ya!"

II
_____

I'll call you, he said.

But Saturday went by, and Sunday, in silence and heat. It was not yet July, but ninety-degree days and terrible humidity were already upon us. Normally, at this time of year I am safely in my cool Sag Harbor house, but here I was, stuck in sticky New York, and by my own will! Sweat dripped down my forehead and trickled into my eyes, burning them; my clothes were damp a half hour after I put them on. If I wanted to move without my skin dripping onto the floor at each step, or write without my arms sticking to the desk, or read a newspaper without the pages adhering to my hands, I had to run the noisy, smelly air conditioner. To add to my discomfort, since all my friends were out of town, no one called, and I felt lonely and abandoned.

Monday came and went, with only a few business calls. Lou and I had a chat about her vacation, to begin the first of July. She had arranged for her friend Lisa to come in for an hour a day to go through the mail and phone me to report on it. Lou simply assumed I would be in Sag Harbor, as in previous summers.

By Tuesday, I decided to go. But I couldn't move. Every time

I thought about leaving the city, my limbs ached; I was an animal caught in a trap I could escape from only by tearing off my
leg or arm. Like an athlete at the end of an endurance test, I was
dulled, hopeless, foggy-headed, yet I couldn't give up and stop,
couldn't sit down on a bench, had to keep moving straight
toward the finish line. My future, my very life, was at stake.

I forced myself to act. I waited until well after lunch hour and
then called *Newsday*, the editorial department, and asked for
George Johnson. He was not at his desk, and I got his voice mail.
I left a light message in a light voice; I said I was prostrate in this
heat and asked how he was holding up. I said I just wanted to let
him know that I was thinking of him and that I was planning to
go out to Long Island for the summer....

I didn't say what day I would go. I didn't mention the Sag
Harbor number. I kept anger, sorrow, and despair out of my
voice. I made it young, calm, sweet. I made it so he could hear a
smile in it. I knew he was at the office; he went in every day. He
must have been at a meeting, or chatting with someone across
the room. He was certain to receive my message sometime that
day.

But he didn't call.

Wednesday morning, I left for the country, my thigh bleed-
ing and raw where my leg had been attached.

I drove out in a blur and settled in the same way. It was good to
be cooler, to be able to throw myself into the water whenever I
wanted to, but I had to tell myself that. I didn't feel much; I was,
almost entirely, numb. I had left in defeat, having lost the fight
for my future happiness. I had lost at love before, several times;
the numbness, the shuddering ache, were familiar. But I could
not recall a time before when I had believed that the happiness

of the rest of my life, of whatever life remained to me, was at stake.

Obsessively, I went over everything I had done or said in our various encounters, finding fault with myself at every point. I should have been less assertive; I should have played harder to get; I shouldn't have asked him about his parents; I should have kept the conversation light; I absolutely should not have kissed him.

I knew it was finished, yet wisps of hope still sometimes blew past my face, softening its strained lines. Liz Margolis came on Thursday, as usual, and threw herself upon me.

"Oh, Hermione! I'm so sorry I took off that way two weeks ago; I'm so awful, I just have no control. And then next time I came, you were gone. I didn't know you were going away! I thought you were here for the summer, like other years. Whenever you've gone abroad, you told me beforehand!

"It was just such a shock, but how infantile of me, how mean! I mean, to assume that people, that a woman, that you couldn't still fall in love at your age. You look great, you know, you don't look old . . . but"—she paused, holding me by the shoulders and pushing me a little distance away from her—"you don't look good." She frowned. She let her sculptor's eye play over my face. "It fell apart, huh?"

"Yes," I said. My face felt tight. She hugged me, held me against her as if I were a small child, patting my back and whispering comforting nothings, like "There, there, poor baby," which did not comfort me, but did make me want to laugh. This impulse I suppressed; but it enabled me to tell her in complete honesty later that she'd cheered me up.

Over coffee, she demanded the details. But one really charming quality of the narcissistic younger generation is their distractability; you can easily deflect any unwanted attention they may direct at you simply by asking them about themselves.

Once Liz was gone, however, I sank back into my stuporous fog. I felt as if my head were encased in plastic, or a bag of flour, or a cloud, while the rest of my body went through normal motions. I swam, marketed, cooked, made telephone calls, and read, all the while using only a pinch of my brain. The novel was finished, but I did not call Molly to tell her. I just let it sit there in the computer, didn't even print it out. I didn't call friends, and I put off those who called me. I didn't feel up to speaking to people. My one sharp perception was that I was driving badly. I worried about having an automobile accident, and the next week, I did hit a car stopped ahead of me, banging my front bumper. In fact, I did it *twice*. The first time, the woman asked only how I was, assuring me I hadn't done any damage to her car (still, it cost me over a thousand dollars to fix my headlight—Porsches are expensive to repair). The second time, the driver claimed I had done over seven hundred dollars' damage to his truck. Although I was only going ten miles an hour, and only scratched my bumper, there *was* a dent in his bumper. That accident raised my insurance rate.

Ah, well.

Actually, George had called that week. Tuesday morning, Lisa phoned to say that sometime Monday, someone had left a message on the New York machine. The caller had not left his name but said he was sorry not to have gotten back to me sooner. A young reporter at the newspaper had been mugged and left with a fractured skull, and he was spending all his spare time at the hospital. He would call me.

Did that make any sense to me? she wanted to know.

"Yes," I admitted, jealousy crawling up my spine. I craved a fractured skull, anything that would make him turn that attention to me.

The days stumbled by. I hardly noticed. I swam a great deal, and I read or reread all the nineteenth-century novels the local library possessed—Trollope, Galsworthy, Austen, Gissing, Eliot, Burney, the Brontës. Just as I could not read anything serious when I was sunk in the misery of my first pregnancy and marriage, I could not read anything now that suggested modern life.

But as I always used to tell my children, nothing good happens without dragging along some attendant misery, and no misery occurs without its attendant good fortune. A version of the cloud–silver lining maxim, but it's true. For during the night, unbidden, two ideas for new novels sprang into my mind. One came as I was drifting off to sleep, listening to the cicadas singing in the grass. The heroine falls in love with a man who is, unknown to her, one of a set of twins. The brothers are identical—no one can tell them apart—but they behave in utterly opposite ways. One eagerly seeks her out, while the other avoids her and is cruel and sadistic when they do meet. To her, the same man appears to take both attitudes. To complicate matters, they are spies, CIA agents in the service of their country (spies can still be admirable in romance novels), and so are required to be deceptive and evasive simply in the normal course of events. Their twinship is of use to them in their work. The heroine's problem is not just to distinguish the lover from the hater, but also to discover their secret profession and the ways the cruel twin is making use of her.

It would be complicated, I thought. But I wanted to be engaged with technical details of plot, intricate conspiracies rather than intense emotions. Also, I could set it in wonderful cities and give myself a nice long trip to research it. I would start it in London, move to Paris, then to Constantinople, and end perhaps in Singapore, a tyrannical state from which the heroine and her lover escape in terror....

Yes. I began to make plans for the trip.

The second idea came to me in the middle of the night. Because of the heat, I was sleeping on the porch regularly. My fantasies had infiltrated my unconscious now, and I would frequently wake up in the darkness from a dream, my body still tingling with a lover's touch, his murmurs of affection hovering in my ears, my entire front alive with crying desire. One night, at such a moment, it occurred to me: what if I wrote a novel about a love affair, filled it with sex, put one or two erotic scenes in every chapter? The heroine and her lover are drunk with desire. They make love near the ocean, under palms and hibiscus; on a sleeping porch utterly surrounded by trees and shrubs, whose leaves brush against the screens in the wind; in a hotel bedroom where the sheets are perpetually damp despite the whirring ceiling fan. Bamboo blinds hang over the glass doors, which open on a view of a pale sky. The lovers, their bodies always wet, call room service and order more champagne.... I would set it in some sleepy, flower-and-frond-bedecked, humid, tropical place, where the water is aqua and the sky a deeper blue. Samoa or Fiji or one of the Caribbean islands. I could spend the winter there, researching it, writing it. Take my laptop.

What would make it unusual is that at the very end, the reader discovers that the entire affair has taken place only in the heroine's imagination, that nothing actually happened with the man, that he rejected her early on, and that throughout the virtual time of the novel, she is wandering listlessly around, helpless with desire, dreaming it all up.... Would love be less real that way? Less intense? Would the sex not still be ecstatic?

Of course, I would have to write this under another name; I could not taint my reputation with a novel like that. I would lose my audience, who did not like their sex explicit. I might even have to go to a different publisher. But it would be fun.

One Wednesday night, the phone rang. I was shocked to hear George's voice on the other end.

"So what are you doing out there?" he wanted to know.

"I always spend summers here," I said. "It's beautiful and cool. I swim every day. You ought to come out and visit." I heard myself say.

"God, I've been too busy. This poor kid that got mugged, it was touch and go for her for a while there. I spent a lot of time in the hospital, all my spare time...."

I wondered at his offering such devotion to a complete stranger—a young reporter, didn't he say? Maybe she wasn't a stranger at all. He went on about her a bit: it seemed she was making a full recovery. "Yeah, well, she's young, you know," he said, as if he did expect me to know.

"Oh," I said finally. "Well, that's good. So what happened? I haven't heard from you in a long time." I hated myself, hated hearing the words come out of my mouth, hoped there wasn't a whine in my voice.

"Well, you know, you really blindsided me!" He laughed.

"I what?"

"Blindsided me. Came at me from a direction I wasn't expecting. You know, I'm not very strong. I can't fight. But one thing I *can* do—I can run and I can hide!" He was laughing. "I sure can run, and I can hide!"

Hide from me?

From me.

My heart was beating so hard in my ears that I was momentarily deaf, and his words passed me by. Only later did I realize that he'd said he was returning to Louisville in August. And not until the next day did I realize that Thursday—today—was the first of August. He'd decided not to take the job at *Newsday,* he said. He'd found New York fun. He'd learned a lot. But he was going back home.

"I'll call ya," he said, and hung up.

August arrived. The green world began to shrivel and dry up. The brilliant pinks and purples and whites of the flowers in my garden turned yellow and brown. The geese began to mass in the fields and flew, evenings, in formation in the sky above my house. At night, they gabbed and quarreled in the fields. So short, summer. August, summer still, foreshadows autumn: it always saddens me.

I lied to everyone who called, saying I was holed up to finish a novel. I could not bear the thought of seeing people, and preferred not to talk to them, either. I swam, read, and perused travel books, making plans for an extended journey to the cities that would figure in the novel I privately called *Odi et Amo.* Of course, that would not be its real title: no one would get it, including, probably, my publisher. No one reads Catullus anymore. But I preferred to think about it from the perspective of its male protagonists rather than from that of the heroine. I knew only too keenly how she felt—like a bug on a pin, legs still twitching. But I didn't understand them, the men who hate and love, hate and love so strongly. To think I had once prided myself on understanding ambivalence! I was a naïf, I! I should reread Catullus before I began to outline the book. I felt lucky to have a new novel to think about, to have anything to think about. I was lucky to have a trip to plan, and I spoke every few days to my travel agent, revising my itinerary.

But of course, I still had to eat, which meant I still had to market, and one day at the butcher's, I ran into Nina Brumbach, who with surprise and enthusiasm reminded me that I had asked her to lunch, and where had I been and why hadn't I called? I was stuck without an excuse. We arranged to meet the following Tuesday.

Nina twirled into Giorgio's in a flowing pink dress, a red cape, and a broad-brimmed red straw hat. Heads turned, mouths smiled and whispered behind cupped palms: she was a local celebrity, the town eccentric—the latter, simply because of her dress. It doesn't take much to make one an eccentric on Long Island.

We each ordered one of Giorgio's little pizzas: prosciutto, peppers, and onions for her; broccoli, mushrooms, and extra cheese for me.

She launched in eagerly. "So tell me all about it!"

I had been dreading this and, before I left the house, had practiced speaking in an expressionless voice. I reached for it now but came up only with a rusty squeak: "Well, it's really over now. It came to nothing. Of course, I still have fantasies that he will suddenly realize what he's lost and decide to call me, but I know they are only fantasies."

"Oh!" Her face fell, bless her. She had really wished me well. She *was* a good soul.

"Do you think he knew how you felt about him?"

I pondered. "No. Not really. Not fully, that is. He had an

inkling. But even that inkling terrified him. If he had known how strong my feelings were, he probably would have fled even faster than he did. I think he flirts and acts seductive without being conscious of it. I think he thinks he's just being friendly, just a friendly country boy, when he's actually being quite provocative. Then he's shocked and disgusted when women respond to his seductiveness. He thinks the women are weird. I imagine it's a pattern in his life."

"So he's a cunt tease." She applied lipstick, blotted her lips, and lighted a cigarette. She was one of my few friends who still smoked. I breathed in deeply: the cigarette smelled wonderful.

"Kind of a willful naïveté," she continued. "But it's pretty cruel to other people."

"Yes. Since he's totally unconscious of what he's doing, he's able to go on feeling he's a good guy. He's intelligent—just self-deluded. It's hard to believe he's as ignorant as he acts."

"It sounds as if he really hates women."

"Umm. That's what he says."

"Really? He admits it?"

"I think he's proud of it."

Nina was silent at that, regarding me thoughtfully.

"You invested a lot in him."

"Everything. I planted all the repressed dreams of my sixty years in this guy. Can you believe it? Someone I hardly knew? It shocked me, what I felt. The nature of it, the intensity of it. Felt. Feel. I can't get past it. All these dreams, these scenarios, these plans, just fermented in my brain, just bubbled up, one after another. I couldn't sleep.... I still have trouble. It's crazy. I'd say I felt like a teenager, except I never felt this way when I *was* a teenager."

"Umm. Doesn't matter. You just had a delayed reaction to

what's been in you all your life. It's part of our upbringing, all of us, girls and boys, in America."

"What do you mean?"

"You know, I've devoted considerable thought to this stuff. I've had to, given the way I feel about Garson. Have discovered I feel about Garson ..."

"Discovered?"

"Well, I didn't *know* I felt this way," she said, a little testily. "How is a person supposed to know a thing like that? I mean, while he was alive, I was annoyed with him half the time, in a rage with him the other half. Oh, not at first. The first years we were together, we talked talked talked, we never stopped, we couldn't get enough of each other's minds; we craved the other's mind. We talked about poetry and dance—we were wild for Martha Graham in those days—we went to hear Auden read, we screeched together about politics: we were both socialists then, we just didn't join the party...

"After a few years, I guess we had to get a little distance from each other, and we began to move a bit apart, but everything we did was done with one eye out for how the other would respond to it, what the other would think....

"And the years went by, and we got older. Our bodies got older: I got thinner, he got heavier, he lost his hair. Then it became terribly important to him that it be known that he was still ...potent. Or attractive. Or sexy. Something. You remember how he was, how he fooled around—everyone knew. All those young women, one younger than the next. It was utterly humiliating to me. But I had to keep my affairs secret, because it wouldn't do to damage his manly ego. And then he got so conservative in his old age! It was really hard to talk to him then."

I gazed at her in shock.

She stared at me with hostility. I thought that for a moment she was seeing Garson, not me. At least, I hoped so. "You look incredulous."

"I didn't understand...," I faltered.

She wiped her hand across her face. "No, I suppose not. I don't understand, myself." Her voice thickened, her eyes filled. "It's just that since he died, all these memories come clamoring back: so many wonderful times we had, such great talk, such magnificent sex.... He was the love of my life. Even the anger, even the arguments—they were part of it, part of the passion. When he was dying, we were having a fight, one of our many. An old girlfriend of his wanted to visit, and I didn't want her to see him in that condition. He wanted her to come, wanted to make her feel sorry for him, wanted to see her cry: I knew him... and I just blasted him. He was such a selfish bastard! I told him he didn't want to see her to see *her*, because he cared about her— because he didn't! All he wanted was to milk her of emotion, the way he always did with women, those young ones especially. To squeeze love and adoration out of them, have them pour it over his head, anoint him with it. And I said he was so self-involved, he never really knew what those young girls were feeling or thinking, but a couple of them had come to me—would you believe it? They had. Weeping about him, his selfishness, his denseness. I wasn't the most sympathetic ear...."

"So then I told him. I told him I'd had as many affairs as he, with young men, older men, all kinds. Of course, I didn't know how many affairs he'd had; I just exaggerated my own. But I recited a whole list—some of his closest friends. Including a priest and a rabbi. That really got him! He was lying there in his hospital bed, he was in a fury, he rose up from the bed, he wanted to kill me, he stretched out his hands to strangle me, but he was too weak to do anything. I laughed. Then he laughed too. Then we both began to cry. We clutched each other's hands. What a pair!"

Nina began to sob.

People at nearby tables glanced toward us uneasily.

"Too bad you didn't have children," I mumbled stupidly. "You might be less depressed."

"There was no *room* for children!" she shrieked. "There was only us. Us, us, us! Don't you understand? Everything we did was directed at the other. The affairs, his and mine! His growing conservatism! Conservatism, hell; he became a reactionary! It was a blow at me. A hostile act. Because my work was starting to get known—I had won a couple of prizes, I was being asked to read here and there—and he had become a little... out of date, a little passé. It was after I won the National Book Award that he wrote that really disgusting book about Jews and blacks."

I laughed.

"It's funny?" She dropped her anger out of curiosity.

"Well...it was an ironic laugh," I apologized, although I did in fact find it funny. "Here you two really lived out the great love affair. And it was so ..."

"Ugly," she muttered. "Yes. But it was magnificent too, you know. We were everything to each other. We ranged the entire gamut of emotion—we had the most intense passion for each other and the most bitter hatred, the uttermost craving need and the uttermost flaming resentment."

I gazed at her with a little animosity and considerable respect. "You have really probed this relationship, plumbed it....Are you going to write a poetry sequence about it? You should."

"Umm," she pondered. "Yes. I should. I suppose I have, really. If I just gathered together fifty or so unpublished poems, it might be already written.... That's a good idea, Hermione," she said, in a cool professional voice from which all passion had suddenly vanished. "You know, come to think of it, it's our generation. Yours, mine, his—well, he was a generation older. He had it even more."

"Had what?"

"The myth. The dream. Prince and Princess, True Love, Love Forever, Happily Ever After. And the truth is, we had it. We had it for real. With all the ambivalence, the rage, the betrayals... I'm often surprised we didn't end up killing each other."

"I don't think that's what most people mean when they talk about True Love and Love Forever."

"No. But they're stupid—because that's what true love, love forever, *is*. It's not some sweet nice pretty hand-holding valentine. It's plowing your whole emotional self—which is far from pretty—with one other person. For a lifetime. It's a bubbling stew, a violent concoction, it's living inside a pressure cooker. One that explodes regularly, spattering the walls and ceiling with blood.

"Love. Hah! We all want true love, love forever. We're raised to want it, educated to want it, brainwashed into wanting it. Only most people are too cowardly to accept it... like you."

Moi!

"Oh, don't blink your eyes at me, Hermione. How many times have you been married? At the least sign of passion rooting itself in you, you run."

I wanted to defend myself, to remind her that two of my husbands had died, one had left me, and the first—well, he was utterly impossible. But instead I attacked. "Well, truthfully, Nina, if what you describe is true passion and love forever after, I'll do without it. It sounds sick to me."

"Oh, it is, no question," she said easily. "It's a neurotic myth. We'd be much better off without it. But we've got it, so we either have to live it out or fail to live it out." She stood up. "I have to go to the loo."

I paid the bill. I wondered if we'd ever be able to be friends again. I couldn't figure out what I'd said or done to arouse Nina's antagonism. I may have been dense, but I'd tried to be amiable. She was a difficult woman to please. I decided to conclude that she was crazy. It was the easiest solution.

Nina reappeared and picked up her cape. "Ready?" She seemed simply to assume that I'd paid the check. Of course, romance novelists earn much more than poets. It was only fair. Or maybe poets don't think about money at all but take it for granted that they will be kept fed and clothed.

"Right," I said, rising. We walked out of the restaurant into midday heat and headed for the parking lot. It was far too hot for heavy clothes, but Nina kept her cape wrapped around her. When we reached my car, I stopped and called out, "Well, goodbye, Nina." She had kept walking, but turned when I called. She walked back to me. Dropping her cape, she grabbed me and hugged me.

"Thanks," she murmured in my ear. "Thanks so much." She pushed me away from her, holding me by both arms. "You are a wonder. There's no one else I could have had this conversation with. No one else would have understood. They would have been shocked, horrified. That I should reveal this stuff about the great Garson Brumbach! But you just accepted it. You saw! Immediately, without argument! I feel so much better! It was a great lunch, Hermione. I'll never forget it. Or you for asking me. And you gave me a wonderful idea for a book. I'd dedicate it to you if I didn't have to dedicate it to Garson." She kissed my cheek.

She dropped her arms, picked up her cape, threw it around her, and walked swiftly to her car. I stood, baffled and battered, watching her cape ripple in the little breeze she made by walking. She did not look back.

I meandered, driving home, gazing at the beauty around me, remembering my first apartment in New York, a seedy place with peeling paint on the walls, the tub in the kitchen, and no bathroom sink at all. It was February 1952 when I moved to Manhattan. Lettice was nearly two and already had a sizable vocabulary. I constantly worried she would tell Bert that "Mommy wites." She jabbered to him, whether he talked to her or not, and she commented on my writing whenever I did it; it fascinated her, and there was no place to hide from her in that apartment.

Jerry had driven us down. He rented a van so he could transport all Lettice's equipment—crib and high chair and diapers and clothes and toys—as well as some things from the apartment. I didn't take much—my books, some dishes and pots, linens—just enough to get me started in my new home. I had quite a time packing them up without Bert's noticing, and that he did not testifies more to his disinterest than to my cleverness. Susan and Merry had found me a fourth-floor walk-up in the East Seventies. It had two bedrooms, a living room, and a kitchen, and was only forty dollars a month.

I left Bert a note, propped up against a tuna casserole. I wrote that if he wanted to see Lettice, he could call Jerry and I'd set up a visit. I wished him a happier future. He did call Jerry that night, yelling about the fact that I'd deceived him, "put one over" on him. He didn't seem disturbed by the fact that I'd left him, and he never asked to see Lettice. In fact, he didn't call again for two years, when he told Jerry he wanted a divorce because he wanted to remarry. I was happy about that—it annulled any residual guilt I felt toward him. I fervently hoped his second marriage was more satisfying than his first. I never saw him again. My summer with Bert had lasted rather longer than I would have wished. I wonder what would have happened if my summer with George had endured into the fall.

After all my daydreams of living in New York, I was frightened and lonely the first year I was there. My sisters saved me: on weekends, we tried to give one day over entirely to pleasure. We sought out every free event in town—and there were lots: walking tours, concerts, readings, even theater. When nothing else appealed, we went to Central Park, which was always a circus on Sundays.

Merry's boyfriend—a graduate student she'd met in the park—made blind dates for me; we'd go together, as a double date. The boys he chose were college boys around my age; they were Jewish, and like him, went to NYU. Most of them had grown up poor, like me. They had strong New York accents, and they dressed horribly. I thought their backgrounds would enable me to empathize with them in a way I couldn't with the tea dance boys. But they were amazingly like the boys from Harvard, Yale, and Brown: they, too, acted as if their experience was something they owned, the purpose of which was to provide a weapon against others. Unlike the boys I'd met at Holyoke, their experience was not of skiing or sailing or riding or voyages to Europe on ocean liners; what they had was knowledge, which they held up for your inspection, so far above your head, you couldn't reach up and touch it. You were supposed to just admire it.

They knew about music and books and politics; a couple even knew about art. They dropped names that left me speechless:

Mahler, Hindemith, Newman, Morris Louis, Proust, Faulkner, Joyce, Malraux, and other names so foreign to me then I can't remember them now. Of the writers they mentioned, the only one I'd read was Faulkner. They were given to pronouncements like "No serious music has been written since Brahms!" or "African art? You call that art? Art didn't begin until Giotto!" or "Western art has been one long deviation from the true path of art, which in no other culture has taken the form of realism." They said such things in tones so supercilious, with facial expressions so haughty, that not only contradiction but even discussion was impossible. I shriveled, feeling stupid and uncultivated, listening in intimidated silence. These boys didn't mind my silence; they seemed to like it—and me. Most of them asked to see me again. And again. But I minded. I minded feeling stupid and ignorant and inexperienced about things that mattered to me; I minded feeling unknowledgeable.

So while I tended not to go out with any one of them more than a few times, these boys inspired me to form educational projects on my own. I took night courses in art and music history. In the afternoons, after a morning of writing, I went to museums. I pushed Lettice through so many, I was sure she would grow up to be an artist. I had to wait until she was a bit older to take her to concerts, but we listened religiously to the classical music on WNYC and WQXR. I took courses in French, German, and Italian; I read Proust, Goethe, and Dante; I read philosophy and history. I wanted to prove to myself that the Millington High School teachers had been right about me. And the first year I was really ahead, I wrote them a thank-you note and enclosed a thousand-dollar check for them to use as they chose. I told them I hoped they would spend it on the library, or another student, like me but less foolish. They wrote back—the ones who were still there; they were really happy for my success and didn't say a single derogatory word about my writing romances.

I pulled into my driveway, smiling about those early years in New York. Although I was often wretched with fear, worried about money and whether the latest book I was working on would be acceptable, would earn anything beyond its advance— and how I would feed Lettice if it didn't—and sad with loneliness, my memories of my first years in New York are dominated by great excitement and pleasure. It was a time of vivid life and emotion, of tremendous learning and deep feeling. It was the beginning of a new life I was creating for myself. I was building it on the ruins of my youth, on top of the ruins of the beliefs and practices that most people held when I was in my twenties. Few people still believe in them. Even Delia is no longer so mean and narrow: she's had to accept one son divorcing, another leaving the church....

I decided that it was in those past events that the notion of Prince Charming was rooted. I'd probably never get rid of it; it was the last vestige of my reptile brain.

My sisters managed to create their own lives too, although it took them a long time. A few years after I moved to New York, Susan and Eldon moved to Long Island, to one of those flat barren towns with identical small flat gray houses and ugly names like Levittown, Hicksville, Amityville. Susan had a couple of adorable kids, a girl and a boy, and devoted herself to them entirely when they were little. But once they were grown, she opened her own advertising agency out on Long Island. She said no one knows more about a business than a good secretary, and that she'd known more about her agency's workings than any of the guys she'd worked for, even the president.

She must have been right, because her own agency was very successful.

When she founded it, she wanted two words to name her agency—one that conjured an image of an honest, moral, healthy America and one suggesting enormous wealth and prestige. After much discussion—and giggling among Susan and Eldon, Merry and me—she chose Kellogg, after the cereals, and Astor, after the millionaire immortalized in the Waldorf-Astoria. To hear the bank manager roll the name Astor Kellogg around in his mouth as if it were something grand and important was pure delight, especially since at first the company consisted of two desks and a set of telephones in a front room! Eventually, Susan moved into commercial offices in Manhasset, and when Eldon lost his job ("inevitable in the advertising business," Susan said), he became her art director. They not only lived happily ever after but are still doing so, with five grandchildren, a plump financial portfolio, and a retirement home in Maine.

Tina, too, had success. For her first few years in Hollywood, she worked as an extra. But someone gave her a part with two lines, and soon afterward, she got a bit part in a film with George Raft. That got her noticed, and she became quite well known; she was featured in eight or ten films under the name Tina Twining. Unfortunately, her popularity didn't last. But she foresaw that, she said in her letters. She knew that actresses become obsolete at thirty-five, and she made sure that before she lost her looks, she married a rich insurance executive. She wanted to be absolutely certain, she wrote, that she would never never never have to work in a bakery again. She doesn't write often, and we rarely see her. It's as if she feels not part of our family, as if we excluded her. Maybe we did; or maybe working all those silent years in the bakery, never getting anything she wanted, not even being allowed to join the Drama Club—maybe all that damaged her somehow.

Merry got married too—well, of course, everyone got married in those days—but her marriage didn't work out too well. Her husband turned out to be a secret gambler, and she was never sure how much money they had or whether their monthly mortgage check would bounce. So she finally left him and raised her two girls alone on a secretary's pay. They lived in some hardship, but Susan, Jerry, and I all helped her. I often think that was our mother's training, the way we always pulled together as a family—except Tina, come to think of it. Merry's girls are grown, and she's retired now, quite content, I think. She lives with a woman, a retired schoolteacher. I suspect they're lovers, although she doesn't let on. So it took her until she was fifty to make the life she wanted, but she did it. And she *still* reads romances! She's my best critic.

Only Jerry, of all of us, didn't take command of his life. He had too much of Mother's self-sacrificing tendency, I guess. He tried to be good for Delia, good in Delia's way. It worked for her, but not for him. They had three boys. Delia stayed young-looking and healthy, guiding her sons toward religion: one of them became a priest, for a few years, anyway. (It nearly killed Delia when he went over the fence, as they say.) But Jerry turned slowly gray over the years, gray and old, and two years ago, he died of angina—just like Mother. I'll never stop missing him.

Over the years, I became successful too. Eda Doyle retired in 1961 and went to live in the south of France. I heard she died sometime in the seventies. Swan Books is long extinct too; Heartbreak House publishes me now. I get a great deal of money for my novels these days, and Molly sells them in England and in other European countries. At least twenty of them have been sold to the movies; eight have made it through production. Of course, by then they were unrecognizable. I don't take that seriously; I don't take what I do very seriously, either. But it has provided me with a wonderful life. I raised Lettice and my other three children, all on my writing.

A few years after I left Bert, I fell in love with a man I was crazy about, sexually—although I didn't reach the peak of sexual desire until I was nearly thirty. In 1954, when I was twenty-three, I met a man at a party, Charles Murano, a freelance artist. We married within a few months and in 1955 had twin sons, James and Girard. Charles did beautiful work and often made high commissions, but there were lean times too. So we lived on my income and re served his for special treats, like trips to Mexico and Italy or renovations to our house. When I met Charles, I owned the two bottom floors of a brownstone on West Twelfth Street. Charles got a huge commission from *Vogue* in 1956, and we bought the third floor and fixed it up as the children's floor—just in time for Stephanie, who was born in 1957. When he got another windfall in 1960, we fixed up the garden behind the kitchen. We made a patio of huge terra-cotta stones and surrounded it with shrubs and trees and an herb garden. We had a wonderful life. But in 1961, Charles died of a heart attack. He was only thirty-six. I was thirty.

It is dismaying how quickly hearts mend. In 1963, I fell in love with and married Andrew Lindsey, an investment banker who knew everything about money and how to sweep a girl off her feet. (We still called ourselves girls back then, even at thirty-two.) He took me dancing at discos and riding at Montauk. He took me and the children out on his sailboat for weekends. I was swept away by him, really. It was with Andrew that I finally understood what it meant to be sexually vanquished. We married, but Andrew proved that sex was not a good ground for marriage. I adored and trusted him, and by the time he left me for a younger woman, in 1968, he had his own company, most of my money, and my brownstone. I had to start over again, almost from scratch, this time with four kids. It was a bitter experience.

I shut my mouth and forgot about having fun—and I worked, come to think of it, exactly the way my mother had in the bakery, literally day and night, turning out novels under three different names. Three years later, I was able to buy the apartment on Fifth Avenue. I hired the architect Mark Goldman to redesign and decorate it. The job got a six-page, full-color spread in *Architectural Digest;* it made his reputation, and along the way, we fell in love. Neither of us wanted more children: Mark was divorced, with a grown daughter. He was very social—we traveled and went to lots of parties. We had almost eight great years together before he fell ill with pancreatic cancer. He died in months, terribly. His death—the way he died, not the fact of his death—made me feel I didn't want to marry again, didn't want to be close to anyone again.

And by the time Mark died, I had had too many losses, too many sorrows. I worked at shutting off my feelings, just soldiering through. My goal was *not* to feel. I've been alone ever since. That was 1979, this is 1991: a shockingly long time. Maybe I needed to fall in love.

No, Molly was wrong. My feelings for George were unique, an experience I'd never had before, one I was unprepared for. It was as if I was finally reaping the punishment for my bad character, or paying the price for having had such a lucky life. Maybe I'd finally let myself feel something I'd denied throughout my life. Maybe I've deceived myself about my emotions all these years. Maybe the punishment for that is being thrust back into adolescence, forced into the humiliating experience of love and longing, here on the edge of the grave.

Friday morning, the phone rang. It was Molly. She was at her country house, upstate, in Garrison.

"I miss you," she said.

"Me too."

"And I'm way up here and you're way down there."

"We both have cars."

"Is that an invitation? Okay, I'll come for the weekend. I'll leave in an hour or so. See you tonight."

"Bring your suit!" I yelled, but she'd already hung up. I knew my bathing suits would not fit Molly, she was so small. But maybe there was a spare left behind by some tiny person. Not worth calling her back for. If she didn't have a suit, she'd skinny dip.

I dressed quickly—I was still in my bathing suit—and drove to the fish market and bought some fresh swordfish. I'd marinate it in soy sauce, hot sesame oil, and mustard, and broil it. I'd serve it with pasta. I wouldn't cook a sauce, just toss the hot pasta into chopped tomato, garlic, basil, and olive oil. Molly would like that—it was her recipe.

I was humming as I prepared the marinade. I was happy Molly was coming. Maybe, I thought, I'd been a bit lonely.

It was dark by the time she arrived, and I served dinner almost right away. We ate heartily, chatted, sipped wine. We were always easy together. I told her about my lunch with Nina Brumbach and her strange story. She told me about a split between two close friends of ours.

We moved out to the porch after dinner. I leaned back in a

chaise, and Molly lay stretched out on the daybed. Although there was light from the moon ascending through the clouds, the porch was very dark. We could barely see each other's faces, except as a pale blur. The blackness was consoling, a curtain draped over us, soft as fog.

"So what's happened with George?" Molly said into the dark.

"Nothing. He withdrew. It's over—the flirtation, or whatever it was. He told me I blindsided him. He said he couldn't fight me, but he could run, and he could certainly hide."

"*Fight* you?"

"I know. Why would anyone want to fight someone who loved him? Unless he didn't love her back, in which case, why keep calling? Eventually, of course, he stopped."

We sat in silence for a while.

"Are you all right?" Molly asked finally.

"Not great. It's painful. I came to feel I couldn't live if the dream wasn't realized, if we didn't get together in this great ecstatic burst and find ourselves perfect companions, agreeable together in everything.... The dream came to seem the only purpose of life, the only possible reason for existing.... I know how absurd it is, but that's how I felt. Feel."

"I'm sorry." She paused, then added, "You know you can't help it. Having that dream, I mean. Don't blame yourself, don't feel absurd. We're all raised on it, and even if we deny it, it's there."

"You can't avoid the entire spirit of an age."

"You think today's girls will be different? With the kind of violent music and movies they're being raised on?"

"Oh, who knows!"

"You think women in India, or in Africa, don't entertain the same sick fantasy?"

"I'm sure not! And anyway, in this country, men have it too. I'm sure of that."

We sat in silence again. The cicadas sang, a comforting sound. Molly's presence, too, was comforting.

"But it's not just a fantasy, a sick sentimental dream, is it? Isn't there something true at the heart of it, something real, something worth wanting?

"You know," I added softly, "lately this image popped up in my head, an image from long ago that won't go away. Once, when I was in Oxford, over twenty years ago, or more, I saw two people walking together up the High Street. They were a working-class couple, short and stocky and graying and shabbily dressed, he in a jacket and cap, she in an old wool coat and tie up shoes with mid-heels, the kind elderly women wore when we were young. And their faces were lined; both their faces had worried a lot. But they had kind faces.

"The thing about them that caught my eye is that they were holding hands. They weren't walking arm in arm; they were holding hands. British couples didn't, on the whole, walk down the street holding hands. Still don't. They're too proper, you know? But this couple—there was such trust and easiness between them, it was like an aura surrounding them. Their lives hadn't been easy, but they'd wrested something fine out of them."

Tears dampened my cheeks.

Molly said nothing. The evening grew cooler, and I was about to get up and fetch myself a sweater, when she murmured—in such a low voice that I had to strain to hear her, "All my life I have wanted, more than anything in the world, someone to take care of me. Someone who would draw my bath and bring me a cup of tea in bed, who would rub my back when it's achy, and even sometimes maybe cook a meal...."

"But *you* do those things!" I exclaimed. "You always do things like that for me when I visit you, or when we travel together."

"I know. I do them because I want them done for me."

"Has no one ever done them for you, Molly?"

"Armand did, a few times. My last husband. But then I think he forgot about it. I never told the first two I wanted them: I didn't have the nerve. It felt so wrong to ask for something you wanted. It felt illegitimate. And it felt as if—if you had to ask—it wouldn't be a genuine gift, you know?"

"I do know."

It was growing cool. August. In a field nearby, a huge gaggle of geese was chattering away. Autumn was here.

"I'm getting chilly, Molly. How about you?"

"Yes. And I'm tired too. I was up at five."

I stood. "Molly. May I draw you a bath?"

I could see her smile in the darkness. "Thanks, lovey. But I'm just going to throw myself in bed. I'm too tired for a bath tonight."

In September, I set off on my journey, which I cut a little short for Stephanie's sake: she wanted to hold a big family Thanksgiving dinner in her house in Kent, Connecticut, and she wanted me there. The twins—my sons, not my characters—were flying in from California, and Lettice was coming from Chicago to be there. So of course I came home early. I was tired, anyway; I can't take long journeys the way I used to. I had enough information on every place except Singapore, which was difficult to get hard facts about. But I had the name of someone who had been in the American consulate there and had retired and now lived in New Milford, who might be willing to talk to me. I'd been told that the only way I could get someone to tell me how bad things were there was by finding someone who no longer worked there. At some point, pinning down the facts of the place began to seem like too much trouble, and I considered dropping Singapore from the plot.

But then I considered the suspense it would generate: the heroine, Nina, and the twins, Whitman and Walter, one of them deeply in love with her, the other, driven mad by a dose of LSD the CIA had secretly given him years before, projecting neurotic hatred for his mother onto the innocent girl, all of them trying to escape from Singapore with highly secret information about its military industry. Therefore, the government and its industrial complex are tracking them all down, and like all totalitarian systems, it has tentacles reaching everywhere.... No, I decided to keep Singapore. It didn't matter whether the facts were true. If I didn't have hard facts, I'd make them up. I could give Singapore a fictional name if I wanted to.

That's the great thing about being a writer: you can make everything up.

Except your life.

Try as I could, I wasn't able to make up a happier ending for my ... what was it? not an affair ... my encounter with George. He remained with me, though, he lingered for months in my body and longer in my heart. One of these summers, he may disappear. He may even be supplanted.

Now, I can't deny that the pull of romance is powerful in me. It is not something I can have a surgeon cut out of me like a wart or unwanted fat or the bags under my eyes. I wonder if it will be with me until I die. Suppose I should by some fluke live to eighty or ninety: will my heart still soar whenever I hear great romantic waltzes, like Ravel's *Valses Nobles et Sentimentales* or the waltzes from *Der Rosenkavalier*? When I hear them, my senses dip and rise so powerfully, my whole body seems to dip and rise. It twirls as the basses boom the beat, the cymbals crash, the violins swirl . . .

and I am young and slender, in a ruffled white ball gown, in the arms of a young soldier wearing blue and red and gold, and we circle the mirrored ballroom in an ordered frenzy of passion. And contained as it is by the beat, by the three-quarter time— the *oom-pa-pa, oom pa-pa*—the passion spills over with longing and loss and the terrible knowledge of the impossibility of satisfaction. This waltz lies at the very heart of my heart, and magnificent and terrible and tragic and terrifying as it is (how the cymbals threaten! how the rhythm speeds up! we swirl faster and faster, nearly out of control! we are approaching chaos, madness, we are liquefying!), it is for me also the dance of life, which is love and sex and body and music. . . .

Maybe most of my mistakes in life were efforts to dance a waltz only I could hear. So maybe they were not mistakes at all but simply me dancing my own dance. Or maybe I was hurling myself, blindly and without thought, into a vivid teeming mirrored room where the drums and basses boom out my own pulse, the violins emerge from my own throat and the woodwinds from my heart, as all the world swings rhythmically in pairs, forever.

I do not know how to think about the fact that I may reach some great age, my face skeletal beneath the wrinkled folds of flesh pulled away from the bone, my eyes sunken into dark pockets of pain, my walk tottery and unsure, my body a tattered coat upon a stick, and still be on the lookout, have an eye out for, be seeking always and ever, a certain voice and eye, a certain look, a hand reached out, breath swiftly drawn, a catch in the voice, an invitation to the waltz. Do I imagine that I will live happily until I die, beloved and embraced? It is humiliating. A better poet than

I demanded to grow old in dignity, to transcend need and desire, to become a golden bird—a goal I scorned, despite my honor for the poem. But now I face the fact, the sorry fact, or is it triumphant? There it is, there it remains: my spirit is still a girl's, trapped inside a deteriorating container. The unending drive, the geyser spurt of desire that is life, goes on and on, will not be stilled, in body or spirit. Till death do us part.

A Note on the Type

This book was set in Janson, a typeface long thought to have been made by the Dutchman Anton Janson, who was a practicing typefounder in Leipzig during the years 1668–1687. However, it has been conclusively demonstrated that these types are actually the work of Nicholas Kis (1650–1702), a Hungarian, who most probably learned his trade from the master Dutch typefounder Dirk Voskens. The type is an excellent example of the influential and sturdy Dutch types that prevailed in England up to the time William Caslon (1692–1766) developed his own incomparable designs from them.

Composed by ComCom, Allentown, Pennsylvania

Printed and bound by Haddon Craftsmen, Scranton, Pennsylvania

Designed by Misha Beletsky